T0357545

ALL'S FAIR

IN

LOVE

AND

FIELD

HOCKEY

ALL'S FAIR IN LOVE AND FIELD HOCKEY

KIT ROSEWATER

**Delacorte
Romance**

This is a work of fiction. Names, characters, places, and incidents either are the product of the author's imagination or are used fictitiously. Any resemblance to actual persons, living or dead, events, or locales is entirely coincidental.

Text copyright © 2025 by Kit Rosewater
Jacket art copyright © 2025 by Sarah Maxwell
Interior hockey icon art by akhmad/stock.adobe.com

All rights reserved. Published in the United States by Delacorte Romance, an imprint of Random House Children's Books, a division of Penguin Random House LLC, 1745 Broadway, New York, NY 11104.

Delacorte Romance is a registered trademark and the colophon is a trademark of Penguin Random House LLC.

GetUnderlined.com

Educators and librarians, for a variety of teaching tools, visit us at RHTeachersLibrarians.com

Library of Congress Cataloging-in-Publication Data is available upon request.
ISBN 978-0-593-89845-1 (pbk.) — ISBN 978-0-593-89846-8 (ebook)

The text of this book is set in 11.4-point Sabon MT Pro.

Editor: Ali Romig
Cover Designer: Angela Carlino
Interior Designer: Cathy Bobak
Production Editor: Colleen Fellingham
Managing Editor: Tamar Schwartz
Production Manager: Shameiza Ally

Printed in the United States of America
10 9 8 7 6 5 4 3 2 1
First Edition

Random House Children's Books supports the First Amendment and celebrates the right to read.

Penguin Random House values and supports copyright. Copyright fuels creativity, encourages diverse voices, promotes free speech, and creates a vibrant culture. Thank you for buying an authorized edition of this book and for complying with copyright laws by not reproducing, scanning, or distributing any part of it in any form without permission. You are supporting writers and allowing Penguin Random House to continue to publish books for every reader. Please note that no part of this book may be used or reproduced in any manner for the purpose of training artificial intelligence technologies or systems.

The authorized representative in the EU for product safety and compliance is Penguin Random House Ireland, Morrison Chambers, 32 Nassau Street, Dublin D02 YH68, Ireland. https://eu-contact.penguin.ie

For my seven twin flames:

C.E.

K.L.

M.S.

J.H.

C.A.

S.G.

D.R.

But mostly for my one half orange:

D.M.R.

CHAPTER ONE

I drag myself through the door, weighed down with every possible layer.

BAM! A hand protector bounces off the lockers.

THUD! A shin guard scrapes against the bench bolted to the floor.

I shuffle into the locker room like the Michelin Man, like a middle school boy who decided at the last minute to be a Transformers robot for Halloween and used couch cushions as a costume. Dad likes to say that when I step onto the field, I have the intimidation and swagger of an NFL lineman, but I don't think that's winning me any more sexy points than looking like a tire mascot would.

"Good practice, ladies." Gloria, our field hockey coach, leans against the wall by the towels. She's a bullish white woman in her fifties, with strong, pronounced shoulders and box-dyed red hair.

"Evelyn," she says with a nod as I waddle past her.

I heave myself onto the bench as my teammates squeeze past each other and skitter inside. They yank towels down from the shelf and crowd their hockey sticks against the wall. They move with the nimbleness of people not weighed down by forty pounds of padding and the crushing demands of blocking perfection. Even their voices are light and bubbly, bouncing off the tile floors like soapsuds.

"Don't you dare take up all the hot water."

"Where did I put my conditioner kit?"

"Hey! That's my towel!"

"God, my toes look disgusting."

"I told you to wrap them after class."

I smile and ease my other hand from its glove, enjoying the slowness that comes with missing the first round of showers. Everyone else slips off their jerseys and flings their skorts over stall doors in seconds. But for me, the transition from *goalie* to *girl* is a process. I have to take my time, removing myself piece by piece until there's just skin. My boyfriend, Caleb, plays football, so between the two of us, we'd give the longest striptease ever.

The truth is, sometimes I'm not in a hurry to take off the uniform at all. It's sort of like a security blanket. A *badass* security blanket.

I'm partway out of the massive chest-protector pad when Natalia pokes her head around the locker bay. Like me, she's still in uniform.

"Captain?" she says, like my title is a question.

I stop fiddling with the side buckle. "Yeah?"

"I'm . . . I was just wondering . . ." Natalia intertwines her fingers and bites down on her lip. Her blond curls are neatly tucked into two braids. She's a freshie, one of the newest members of the team, and definitely knows how to work the help-me-I'm-a-baby-deer look.

I sigh and pat a spot on the bench. Natalia totters around the corner, but stops, and stands right in front of me.

"What's up?" I ask.

She twirls one of the braids around her finger. "I can't . . . I can't do back passes."

"Ah."

I grab my stick from behind me and stand next to Natalia. I'm about to place it in her hands when I pause, holding the stick just above her palms. "What did I tell you about the phrase *I can't*?"

Natalia rolls her eyes. "That it always comes with a *yet*," she says in monotone. "But seriously, Evelyn, I've tried so many times on the field. I can't aim anywhere with back passes. And with the Van Darian game coming up next week, I know that I'm going to shoot the ball into the stands or accidentally score a point for Van Darian and everyone's going to hate me and—"

"Whooooa, hold it!" I squeeze Natalia's hands until I feel her pulse settle.

I get why she's freaked out. Van Darian's our fiercest rival in field hockey, mostly because they're the second-best team in the district. It's an all-girls boarding school, and the players have a reputation for taking their repressed sexual energy out on hockey sticks. But they're second-best for a reason. And that reason is us.

I help Natalia take a step away from the benches.

"Like this," I say gently. I reposition the hockey stick in her hands and turn her shoulders at a slight angle. "Now relax."

Natalia goes stiff at the pose, then breathes in and out, softening with each exhalation. Finally I see the connect, the moment when the stick becomes an extension of her own arms. I grab an extra ball from my locker.

"Now try a back pass. Aim for the towel basket."

She nails it on the first swing.

"Yeah!" I pump a fist in the air. Natalia breaks out into a huge grin.

"Oh my gosh, thank you! Thanks, Evelyn! Oh my gosh. Oh my gosh!"

She squeals and throws the stick to me, then skips back around the locker bay. I smile and return to my chest pad.

Another set of footsteps comes squashing around the corner.

"Hey, Katie," I say without looking up.

Katie Lu, center midfielder and my ride-or-die field hockey wife, opens the locker right next to mine. Her towel is tucked around her torso, and her jet-black hair drips water onto the floor. She reaches for her phone and scrolls through.

"Shit," she mutters.

I pull off one of my shoes. "What is it?"

"Shiiiiiiit." Katie throws her head back and slumps onto the bench. "Mr. Figuel doesn't think I should get to play next week."

"What?" I pause at the other shoe and read the email over

Katie's shoulder. "Academic probation? We've only been in school for a month."

Katie looks at me dolefully. "I sort of failed the last three weekly quizzes."

I blow a raspberry and grab the phone from Katie's hand. "All right," I say, already typing. "Here's what we're going to do. We're going to email Mr. Figuel and ask for a retest next Friday."

Katie's eyes go wide. "But—"

I hold up a finger. "Melanie's in advanced calculus. She aced Mr. Fig's class last year."

I hop on the bench and shout over to the showers. "Melanie!"

"What?" Melanie yells back. She sticks her head out of a shower curtain. Soap slips down her copper hair and onto her thick, freckled shoulders.

"Can you tutor Katie next week after practice?" I ask. "She can't play the homecoming game unless she passes a trigonometry test on Friday."

Melanie rolls her eyes and disappears back behind the shower curtain. I grin down at Katie. When it comes to Melanie, *no* means *Hell no* and silence means *Fine, but you're a pain in my ass.* Which is technically still a yes.

Katie takes hold of her phone. "You think this will work?"

"Definitely," I say. "Melanie's a math genius. And as long as Gloria sees that you're trying, she'll make sure you're in the game."

"Thanks, friend." Katie smooshes her head into my shoulder. She pulls back and looks at me. "You smell super sweaty."

"Yeah, and hugging you is like hugging a wet sponge."

She flips her hair into my face and we both laugh.

Katie dresses next to me while I continue to remove the last of my gear. Our teammates leave in twos and threes, drifting out the door until there are only a few of us left.

Just as I get down to an undershirt and shorts, Katie slams her locker closed and slings her bag over a shoulder.

"You seeing Caleb, or you want me to wait?"

"Um . . . no need to wait," I say with a cheesy grin.

Katie smiles.

"Have fun, lovebirds!" she sings as she disappears down the hall.

The door closes and I sigh, then turn for the showers.

The truth is, I'm not meeting Caleb anywhere. He and I don't really hang out beyond breaks at school or the occasional hookup in his truck. But Katie's the type of friend who will talk over the shower curtain the entire time I'm scrubbing down, and let's face it: sometimes getting the sweat and grime off *everywhere* requires a little more privacy than having an incredibly energetic best friend affords.

I latch my stall closed and hang up my towel, praying there's at least a tiny bit of hot water left as I reach for the faucet.

But the water's cold as fuck. As usual.

Goose bumps rise on my arms and legs as I slap soap all over my body. I can hear the few remaining teammates blow-dry their hair, laugh over inside jokes as they get dressed, slam their lockers closed, and burst out the side door. The steady slowness drifts back into the locker room, settling around me.

There's a calm I get from being the very last one out. Some-times it seems like every other member of the team is always spinning around, freaking out over school or practice or flaky boyfriends or clingy girlfriends. But I get to stand in the cen-ter of the hurricane, helping everyone else stay on track. It's nice to have that kind of role on the team. Whenever I'm on the field, or even in the locker room, I know I'm exactly where I'm meant to be. That I'm doing what I'm meant to be doing.

The water finally gets too cold to stand, and I switch the showerhead off. I hang back in the stall, wringing my hair out, when two voices slowly rise from over by the sinks. It's August and Jade, two juniors the rest of the team nicknamed The Twins when they first started back as freshies. Techni-cally they don't look like twins at all. Jade has dark brown skin, whereas August is white, and ridiculously pale. But the two spend so much time together, they might as well be conjoined.

"Did you hear about Van Darian's new forward?" Au-gust asks.

"Oh yeah . . ." Jade's voice trails off. "That's the profes-sional recruit, right?"

I freeze, still halfway hunched under my towel.

Professional recruit?

"Uh-huh," August says. "I heard they got her from the Southwest. Paid her to move here and everything. She's scored every Van Darian goal so far this season."

Jade laughs. "Which is, what, like, three goals?"

"Nine," August says.

My breath hitches.

"Nine goals in four games is insane and you know it," August continues. "We're going to get our asses kicked at our own homecoming."

Jade clicks her tongue. "I don't know. . . . You know how hard-core Evelyn is. Nothing gets past her—she's a wall. Why do you think Gloria gave her that stupid 'No-Goalie' nickname last year at regionals? No one can score against Evelyn when she's on."

"I guess we'll have to see if she's 'on' at the game," August says. I can hear a weirdly amused tone in her voice, as if the thought of me failing the team would somehow, in some universe, be funny.

Their conversation dies down as each girl grabs her bag and heads out.

I do my best to slow my heartbeat, to keep the sudden wave of worry from pounding in my ears and stinging my fingers until each one goes numb. I force myself into a straitjacket of silence, smothering away any fear, any doubt, any feelings at all. It all gets tucked away, down, down, down.

The curtain barely makes a sound as I draw it to one side. I step out from the shower and into a now totally empty locker room. No one's around to ask my help with field hockey passes. No one needs my advice with school. No one has a broken heart, or problems at home, or sadness they can't seem to shake no matter how hard they try.

It's just me.

I catch my reflection in the mirror over the sinks. As goalie, getting in uniform basically means doubling in size. Sometimes it feels like I've multiplied into something bigger than myself. Almost like I'm wearing someone else's body over my own.

But as I look in the mirror now, all I see is a gangly girl with thick-ass wet hair that trails like ropes over her shoulders. I see gray eyes that act more like closed doors than windows into what I'm thinking. I see a teenager who wants to seem as cool and collected as everyone thinks she is, but really, secretly, she plays field hockey like her life depends on it.

Or like someone else's life *did*.

"Nine goals in four games," I say, shaking my head.

Nine goals in four games.

All made by a girl I've never played against. Recruited by the team we *cannot* lose to. The one year it truly matters.

The year when I either make—or break—my promise.

Shit, as Katie would say.

Shiiiiiiiiiiiit.

CHAPTER TWO

There are a million things I love about field hockey, but one of the best parts has got to be the time of year we play. If there's one season to spend every day outside in New England, you can bet your ass it's the fall.

Butter-yellow leaves drip from the sweet birch trees lining Heathclef Prep's central quad. Last week the temperature finally dipped into the high sixties, meaning nearly every person at school dragged the obligatory Ralph Lauren pullovers and L.L.Bean boots from their closets. Ralph Lauren isn't really my thing, but I do have a cool vintage field hockey sweater from the eighties.

Thanks to homecoming week falling within the magical season of hayrides and apple picking, Heathclef's student council has managed to turn collective pumpkin latte obsession into a form of school spirit.

Heathclef Homecoming Mocktails
Handcrafted beverages repping each fall team
Come say "Cheers!"
Monday morning break, central quad

"Cider? Cider!" Katie flaps her arms in the senior commons. "Who the hell decided to pair the football team with the best drink of the season? They never even make state playoffs!"

I close my locker door, cradling a laptop, notebook, and oversized water bottle. "It's a popular drink. They're a popular team. Makes sense to me."

"Says the girlfriend of the quarterback," Katie quips.

I shrug. "What can I say? I like being with the most loved guy on the school's most loved team. Makes me feel like I've won a prize or something."

"Are you calling Caleb a trophy boyfriend?"

"I think that's exactly what I'm calling him," I say, laughing.

The smells of newly mashed apples and caramel syrup swirl through the halls. Students tromp in from the quad, carrying paper cups of frothy golden liquid and foamy milk sprinkled with cinnamon. I try to peer through the glass door leading outside, wondering if Caleb's out there with the others. Meanwhile, Katie goes on about the horrifying mocktail chosen to represent the field hockey team.

"Eggnog!" she yells. "They're fucking with us—they have to be. Eggnog isn't even in the roster of fall! It's a winter drink! Thanksgiving at the very earliest!"

I switch my water bottle to the other arm and lay my hand

11

on Katie's shoulder. "Kay. Breathe. We'll survive this atrocity somehow. Maybe the eggnog thing is supposed to be nice."

"Nice?!" Katie sputters.

"Yeah! Maybe it's a commentary on our predicted long season. Nationals won't be until December."

Katie gives me a pointed look. "All right, smoothie. We both know that's bullshit, but you get partial credit for reasoning."

I grin and reach for the door handle to history class. The room is pretty much empty, so I drop my things on my desk and head to the door. Mr. Mendenhall, my teacher, looks up from his computer.

"Have anything for me, Feltzer?"

I hitch my thumb behind me. "Class doesn't start for another twenty—"

"I'm aware of when class begins. Are *you* aware of your missing assignment on the rise of Industrialism?"

The air squeezes out of my lungs.

I was supposed to get the essay done on Sunday. I knew it was due last week. But the news of Van Darian's recruit sort of pushed everything else off the agenda. Every waking hour last weekend was spent practicing saves in my backyard. I have to beat this new girl come Saturday. I have to be *on*.

"I . . . need more time," I mumble. "With homecoming and everything else—"

Mr. Mendenhall sighs, not bothering to hide the look of reserved disappointment that every teacher at Heathclef seems to have down to an art form.

"Next Monday," he says. He adjusts the thin glasses over

his nose and turns back toward his computer monitor, where I can see he's secretly propped up a well-creased paperback copy of a romance novel.

"Next Monday!" I echo, nodding like a bobblehead. Everything will calm down once we get past Van Darian. I can pull the paper together in a day. I have to.

Katie and I burst outside into the quad. We kick through a pile of dried leaves and wade to the student council table.

"Spiced chai?" A council member in a pink houndstooth blazer gestures to the drinks sign like a game-show hostess.

Katie's eyes bug out as she reads over the menu. "Golf gets to be chai?!" she cries. "Did the *golf* team bring home a giant regionals trophy last year?"

I swing my arm around Katie's middle.

"We'll each take an eggnog," I tell the council member.

A few minutes later, we shuffle through the quad, ducking under the heavy branches of maple trees that haven't yet changed color. We approach a cluster of broad-shouldered letter jackets at the northwest corner. Two of the guys sit on a wooden bench, checking their phones, while four others jostle around over on the grass. I watch the bench guy on the left, waiting to see if he'll look up. He has thick, wavy blond hair and cheeks that bloom pink at the center. His brow crinkles as he scrolls through his phone. I slide onto the edge of the bench, holding out my cup of eggnog so it doesn't spill. My hip juts gently into the boy's side.

"Cheers to winning."

Caleb looks up from his phone. The little crinkle at the top of his nose goes smooth and his pursed mouth opens into an easy smile. He grabs hold of my offering and takes a swig, then quickly blanches.

"Ugh. Eggnog?"

"Official beverage of the field hockey team," I tell him. "Apparently."

Katie ducks her head into her sleeve. "P"—*cough*—"ularity"—*cough*—"test."

Caleb tosses the cup, which I'm pretty sure was still half full of eggnog, over my shoulder. He grips my hips and pulls me onto his lap in one fluid motion.

"Hey!" I say, my breath catching in my throat.

Caleb's hands feel strong and steady against me. I love how easily he can pick me up, whenever he wants, and set me someplace new.

It's weird, because sometimes when I look at his hands, when I feel the lightness of my body against the heaviness of his, I sort of get . . . jealous. Like maybe I wish I was the one swooping someone onto my lap. I get jealous of Caleb a lot, actually. I think jealousy and attraction are sort of meant to sit side by side in that way. Do I wish I could *be* that person, or kiss them until my lips chap? The feelings curl together in my stomach, tangling around each other, making my mouth water with the taste of wanting.

I let Caleb dig his palms into my sides. I catch the swoop of hair just over his forehead and tug it lightly as he leans in to kiss me. His mouth presses into mine, our teeth knocking slightly the way they always do when we're in too much of a rush to aim properly.

After a minute or two, I pull back to gulp some air.

Caleb glances at the strewn cup of eggnog and shakes his head. "Damn. I can't believe they put your game on the same day as ours."

I laugh, but I can't tell if he's joking or not. Of course all the major fall teams play on homecoming. Did Caleb really think the day was entirely about football?

"Maybe you can sneak away for a bit," he offers.

I raise an eyebrow. "You think I can just sneak away from my own goalposts?"

Caleb smiles sheepishly. "I always play better when you're watching."

He pulls me in again, reeling me close. I can feel my body wanting to burrow into his chest. I see the place just above his left collarbone that's a perfect fit for my head. I let myself go to him, inch by inch, until our noses touch, tingling with electricity.

"I think we'll have to settle for celebrating both our wins at the dance," I whisper.

Caleb juts his chin into a pout, but I can tell he's being playful.

"Okay," he says, relenting.

He squeezes my hand once, then pulls his phone out of his pocket, is already back to scrolling through whatever he was reading before I got there.

I pop back up from the bench and loop my arm around Katie's. "Come on. Let's grab seconds before class starts."

We leaf-kick our way back across the quad.

I love how easy it is to be with Caleb—how I can come and surprise him around his friends and then float away, just like that. We hang out with our own people, do our own things, and we still get to make out whenever we want. No drama. No missing each other in between meetups.

Total dream team.

Three periods later, with a stomach full of football-themed cider, I gather my stuff for study hall. Study hall is always the last block of the day, reserved for athletes while everyone else takes phys ed. I slip into my usual chair at the designated field hockey table in the dining hall and pull out my laptop, checking the online dashboard for assignments.

Since I can't be trusted to think about anything other than game strategy most of the time, I've had to develop a system for juggling homework alongside field hockey duties. Every school-related thing gets arranged by due date instead of assigned date, which means I don't have to worry about any assignment unless it's due the next day

I'm always going to be a little behind, of course. There's just no way to stay on top of college prep–level amounts of homework, even in the offseason. But I tend to function best as a student when there's a gigantic flame under my ass forcing me to get math problems and English readings done in one night *or else*.

I need that *or else*.

I click and sort through various notes from teachers. By now I pretty much know which ones are sticklers for due dates and where I can get some wiggle room. An email from Mr. Mendenhall sits unread with the subject heading: *INDUS-TRIALISM ESSAY DUE.*

I hum and drag the message over to my file for next Sunday's homework.

A new email dings in the inbox.

Subject heading: *Duke rep Monday 9/22. 3:00 p.m.*

I gasp. This isn't an email—it's a calendar notification. I could have sworn the rep was coming next week. I look at the clock on my laptop screen. 3:01. *Shit.* I shoot up and bang my knee hard on the table.

"Sorry," I hiss as everyone's stuff tumbles sideways.

I gather my things and stuff them all into my backpack, cramming heavy books on top of loose-leaf pages and knowing I'll regret it all later, much later, but right now I have an entire future to worry about.

I sprint down the main hallway for the college counselor's office. A bulletin board sits to the right of the door, showing off a fresh map of the United States. Over the next seven months, as seniors receive acceptance letters and choose where they'll head off to next year, pins will start to form constellations across the states. By graduation, the entire map will be riddled with holes and decisions. For now, it still looks invitingly smooth. Only a handful of students are applying early decision, and I'm one of them.

It's easy to choose a college when there's always been only one option. It was the only option when I was twelve years old and made the promise, and it's the only option now.

I just have to get in.

Ms. Williams, the college counselor who looks like she's still in college, sits behind her desk. Her hair is braided in a new style, with cornrows crisscrossing from one ear to the other. In one of the two chairs across the desk sits an East Indian woman with a bob of black hair that ends abruptly at her chin. She looks up and smiles politely as I suck down all the air in the room. Ms. Williams glances over my shoulder.

"No dad today?"

I shake my head. "He had to work."

More like I forgot all about this appointment until ten seconds ago, but it doesn't matter. Dad's not really on the college scene. He doesn't need to be. I have things totally under control.

I set my backpack on the floor, trying to slow my heart down. My hand squeezes the life out of the armrest as I lower myself into the chair next to the woman.

"I'm so sorry I'm late," I say. "This meeting is really important to me. Really, really—"

The woman holds her hand up. "Please," she says. "You're fine, Evelyn. Ms. Williams was just telling me about your impressive goal-saving record. I'm Coach Rampal."

"I know!" I say, my voice dangerously on the edge of gushing. "You're amazing—erm, well, an amazing player. And a great coach, I bet. At Duke. At the school I'm trying to . . ." I wave my hands uselessly in front of me.

Coach Rampal laughs. "Yes. Well, that's why I'm here. You know that Duke's field hockey team is nationally ranked. We've been eyeing the number one seat for a few years now, and part of my job is to see that goal through. Your performance on the field is quite impressive, Evelyn. I think you would do well on our team."

My breath hitches. I've imagined this conversation so many times—way too many times—and in every single one of those fantasies, it hasn't gone nearly this well. I'm a perfect fit for Duke's team. Even the coach says so! I try to stop myself from mentally choosing which Duke sweatshirt to order from their online bookstore and show off the rest of the year. Zip-ups are nice, but the logo really pops on the hoodies with front pouch pockets. I remember seeing a pretty blue hoodie with the Blue Devils' *D* come out last week. . . .

"But—"

The royal blue pullover disappears. I blink, trying to focus on the coach. "But?"

Coach Rampal frowns. "Unfortunately, I have only so much say over admissions. I've seen your SAT scores from last spring, and Ms. Williams caught me up with your current standing in class. Duke is an extremely competitive school. We want every student to thrive . . . academically."

Silence trails after the coach, hovering between our chairs. I'm absolutely mortified. The head field hockey coach at Duke—Duke!—came all this way to meet me, and I can't even pull a report card together to make her trip worthwhile.

I sigh into my hands. Getting into college feels like such a trap sometimes. Everyone's always encouraging me to keep going at the things I'm already good at, to spend all my time on the field, getting better and better and better. Then I'm just magically expected to do great in school, too.

"I understand there's a legacy status at play here," Coach Rampal says gently. "And I know you're a hard worker, Evelyn."

Rampal's voice is heart-wrenchingly soft. It twists in my

gut, grating against my organs. I don't want to be talking about the legacy thing. I don't want to be the idiot who only gets into her dream school because someone else earned it for her. I want to earn this on my own.

I clamp my teeth together.

"Which is why I've come here with a possible option for you." The coach picks up a piece of paper from her lap I hadn't noticed before.

"Every year, Duke holds one scholarship for a field hockey player on the winning team at high school nationals," she says. "Heathclef hasn't yet taken home the title, but from what I've seen in your last few seasons, it's only a matter of when. I understand your coach expects you to do well there this year. I'm not allowed to make any promises, of course. But if your team *were* to become eligible for that scholarship, and from what I know of your personal interest in attending Duke . . ."

Coach Rampal lets the sentence go unfinished. She nods once and rises elegantly from her chair. I go to stand after her, then realize I've gripped the armrests so hard that my fingers are now cramped into weird little claws. I pry them off and raise my stiff arm to meet the coach's handshake.

"Well! I'd say this was very helpful." Ms. Williams stands with Coach Rampal and walks her to the door. "I'll be adding this to Miss Feltzer's file. We have our homecoming game this weekend, if you're interested in sticking around the Northeast for a few more days."

"I'm afraid Duke has its own game this weekend," Coach Rampal says. "But I will be attending nationals." She raises her eyebrows at me and smiles. "See you there, Evelyn."

"See you," I wheeze. My voice sounds exactly like the air being let out of a squeaky toy.

The door opens and closes, and then it's just me and Ms. Williams alone in the office. As promised, Ms. Williams tucks the paper from Coach Rampal into a red file marked *FELTZER* in all caps. The paper sits atop a pile of subpar test scores, mediocre grades, and a few depressing recommendations from my teachers about my "winning" attitude in class.

But it also sits on top of the essay I first sent to Heathclef for admissions, the one marked *greatly touching* by the head of the school. It was an essay about my personal hero, which sort of turned into a persuasive argument for how I needed to get to Duke, and all the things I was planning to do there after graduation. I can see the dog-eared essay poking out from the bottom of the stack. I know Ms. Williams can see it too. Which is probably why, when she grabs the red folder, opens the file cabinet drawer, and asks "Would you like to discuss backup options?" we both already know the answer.

"No," I say. "I'm going to Duke."

I grab my backpack and leave before the drawer closes.

CHAPTER THREE

The flame under my ass grows throughout the week.

Over the next four days—the last four days until homecoming—I blow through every mandatory assignment I have during athlete study hall. Unfortunately, one hour isn't nearly long enough to cover the insane amount of homework we get daily at Heathclef. But I'll just have to go a week without finishing every practice problem in math or reading the actual text versus skimming SparkNotes for English. This week, I'm going to have to settle for bare minimum.

I need every spare moment outside of school and practice to get ready for nationals, which means a perfect season, which means this game against Van Darian absolutely cannot go wrong.

Forget a single flame. By the time I make it to Friday, I'm basically sitting on a full-on bonfire.

I've ridden this level of pressure before, of course. Ever since I made The Promise.

Vowing to make it professionally in field hockey obviously comes with some hefty expectations. The tension's always there, lying low most of the time. But then a hard week comes along, and the pressure creeps up and up and up until it's a constant pulse in my shoulder, throbbing and angry. And, okay, yes, the night before a big game my fingertips tingle, my arms go numb, and I usually vomit until I'm dry heaving and clutching a toilet for dear life.

But then game day arrives, and I calmly stand in front of the goal line and let my head float far away where it can watch the whole field at once, and I dominate.

That's how I work.

I pull the chair up to my desk on Friday night and open my notebook halfway in, where I left off taking notes last night. A recorded field hockey game is cued up on the screen: Van Darian versus Honesville. I hold my pencil ready and hit Play.

There isn't a lot of money in sportscasting high school field hockey games, which means the recordings are mostly from shaky phone cameras with the odd aside from a mom asking where she put the giant Ziploc bag of orange slices for after the game. Still, I'm thankful the recordings exist at all. I can narrate the action well enough in my head.

I watch the opening passes as Honesville pings the ball back and forth toward the goal. Every now and then Van Darian intercepts a pass; then Honesville gradually wins back possession. So far, so good. Gameplay as normal.

Then a blur of a person suddenly darts into a pass and scoops the ball up.

"Whoa!" a voice calls from behind the camera.

The blurred player is tiny—all long hair and legs that spin like car wheels. She zips by everyone else as if they're in slow motion. The ball clacks rhythmically against her hockey stick as she dribbles it down the field.

"Alvarez," I whisper.

Rosa Alvarez. The Van Darian hotshot recruit from New Mexico, where apparently amazing field hockey players are being secretly incubated. Over the last four days I've filled page after page with notes on my new, albeit temporary, adversary.

#1: Rosa Alvarez used to play soccer.

Irony of ironies, it turns out that while I was sliding into goalie gear in tenth grade, Van Darian's superstar wasn't even swinging a hockey stick yet. According to an article in her old town's paper, Rosa's sophomore year was spent on the soccer field, playing striker on her high school's varsity team in New Mexico. She was poised to win state as a junior, but a week into the season her whole family up and left when one of her dads was offered a huge pay raise up here in Pennsylvania. I thought articles were supposed to be objective, but you can tell even the journalist was bummed to see Rosa leave. I guess a sophomore striker on varsity was a pretty big deal. Maybe almost as big a deal as being named goalie at fifteen.

#2: Rosa Alvarez didn't try out for field hockey.

Van Darian might have recruited their latest prizewinner, but not over state lines. Thanks to her dad's move, Rosa was already attending the boarding school last fall when their field hockey coach asked her to join the team. They were further in the season by that point; our annual game against them had come and gone. But adding Rosa to the roster shot Van Darian's ranking through the roof in their last month. The school website published a spotlight piece on her in December.

"Soccer Star Shines with Stick," the headline reads, which might be the stupidest alliteration I've ever seen. There's a photo next to the article of Rosa holding a soccer ball under her left arm and gripping a field hockey stick with her right hand. The portrait looks weirdly like some medieval painting of a knight holding a helmet and brandishing a sword. As if one decent season makes someone a damn hero.

#3: Rosa Alvarez is an Aries.

Okay, so maybe no direct source confirms this. But Rosa's Instagram account—which is mostly a collection of laughing friends and family members squeezed into every last millimeter of the 1:1 frame—has a photo of her in front of a glowing cake last April. Plus, I could guess that Rosa's an Aries from her field play alone. Most field hockey players watch and wait for openings before diving in to intercept the ball. But Rosa never waits. She runs before the opening. And if that isn't Aries behavior, then I don't know what is.

#4: Rosa Alvarez shoots left.
#5: Rosa Alvarez hits with ridiculous accuracy.
#6: Rosa Alvarez has stupidly pretty brown hair that looks like gold in the sun.
#7: Rosa Alvarez fakes passes.

I return to the video and watch as Rosa slides up and down the field. She's playing the game in a totally different form than I've ever seen it played. *She's* different. As she darts and spins and pounds her stick into the grass, the rest of the field starts to lose focus. She's this force, this brightness that pulls attention away like a magic trick. Like people have no choice but to stare, open-mouthed, at her.

I return to the note about her hair glinting in the sunlight. *Diversion tactic??* I scribble along the side.

As I scan the pages, I start to realize that every field hockey note I've taken this week has only been about Rosa. There's nothing in here about Van Darian's coach, or their team's goalie, or even wind patterns projected for Saturday. But I've played against Van Darian's goalie before. I know their coach. I can play in wind or rain or hail. Alvarez is the unknown factor. She's the one I need to beat to make the big plans happen.

A knuckle raps on the other side of my door.

"Coming," I call. I pause the Van Darian versus Honesville game and get up from my desk.

I'm hoping it's Dad asking what we want to order in for dinner tonight. But when I open the door, I see Seth standing in the hall.

Seth's my older brother. He's a college senior over in Boston and comes home every now and then to build random stuff in the shed with Dad, or whatever silly dude-bonding thing they have going on at the moment.

Seth's dressed in his usual combination of tailored button-up shirt, jeans rolled at the ankles, and styled curly hair. He only came out and changed his name a few years ago, but with the way Seth carries himself, it's like he's been a suave ladies' man his whole life. Well, technically, he *has* been.

"Got a hot date?" I ask.

"I might," Seth says slyly. He pushes a section of hair from his forehead. "You never know. I heard Mrs. Pellington next door was looking for a square-dance partner."

I cock my head. "Isn't she ninety-something?"

"Yeah, but rumor has it she dances like a spry sixty," Seth says, wiggling his eyebrows.

We both instinctively laugh into our hands, our go-to move when we were little and supposed to be sleeping instead of making fart noises at each other across the hall.

The laughter dies down, and I try to disappear back into my room. But Seth leans against my doorframe.

"You're the one who should be out on a date," he says. "Why are you home?"

I look around. "Because I . . . live here?"

"Eve. Come on." Seth sighs heavily through his nose. "Home-coming's tomorrow."

"Right. As in not today." I wave vaguely inside my room. "I've got the dress and everything, don't worry."

I start to close the door.

"That means Heathclef is doing skits tonight!" Seth says. "And s'mores. And running around campus like drunken idiots. Okay, maybe the school doesn't officially sanction that last one, but it's practically a rite of passage! You have to get over there."

He ducks under my arm into the room. I immediately reach after him. "Wait!"

"Whooooa. What's all this?" Seth picks up my notes on Rosa. I quickly snatch the notebook and shove it under my arm.

"I have to be ready," I say. I swallow and set the notebook, now deliberately closed, back down. "One of our biggest games is tomorrow, and there's a new player at Van Darian who's been scoring an insane number of goals, and I have to make sure we get to finals or else I won't get this Duke scholarship, and . . ."

I trail off as it becomes apparent that Seth isn't actually listening to me anymore. Instead, he's looking around my room, taking in the slightly grainy framed photographs and old hockey medals dangling from hooks. He picks up the cuff on my vintage field hockey sweater, squeezing it gently for a moment before letting it drape over the bed frame again. He turns back to me, eyebrows raised.

"Sorry it's a mess," I say, shrugging.

I push my chair back in to my desk, then grab the sweater, along with the other clothes littered around my floor, and shove them into my hamper. My bed is beyond help, but I pull one corner of the quilt taut anyway.

Seth shakes his head. "I can't believe you still have all this shit up."

"What are you talking about?" I do my best to feign nonchalance as I wipe some dust from one edge of the bookshelf.

But Seth won't take the hint. "You don't have to keep all her junk out here anymore."

I stop and look at him. "It's not junk. This is my stuff."

Seth tilts his chin, his eyes deep and fixed.

"Eve, come on. You're a senior now. You're supposed to be your own person. That's like the definition of a seventeen-year-old. Latin root: dead opposite of the person your parents want you to be." He pulls the blue pennant from my shelf and faces it toward me. The word *Duke* is screen-printed over the skinny triangle flag.

"You don't have to keep pretending to be Mom."

I stare down at the floor, my cheeks burning. It must be so easy for him to take a quick glance at the million little pieces that make up my life and reduce them to something as simple as playing copycat. But Seth doesn't understand. *He* wasn't there at the very end. He was off hiding in his room, pounding Rage Against the Machine songs at the walls like he was the only one in the family whose life was falling apart. He didn't have to hold Mom's hands and feel her pulse fading and promise her, swear-on-his-life promise, that he would keep going for the both of them.

I have to go to Duke and play all four years. I have to at least try to make it pro, the way Mom always wanted to. It's the one thing she asked for.

Dad gets it. He never questions any of the shit I'm doing. But then Seth comes along every few months and acts all high-and-mighty just because he gets to have a blank slate and do whatever he wants. He doesn't know what it's like to carry someone else's dreams on top of his own.

I press my lips tight and take the college pennant out of Seth's hands.

"You have no idea who I am," I say flatly.

I arrange the flag on the shelf over my desk where it belongs and sit back down in front of my computer.

Seth doesn't move from where he's standing. I feel his palm settle over the top of my head. I used to love that when I was younger. It was his way of protecting me, of keeping me tucked under his wing. But these days I'm basically as tall as he is.

"I *do* know you deserve to have your life to yourself," Seth says from behind me. "Not be some wish fulfillment for someone else."

A voice inside my head—the one I've kept safe for the last six years—screams, as if in pain. I jerk away from Seth's hand and look up at him.

"Get out," I say. "Right now."

Seth looks at me sadly. I get the sudden urge to pinch him, just to rip that pitying look off his face. Finally, he backs away toward the hall. My door closes with a small click.

Good, I think. *Back to work.*

I open my notebook and pull up another game recording. Seth's words get shoved right out of the room with him. I don't have time to think about any of that. I'm in a hurry. There are only a few hours until the game, and even fewer hours until my regularly scheduled breakdown begins.

I have to make the time left count.

CHAPTER FOUR

Our hands vibrate as the team's crisscrossed web of hockey sticks pulses together.

Clackclackclackclackclackclackclack.

It's the kind of noise that drives you nuts unless you surrender yourself to it completely, letting it fill you up from your fingertips to your toes. A lot of people think starting huddles are this childish touchy-feely hug thing, but done right, they're the last big jolt of energy before hitting the field. Each person on the team pours every ounce of energy they have into the circle, then gets it back twice over.

Katie arches her eyebrows across the way, and I nod. We start the chant, call-and-response style.

"Right, left—"

"*Sweep it under!*"

"Right, left—"

"*Bring the thunder!*"

"Right, left! Right, left! Who are we?"

"HEATHCLEF!"

We tap sticks once low, then high in the air. I choke the handle of my stick and hold it close to me.

Time for another one.

The team turns from the huddle and disperses across the field. We'll have first possession, which means our forwards and midfielders need their own moment to strategize starting plays. I stretch my arms overhead and survey the spectators gathering in the stands.

Most weekends, field hockey doesn't pull much of a crowd. I try to get Caleb to bring his football buddies when he can, but we're lucky to get even a handful of moms and bored younger siblings who keep their eyes firmly on their phones, almost as if to prove we're so much less interesting to look at than a gaggle of grandmas dancing in sync to Rihanna.

But on homecoming weekend, everything changes.

I watch as families cram into the stands, jostling over each other while holding hot coffee and doughnuts carefully cradled in wax paper. Nearly everyone is decked out in Heathclef's colors of gold and purple. I wish I could say that homecoming shakes some sense into all our classmates and they realize that field hockey really is the most kickass sport in the fall lineup. That doesn't actually happen, but the truth is almost as good.

What happens, really, is that tons of Heathclef field hockey alums show up. They must make a pact when they graduate or something. I can see a group of girls in their twenties clustered on the benches. A few scattered couples snuggle close.

Moms tote babies on their hips and chase little kids up and down the stairs. Old ladies giggle and point at different parts on the field, probably finding their old positions. I see a mom laughing with her daughter, both wearing matching Heathclef sweaters even though the girl can't be older than eleven. I swallow and turn away.

"Evie!"

Dad bounds from the sidelines toward me, holding out his arms for a hug even though he's still at least thirty yards away. Back when he was in high school, he had thick hair that swooped over his forehead like the perfect squirt of toothpaste in a commercial. These days the swoop has turned into more of a thinning flap, even though he styles it exactly the same way he did back at his own homecoming dance with Mom.

One of my favorite things to do with Dad on a lazy Sunday afternoon is throw all the pillows on the living room floor and pore over his and Mom's high school yearbooks. Prom king and queen. Male and female athletes of the year. Dad loves looking at old pictures of them together nearly as much as I do. We burn through their nostalgia like a candle.

"Hey, Dad." I give him an awkward hug in all my goalie gear. "I'm surprised you're not with your brethren across campus."

Dad furrows his brow. "Do I look like the kind of dad who would miss the chance to see his baby girl in action?"

I smile. "No, but you *do* look like a football alum who's missing his own game."

Dad shakes his head, but I can tell that a part of him really does want to catch up with his old teammates and cheer on Caleb and the others over on the main east field. He won't take off, though, not even when we're down to the final minutes and everyone knows we have the game in the bag. He thinks I look at him like a stand-in for Mom, that if I search through the bleachers and find him and Seth, it will be like she's there too. But my dad and brother taking up room on the bench doesn't fill in the empty space beside them.

The referee blows the whistle for positions before the initial center pass.

"Good luck, kiddo," Dad says. He squeezes my shoulder and lumbers off the field. Seth waves to me as Dad catches up to him, and together they go off to find seats.

I take a deep breath, enjoying the sting of morning chill, and jog over to the North Chamber.

I've named both goals on our field. North side is unofficially the North Chamber, and the south side is the South Wing. I'll be cozying up to North first, then switching to South in the second half—but I'd like to think that from start to finish, the whole field belongs to me.

The field is your house. Protect the house.

Mom's advice echoes in my head like an omniscient narrator.

I close my eyes, and with my next step, her voice spools out of memory and becomes something whole and complete. There she is, standing a few yards away. Her hair is knotted into the perfect messy bun centered at the top of her head. Her arms are folded over her field hockey jersey. And I'm there too, barely up to her chest in height and trying my best not to fall over as I wobble in her old goalie padding.

"How can a field be a house?" I ask, my voice high and uncertain. I'm only in fourth grade, trying to charge my way through growing up as fast as humanly possible so I can leapfrog right into high school and play field hockey just like Mom.

She exhales, her breath curling in the cold.

"It's not literal," she says. "The problem is your focus. I saw the way you flinched on that last hit."

My cheeks burn behind the caged helmet.

"I didn't flinch."

"It's all right," Mom says, her voice soft, forgiving. "I was the same way. Everyone is when they start out, and a lot of goal-keepers never get past it. A ball comes flying and you want to swat it away so it doesn't hurt *you*. But check this out."

Mom pokes me hard in the chest, her finger digging into my padding.

"Did that hurt?"

I shake my head.

"Exactly," she says. "Because you're made to protect the house. The ball isn't going to hurt if it knocks you. But if it knocks that precious space behind you, it hurts the team. That's what being a goalkeeper is about. You have to be a wall."

I blink and glance at the slivers between my pads.

"But goalkeepers do get hurt, don't they? They get bruises all the time."

Mom smiles. "Walls get scratches and chips, but they

don't fall down. I know you're strong, Eve. You'll protect the things that need protecting."

Her hand falls over my shoulder, and I can feel the warmth from each finger radiate all the way down past skin and blood and bones.

My eyes pop open and she's gone again, but the warm lines of her fingers still sizzle on my skin. I smile and nod at the dingy white netting in front of me.

"Morning," I say to the goalposts.

I know Mom told me not to get too literal with the house analogy, but I can't help what makes me play better come game day. As my teammates line up across the field, I go through the usual mental practice of moving in and unpacking my boxes. All my favorite things come out one by one, then perch on top of the invisible shelves within the goal box. Pictures of Mom in school. Old awards. All my irreplaceable mementos. Up they go behind me, where I'll have to keep them safe.

"I'm a wall," I whisper. Unpassable.

Even if it is mostly Mom's strength propping me up from the inside.

The referee blows the starting whistle. I crouch and stare across the field.

Since Heathclef has first possession, my teammates will have the other goalie cornered, at least for a little while. That gives me plenty of time to settle in and get cozy. By the time the ball makes its way to me, I've already sized up each player, studying their gait, their swing, the way they wear their hair or rock their hips from side to side while waiting for a pass. Anything that could be useful.

From what I can see, we're doing a pretty good job at keeping the pressure on. The ball bounces back and forth within Van Darian's striking circle like a pinball machine. The other goalie lunges across the South Wing with every pass. She's getting tired already. Not much longer before we break her in.

As if on cue, Natalia makes a perfect back pass and Melanie slams the ball into the net. A shrill whistle cuts through the air.

"Woooo!" Katie pumps her arm and twists to throw me a grin.

"Yes!" I say, raising my gloved arm like I'm making a toast.

I watch as Van Darian's goalie angrily hooks the ball out from the goal box. Now that we've scored, I know the action on the field is about to make a hard turn onto me.

I knock the heel of my hockey stick into the ground twice and watch the pack approach. At first, it's all a bunch of ponytails and braids in varying shades of brown and blond, and I can't tell any of the Van Darians apart in their green polyester skorts.

Then one girl suddenly jets out in front of the others, and I know exactly who she is.

Field hockey teams usually move with precision. We're pack animals, like wolves. We don't go anywhere without a carefully coordinated plan.

But Rosa's a freaking unicorn. She's already made a name for herself by crashing right through plans.

She yells something to one of her teammates, revealing flashes of her matching green mouth guard, and signals to the left. Luckily, I've already seen Rosa pull that fake-out play, two weeks ago against Honesville. I don't move from my stance.

Van Darian juggles the ball back and forth as they sail down the pitch. But I keep my eyes trained on Rosa. She's the team's shooter—they've made it obvious by now. It's almost stupid to think I'll turn my attention to anyone else.

Rosa jumps into the striking circle and whacks the ball to another forward on Van Darian. She keeps passing, trying to trick me into looking away. I watch her sigh heavily enough to blow her bangs up in frustration. The gesture would be cute if my entire reputation as No-Goalie didn't hinge on this game.

"Come on," I murmur, my voice low and gravelly.

I've put in countless hours practicing every possible lunge and kneel and spread across the goal box. I know how to stay a second ahead of the ball, how to read the girls' faces to know where they want to send it. When they come into my house, I'm the one who knows every corner and angle. I'm ready for everything Van Darian's got.

Rosa has the ball again. She slides it forward and runs full speed across the circle. I see her look up repeatedly at me, checking for an opening. But I'm locked in on her. All my focus is dead set on the ball, and Rosa's hockey stick, and—

A tattoo?

I blink and shake my head slightly. That can't be a tattoo. Everyone I know with tattoos at school gets them on their arms or shoulders, someplace they can show off exactly how cool they are or how much money they have, or the way needles don't scare them at all. But the two curving lines trailing down this girl's thigh don't show off anything. They're all mystery, winding up farther under her clothes where no one else is ever going to see what she decided to get inked.

Rosa changes directions and runs back toward me again. I can tell the two curves are earrings now. And there's a neck too, stretching up and proud, and a chin barely peeking from the top of her thigh—

The referee's whistle shrieks like an alarm.

"Goal!" somebody yells.

Every other noise suddenly goes quiet.

My brain swerves and recoils, trying to back up, start again, press Undo. Whoever yelled out was wrong. They have to be wrong. I don't miss saves. I'm always watching, always ready. Rosa hadn't even shot yet. She didn't . . .

Oh God.

My stomach drops like lead as I turn to see the small field hockey ball gathered in the net behind me. I didn't even try to stop it. I must've been standing there like a zombie idiot.

Rosa's hugging and high-fiving the two other Van Darian forwards in the circle. I shake my head. This isn't happening. It was a second—literally a split second. I was watching her the whole time. My feet drag horribly, and I feel every ounce of the forty pounds of gear as I fish the ball out from behind me.

Katie's already smacking another ball in from the sidelines.

Usually we catch eyes in the game and nod to keep each other going. But she doesn't turn my way at all. The three Heathclef defenders do, though. Before jogging away, they look over at me like I've just walked onto the field wearing a catsuit and heels. They look at me like they don't even know who I am.

And right now, I don't know who I am either.

CHAPTER FIVE

"Eve? Eve! I know you're not showering in there. You never even turned on the water."

"Hmph." I squirm to one side and stuff another marshmallow in my mouth. "Gro awwy."

The handle on the bathroom jiggles back and forth.

"You know I know how to get in there, right?" Seth calls. I hear something small scrape the other side of the wall. "Aha! Mom's quarter is still over the doorframe."

The narrow crevice in the doorknob slowly turns from horizontal to vertical. I swallow my marshmallow and sit up a bit higher.

"I could be naked in here! You really want to see your sister naked?"

Seth sighs as he presses the door open. "You're not naked."

He marches over and jerks the shower curtain the rest of the way back in one violent motion.

"Jesus Christ, half your padding's still on!"

I clutch my bag of marshmallows and watch Seth drop onto his knees and push his sleeves back like he's about to deliver a baby.

"All right, up you go."

"No!" I fold my arms and curl as much into myself as is possible while decked in shoulder pads. Seth reaches for my side and I shift the other way. "Leave me alone!"

He rocks back onto his haunches, clearly annoyed.

"It's one game, Evelyn. You think Mom didn't lose one game?"

"Wrong," I say, and now I grunt and heave and push myself so I'm sitting all the way up. "It's not one game. It was *the* fucking game. Senior year. Homecoming. Us versus Van Darian. Nationals qualification. It was the one game I needed to dominate, and instead I got my ass handed to me by a goddamned SOCCER PLAYER!"

I grab the shower curtain and yank it closed so hard that for a second I'm afraid the whole rod will come down on top of me. But it doesn't, and instead the light from the bathroom softly dims as I remember everything from this morning.

I've seen it happen in games before. The veteran player—the one who never missteps on the field—suddenly makes a stupid mistake out of nowhere. And then another one. And another one, again and again, until the game is shot to hell and they're slouching off the field with their head so heavy their chin is practically glued to their chest.

"Psych out," Dad always murmurs when he sees it while watching football. As if that explains everything.

But blaming an entire game's performance on being "psyched out" is a non-explanation. Obviously the player got psyched out. The deeper question is: what the hell short-circuited in their brain that kept them from getting their shit together?

I suck on the question and close my eyes, seeing myself on the field pulling ball after ball from my goal box. Rosa scores on me so many times that it must look like she's been given endless access to free hits. Meanwhile, all the invisible precious things I've lined up behind me get smashed with every goal. My framed photos of Mom shatter. Her old medals tumble and sink into the mud. Everything I was supposed to protect breaks.

And how do I even explain it? I got tricked by a stupid tattoo the first time, and then what? Every other high school senior has some idiotic tattoo. I knew this by the time Rosa came rushing down the field at me again. I should've been ready.

The second time around, I wasn't even looking at her legs. I was following her swing, step by step, watching her field hockey stick as it shifted back and forth, getting ready for her shot.

Then I noticed the engraving.

There was something carved into the shaft of her stick. I could barely make out the words, but that wasn't what concerned me. Nobody writes on their gear—and field hockey sticks are supposed to be team-issued. Why would this girl carry around something so unique? What did it say? I thought that, at the very least, maybe I'd be able to report it. I could wave down the referee or something.

The whistle sounded before I could call out.

The ball sank into the net as if in slow motion.

The next time it was the bright coral color on her nails. Then the shimmery ribbon she braided through her dark hair. I was running out of places to look. On the last play, I stayed trained on the ball—just the ball. Until Rosa flipped it in front of her and added the cherry on top of the morning's shit sundae: the soccer-player-turned-field-hockey-virtuoso actually *winked* at me before she made her last shot.

By that time, no one on Heathclef seemed to acknowledge I existed. I fished out the last ball and knocked it to the sidelines. If I had tried looking at Gloria, I probably would have seen her rolling back and forth in the fetal position, cursing herself and all the field hockey gods for not thinking to train a backup goalkeeper. I didn't look at her. I didn't look at the scoreboard, which announced to everyone that Van Darian had just soundly beaten us six to two. Rosa literally made a double hat trick in one game. I didn't even think a double hat trick was possible in field hockey. And yet, here we are.

I didn't look at Katie, or my dad, or any of the Heathclef alums I had just let down. And I especially didn't look at the empty space next to Dad. I dragged my ass off the field and straight home into my bathtub. I don't even know when I managed to look up enough to grab the marshmallows from the pantry.

Seth rips the curtain open again.

"Stop feeling sorry for yourself," he orders. "You're not an idiot—you know it doesn't matter if you lost by one point or fifty. It was one game, one loss on the record, which means it doesn't disqualify you from shit."

I grunt and glare at him, but he seems entirely unfazed by the lump of sweat staring daggers over a bag of marshmallows.

"It's the dance, and you promised you were going. Now, get up and take off your gear or I'll just start the shower on you."

"I'm not going anymore," I grumble.

Seth gives me what looks like a sympathetic nod, opens his mouth—probably to give me a sweet pep talk—then thinks better of it and cranks the shower on full blast.

The windows of the Heathclef music building rattle and shiver as the bass pumps through the hall. I march to the check-in table, right up to Ms. Williams, who seems tragically unaware of the morning's screaming failure. Either that or she's doing a hell of a job pretending not to know about our game.

"Evelyn! You look stunning!" she says, gesturing to my floor-length navy dress. "Where's the posse?"

I look over my shoulder, as if Katie and my other teammates were there only seconds ago.

"Um. We came separately," I say.

Ms. Williams nods. "The group limo thing is completely overrated," she confides. "I've been in them enough times. Way too sticky."

I have approximately zero interest in finding out what sort of stickiness Ms. Williams is referring to. I scrunch up my face and try to move past the table, but she stops me with a fan of five playing cards, all held face down.

"Pick one," she tells me.

"What?"

"For the Breathalyzer. It's a random check. Pick one."

I hesitate a moment, which is especially stupid considering the only thing I'm currently drunk on is self-pity, then draw the queen of spades from her hand.

"Not this time," she chirps. "In you go. I think Caleb's already inside."

I don't wait for another nanosecond of small talk before pushing my way through the foyer and into the main music hall.

The entire Heathclef student body has melded into one blobby form, undulating and grinding to last year's trap music. I see arms waving and hips shifting at every angle, and for a second the blob looks so complete and whole that I'm positive there's no room for me and I want to turn around and race back home to the bathtub, or, better yet, my bed. Then someone tall and confident breaks from the formation and strides toward me, capturing my hand in his.

"You came," Caleb says.

His voice tilts in surprise, and I'm hit with a tidal wave of embarrassment. He knows—of course he knows—about this morning. Without a word, I turn and lead Caleb back onto the dance floor. We disappear into the bodies, but it's not enough. I want to disappear entirely.

Caleb's palms slide over my dress, carving out the dip of my waist and the curve of my hips. I turn and press my back into his chest. His breath comes urgent in my ear as he leans in to me.

"You're so hot," he says.

The words seem to slide past, like they know I'm not really the person Caleb thinks he's holding. I'm not the hot, sexy girlfriend of the quarterback that he wants. I'm just a shitty goalkeeper who let a freaking thigh tattoo torpedo her entire senior season.

But I grab hold of the compliment anyway, stretching it over me like a dress that's too tight. I want to be hot. I want to forget I've ever been anything but hot. I arch my back and let my body dig deeper into Caleb's hips. He moans softly, and that plus the thumping music are the only sounds I want to hear ever again.

We dance to the next five songs—jumping and shaking together, but mostly grinding and twisting and sweating until our hair is slicked back and our breath is heavy. A slow song comes on next. Caleb reaches for my hand, but instead of letting him pull me into another dance, I go on tiptoe and press my mouth onto his, parting his lips open with mine. My tongue taps the edge of his and he moans into me again. I feel the mass of his hands over my back, gripping the parts of my dress that have puckered at my thighs.

What the hell, I think. *Who cares if someone sees. Who cares if we get told off by a teacher. I don't care about anything anymore.*

My eyes are still closed, lips still open, taking Caleb in. I can smell his aftershave and feel the thickness of his shoulders. I can hear the way he almost growls when he wants me. I can see the way she winks at me when—

"Are you okay?" Caleb asks.

I suddenly realize I've pulled away.

"Oh, yeah," I say. I lean in again and kiss him hard enough to block out the image of a tiny, dark-haired field hockey player.

It works for maybe ten seconds.

"Dammit," I whisper.

Caleb drops the fabric of my dress. "You still upset about the game?"

I wince. I don't want to talk about any part of the game from this morning. But I especially don't want to acknowledge the girl-shaped piece of it that I can't seem to shake from my head.

The song changes and the strobe starts back up, turning the gym floor back into a blur of flickering light and gyrating bodies.

"I just want to dance!" I yell out.

Caleb seems happy enough to exchange making out for grinding. He grips my hips against him and I try to focus on some corner of the room, some group dancing or detail in the decorations, anything to get my bearings. But no matter where I turn, I only see the same person, the same wicked grin, that same wink over and over and over.

CHAPTER SIX

The next week, I show up for school armed with oversized sunglasses, a shitty paper on the Industrial Revolution, and shame wafting all around me.

"Hangover?" Mr. Mendenhall asks sarcastically as I hand in my paper. He doesn't look up from his computer.

"I wish," I say.

I slink down into my usual seat near the back and bury my head in my textbook. I know I can't go on hiding from the world forever. But maybe I can fake some memory loss to get me to winter break.

After history, the halls slosh with a sea of students and backpacks. I'm hoping that maybe if I show up to all my classes early and stay late every day for the next month or two then I'll only have to squeeze through the rest of the campus during the passing period rush hour. That way I won't have to talk to anyone.

Katie suddenly grabs the edge of my shirt.

"Hey!" she says, and I flinch because even the word sort of feels like a punch.

"Oh, hi," I say meekly. I stare down at my shoes. I can't imagine how pissed off she is about the game. Cannot imagine.

"You're avoiding me."

"Am I?"

Katie presses on her fingertips. "I called your name at the dance on Saturday, which you soundly ignored as you grinded the ever-loving fuck out of your boyfriend. Then your phone was off all day yesterday. And just now you tried to push past me like I was an actual door. What the hell?"

My toes flex up and down as I chew on my thoughts. I was never going to be able to avoid Katie forever. I may as well let her hand me my ass so we can move on.

I look up and sigh.

"I messed up, okay? I ruined the team's chances this season, and it's our last season together, and I didn't want to face that by seeing you. I feel like shit already, but you deserve to air out your problems with me too. So let's have it. Tell me what an absolute loser I am."

Katie blinks at me for a moment. I'm guessing she's trying to choose her insults wisely. We only have fifty minutes of lunch period, which means she'll need to dig deep for her best material if she's going to give me the tongue-lashing I deserve.

She opens her mouth to speak and I'm ready to hear it, but then she closes it again and grabs my hand instead.

"Where are we going?" I ask.

"The field," she says over her shoulder.

Oh God, she's probably staged the whole team there, waiting for me. Here we go.

Except when we get to the field, there's not a whole team of people armed with overripe tomatoes and blackened bananas. There's just Katie and me and the unbearable sight of the goal boxes. Katie frog-marches us to the arch of the South Wing. She lets go of me then, plopping down on the grass. I watch as Katie digs through her backpack, takes out a flat plastic tub, and produces two sandwich halves from inside.

"Here." Katie sticks one triangle of peanut butter and jelly in my hand.

"Is it poisoned?" I ask.

Katie snorts but doesn't really smile. She takes a large bite out of her half of the sandwich. After a moment, I sit next to her and do the same.

"You didn't ruin our chances this season," Katie says finally. "Van Darian was ridiculously good. That probably means they were our toughest game in the region." She gives me a pointed look. "You don't lose games normally, Eve. You know that."

I can't tell if she's trying to make me feel better or worse.

"I know," I echo.

"But what sucks is that you didn't come to me, or to any of us. You didn't even come change out with us. Don't you think we *all* had a tough game? Don't you think we needed our captain?"

I wince. I hadn't thought of this, not really.

"It was just a game," Katie says, eyes down on her sandwich. "Everyone knows it's not the end of the world. But walking off that field alone sucked ass. We needed you." Her voice gets quiet. "I needed my best friend."

I shrink into myself. "I'm sorry. I . . . I didn't know how to talk about it. I was so embarrassed."

"Embarrassed of what?"

My skin starts to go hot. How am I supposed to explain the weirdness about Rosa? It would sound crazy. It is crazy! I wouldn't expect anyone else to understand something I can't even understand myself.

Katie moves closer to me.

"It's that girl, isn't it?" she asks.

I nearly jump. "What?"

"The Van Darian forward. I saw the way she teased you during the game. She was a complete ass about the whole thing. The team talked about it when we were in the locker room after. She was trying to mess with you, nonstop. The entire game."

My mouth hangs open. I'm so filled with relief that I don't know what to say.

"You saw it too?"

"Uh-huh," Katie says, swallowing another bite. "We all did. She was definitely playing mind-fuck games with you. She must do it on every goalkeeper."

This thought hadn't occurred to me before, and for some reason it makes me incredibly pissed off. The girl was playing dirty. She wasn't just focusing on the ball and passing and aiming. She was focused on making me look bad. On *my* homecoming. And it worked like a charm.

"I thought that I was crazy," I say. "Like, I was afraid you would think I was obsessed with her or something."

Katie shakes her head, and this time she finally smiles at me.

"Girl, I know you better than that. Your eye is always on the top prize. And we're still going to get there," she adds. "We'll wipe the field with everyone else and it will still be us at nationals. I know it."

I grin back at Katie and cheers her with my half of the sandwich. Thank God I have the best hype woman ever for a friend.

By the time practice rolls around later in the afternoon, I feel solid enough to show my face to the rest of the team. Of course I don't expect anyone else to be as nice as Katie—she is my best friend, after all. But when I walk into the locker room, nearly everyone gives me a nod or a supportive shoulder nudge.

"Hey, Feltzer."

"There's our captain."

I catch eyes with Katie and she widens hers a little, as if to say *See? I told you we all get it.* The more I look around the room and take in my teammates, the more it hits me that Saturday's game was hard on everyone. I shouldn't have run off like that. I thought I had singlehandedly torpedoed our own homecoming. But it turns out Miss "Soccer Star Shines with Stick" was the real reason behind the loss.

I find Gloria scribbling over her clipboard in the hall outside the locker room. I've seen her like this before. She's planning our next gameplay, checking all our positions on the field, looking for weak spots. I fight the thought that she's specifically looking for goalie replacements as I approach her in my gear.

"Hey, Coach," I say gruffly.

Gloria doesn't look up. "Feltzer."

My eyes briefly slink over to the paper under her pencil.

"I, uh. I wanted to apologize. About last weekend's game."

"Apologize for what?" Gloria says without any hint of a question.

She keeps scribbling. I just *know* she's swapping my teammates' positions into defense, pulling them over the field, closer and closer to my goal box. She's probably figuring I can't seem to hold the fort down on my own anymore. I imagine her going over the roster, finding people taller than me, stronger than me, braver than me. I see her yanking me right out of Mom's dream, all because one Van Darian girl made me look bad.

I start sweating under the padding. Gloria has to know she can still count on me. She has to understand that last weekend was a one-time fluke.

"I'm sorry about Alvarez," I blurt.

Gloria stops writing. She blinks at me. "Who?"

"Rosa. Alvarez. The girl with the . . ." I trail off, thinking of Rosa's tattoo, her braids, the megawatt smile under her mouth guard. I shake the images loose from my brain.

"Van Darian's forward," I say, clarifying. "I'm sorry I let her—well, she was messing with me the whole game."

Gloria furrows her brow. She squints at me, looking either confused or disappointed, or, knowing Gloria, both.

"You're telling me we lost . . . because a girl was messing with you?"

"Yes!" I say. Thank God, Gloria gets it. "Yes, exactly. But that's never going to happen again. It was a super random, super stupid thing. And it's completely over now. And I have the goal box covered. Completely covered! So everyone can play their normal positions, yeah? Because I don't want to be the reason Katie gets pushed to defense and—"

Gloria tucks her clipboard under her arm. "You're rambling, Feltzer. I'm not making anyone change positions. Not yet, at least. You got knocked on your ass last weekend. Show me you can get back up."

She doesn't have to tell me twice.

I nod and head toward the main doors as Katie and Melanie slip out of the locker room and catch up on either side. Katie eyes Gloria and turns to me.

"Everything good?" she whispers.

I half nod. "Yeah. But the sooner she forgets about the Van Darian game, the better."

We press open the gymnasium doors and trail out into the haze of low afternoon sun. For home games, the team plays on the south field, with rows of stands and even a little refreshment cart in the corner that sells gigantic pickles and over-salted popcorn. But for practice, we're relegated to the lower west green.

Unlike the pristine, even grass on the game field, the lower green is filled with random dips and unkempt mounds of wild meadow grass. It's surrounded by haunted-looking trees on one side, a chain-link fence on the other, and spider-infested hedges in between. Gloria's tried switching us a million times, has put in a million complaints about potential injuries, but every year Heathclef admin shrugs and points us down the same hill. Personally, I don't mind the practice field so much. Between the dips and the spiders, we *have* to stay focused and in the moment.

Katie and Melanie link arms and skip down the path past the science building.

"Since when did you two become obsessed with each other?" I call out.

Melanie whips her head around. "You're the one who paired us up for math tutoring."

"Oh yeah." I rub my neck. "Dang. That was me."

I hold out a finger in warning. "But I'm still the captain, and I'm telling you, Mel, Katie's mine. Trust me, you don't want her for a best friend. She falls asleep thirty minutes into every movie. She steals all the red and purple Skittles. She's bad news."

Katie grins and sticks her tongue out at me.

I laugh as I tromp down the hill behind them. The rest of the team filters out of the gym and fills the pathway. Our sticks knock into the pavement every few steps. We're like water rapids rushing down and down. It's impossible not to get swept up in the team energy.

I start our chant.

"Right, left—"

"*Sweep it under!*"

"Right, left—"

"*Bring the thunder!*"

My teammates wave their hockey sticks high in the air with each response. They pass me by on either side, running as I waddle, taking off to the field like they're desperate to prove themselves, to start the season over again. They're shouldering my loss, I realize.

I don't deserve this team.

My chest swells with an unholy amount of pride as I watch my friends disappear behind the bend, past the line of spooky trees separating us from the rest of the school. I cup my hand over my mouth and call out the final line.

"Right, left! Right, left! Who are we?"

No one answers.

I stare ahead at the last few yards of empty path.

"Who are we?" I yell again, this time sounding a little uncertain.

I swing around the corner.

The team stands butted up against the side of the field, staring out at the green with disbelief. Red Solo cups are littered everywhere. Half-torn streamers wave from the goalposts. Paper plates pile up over the grassy mounds, and crumpled napkins roll across the green. I thought our practice area sort of looked like a dump before . . . but now it's become an actual landfill.

"What. The. Hell." Katie barely gets the words out through her tightly clenched teeth.

My teammates shake their heads and trade looks with each other, each player falling somewhere on the spectrum of furious to heartbroken. One way or another, everyone looks like they've been personally punched in the stomach.

As I scan the field, every muscle in my body tightens into one hardened knot. Getting pummeled last weekend was bad enough. It isn't right that on top of everything else, now we have to deal with the aftermath of some idiot classmates' homecoming party.

But it's on me to pull the team together and get us through shitty things like this. I toss my stick to one side and take off my gloves.

"All right!" I say, trying to sound a lot more cheerful than I actually feel. "We can clear this out in twenty minutes. Defense, take that side of the field. Forwards, the other side. I'll get the goal boxes."

I start to lumber forward when Melanie grabs my arm.

"You seriously want to ignore this?" she asks.

"No," I say, shrugging. I reach down in front of me and grab a plate smeared with frosting. "That's why we're cleaning it up."

Mel shakes her head. "But this is too much, Eve. It's freaking humiliating. You *know* those assholes left it for us to see."

I freeze with my hand on the plate. How does she know who was partying here?

"What assholes?" I ask.

Melanie directs my gaze to the chain-link fence directly

behind my goalpost. Red cups have been stuffed into the gaps, forming the number fifteen on either end of the fence. One word sits between the numbers, spelled out in garish, shiny bubble letters.

ALVAREZ

CHAPTER SEVEN

I start to put the red Solo cup dots together.

Van Darian had the party here.

Van Darian left all this trash for us to clean up.

I read the chain-link fence across the field over and over.

15 ALVAREZ 15

The message feels cryptic, like some kind of riddle. But I'm not playing Rosa's stupid mind games anymore. None of it matters. What matters right now is the anguish on my teammates' faces. What matters is that I'm in charge of protecting these girls both on and off the field. Rosa needs to know she can't just barrel through me and hurt my team like this. I may have royally messed up last weekend, but I'm still a wall.

"Right," I say to myself.

I drop the paper plate and turn on my heels back up the path.

"Evelyn! Wait!"

Katie jogs next to my side. "Where are we going?"

"Take the soccer field today," I mutter. "They're off. Our field will be ready by tomorrow."

Katie leaps a few steps ahead. She twists and looks at me, her feet hopping in a backward prance. "But where—"

I stop. "Katie. The team needs you today. I need you today. Lead practice, *please*."

"And what about what I need?" Katie folds her arms. "Is this going to be an Evelyn pity party, part two? You go off to sulk and grind up on your boyfriend again?"

The question stings, but at this point, it's more than fair. I swallow and do my best to keep my expression measured.

"No. I'm going to Van Darian."

Katie gestures down the path. "Then grab the whole team! Let us all show up!"

I shake my head. "Did the fence say: *Boo, Heathclef. Yay, Van Darian*?"

"No, but . . ."

"But this isn't a team thing," I explain. "It's Alvarez, and she put her name behind *my* goal box for a reason. This is between me and her." I tap Katie's hockey stick. "Lead practice. Trust me on this."

Katie rolls her head back and groans. "Ugh. Fine. You better get your ass back here soon."

"As soon as I can," I say, already walking past her.

I mean it, too. My heart thunders in my chest with each step. The static energy from Saturday's game is already coursing back through my veins, already churning the blood in my ears loud enough to block out every other sound. I close my eyes and all I can see is her. That stupid wink on the field. The tattoo. Her legs. Her hair. Her nails. Everything, every inch of this girl, is under my skin.

I can't get this over with soon enough.

I rush right past Gloria on my way inside the gym.

Gloria waves her clipboard. "Excuse me?"

My hand's already on the locker room door. "Our field got trashed. Katie will explain."

"Feltzer! Hey! I'm not finished with you!" Gloria's voice fades as the door closes behind me.

Usually I know better, way better, than to pull rank over Gloria. But Gloria won't understand. She'll think the party was some silly prank. She'll tell me to let it go and focus on the next game.

She won't realize that Rosa is standing between us and the rest of the season.

I shrug off my pads in the locker room, leaving them scattered on the floor. My shirt goes on backward. One sock gets put on inside out. Laces go untied. By the time I march up to my car, I look like I had a fight with a laundromat and lost.

"Doesn't matter," I tell myself as I unlock the door.

It's not like I'm heading out on a date.

I fiddle with the ignition, twisting the key over and over. Seth bought this car—an ancient teal Buick—the second after he turned sixteen. He likes to call her The Mermaid, but most of the time I refer to her as a piece of junk. After three tries, the engine starts.

The only times I've been to Van Darian are for field hockey games, which means I've only ever sat in the back of a school bus and talked over the rows of seats to Katie, or closed my eyes with my earbuds in and music turned all the way up. Getting there on my own turns out to be so much freaking harder. I end up circling the outer perimeter of the campus for three entire laps before I figure out how to get inside. The main gate is surrounded by a thick army of trees, hidden off the roadside in a blink-and-you'll-miss-it spot. My tires squeal from the U-turn when I finally catch it. I drum my fingers on the steering wheel, waiting behind a white sedan to get through security.

The gate looks old and Gothic, the iron-tipped spikes puncturing the blue of the sky. I click my tongue at the complete pompousness of it all. I mean, I know Heathclef isn't exactly the most down-to-earth school either, but this might as well be a fortress. I remind myself that maybe all the "stay the hell out" fanfare is because Van Darian is a boarding school, but that only makes the whole vibe seem even prissier.

Send your girls to Van Darian and we'll protect them from the scary, outside world!

Please.

At least the guard waves me through as soon as he sees me, probably thinking I'm just another Van Darian student who spent the weekend trashing other school campuses and torturing rival team captains. I nod and coast inside, trying hard to pretend I know exactly where I'm going. It would be easy enough if I could just drive up to their field hockey practice. But the only green I can see from the road are rolling fields of meadows.

A bell rings in the distance—not the alarm kind that blares, but more like a church bell. There's a song I don't recognize hidden in the chimes, and as the melody plays, it draws streams of students out from the buildings. The girls stroll along the sidewalk parallel to the road, clutching books and bags and laughing in the evening sun. They all look strangely . . . normal.

One girl pauses in her conversation and stares up at me, and I suddenly realize I've gone from casual coasting to foot-all-the-way-on-the brake in the middle of the street.

Somehow this does not seem like something a typical Van Darian student would do.

More people are pausing their conversations as they stare through my windshield. I should just hit the gas, or even roll down the window and ask someone for directions. But I stay completely motionless. It feels like in this moment everyone knows exactly who I am and what I'm here for. I'm the spy in enemy territory.

Another girl looks over, and at first my heart catches with relief because I actually know this person. I smile at her, then immediately want to smack myself because of course, of *course,* the girl is Rosa—complete in her field hockey jacket, no less.

She's holding a stack of books in front of her chest. It's not even the normal amount of books someone would take to class, but more like a librarian who decided to forgo wheeling the return cart around. The top book slips off and hits the pavement on its spine. Rosa studies it for a moment, weighing what to do with the other ten books in her hands to get the tumbled one back. I sigh and jump out of my car, then scoop the book up off the pavement.

"Thanks," Rosa says. She grins at me, her eyes sparkling with recognition.

How great for her that I get to be the reminder of the best field hockey game she's ever played in her life. Unfortunately, for me, looking at her is a reminder of the dead opposite.

"That was a fun weekend," she chirps.

"The big game or the big party?" I ask dryly.

Rosa scrunches up her mouth, considering. "The game. Definitely the game."

She winks at me again. The fucking audacity.

"How'd you know about the party?" she asks.

I shake my head. "Don't play dumb—"

BEEEEEEEEEEEEP!

We both turn toward the road to see two cars now lined up behind mine. All the bravado I've been building deflates as I give a "one second" wave to the car behind me.

I run back to the driver's-side door and point at Rosa. "I'm not finished with you."

I try to say it mean, exactly the way Gloria barked the words at me earlier. But Rosa only rolls her eyes and steps to the passenger door. She leans the stack of books against her hip and reaches one hand out for the handle.

"What are you doing?"

She slides effortlessly into the seat. "You're lost, you're in the way, and, as you said, we're not finished. So start the car and I'll get you to visitor parking."

I open my mouth to argue, but another blast of a car horn comes out instead of words. The driver behind me raises both hands.

"Fine. Fine!"

I turn the ignition and drive around the old brick buildings, winding down the elegant, tree-lined road. Rosa sets her stack of books in the footwell and shrugs off her jacket. We drive silently, with Rosa pointing every now and then until we make it to a small parking lot at the far end of campus. I put the car in park. Slivers of lake shimmer just over the tree line. The prettiness of everything just pisses me off even more.

"You need to stay the hell away from my team," I say, pulling the keys. "It's one thing to go after me, but—"

Rosa looks at me teasingly. "You think I'm going after you?"

I squint at her, trying to figure out her angle. The game's long over. Van Darian's already danced on top of our loss. What can this girl possibly get out of tormenting me? Why can't she just drop this and leave it behind her?

"Stay away from my team," I say again. "You want to make me look stupid, fine. Saturday was on me. But you're not going to slither back on our campus and throw yourself some vanity party, then leave every last scrap of trash for us to clean up. That shit is not okay."

Rosa's mouth opens and closes without a word, like a gasping fish pulled out of water. She stares off into the trees.

I glance down at the jacket bunched up by her feet. The number *17* sits under the arched *Alvarez* lettering. "You didn't even get your jersey number right, by the way. It said *fifteen* on the fence."

"It was a quinceañera," Rosa murmurs.

"A what?"

"A quince. It's like a sweet sixteen party, but for fifteen."

I press the crease between my eyebrows, trying to make sense of this. Rosa can't be fifteen. "Wait. So last weekend was your birthday?"

"No." Rosa shifts uncomfortably. "It was my fifteenth goal of the season. My teammates—we wanted to have a party for it."

"On *our* campus," I finish.

Rosa says nothing. She twists her fingers together and sighs. For the first time since Saturday, she finally seems human. Like I've managed to wrangle her away from Fun Land and back to Earth. The pressure starts to ease in my neck. The pulsing in my shoulder slows.

"Well, you need to get your team to clean it up," I tell her.

She looks up at me suddenly. "No."

I cock my head. "No?"

"No," she says again. "I . . . can't do that."

"Can't or won't?"

Rosa rolls her eyes. "What does it matter?" she asks. "It was just a party. It's just trash. Drive us back there and I'll help you do it now."

"No!" I yell. I can already imagine her sneaking photos of me balancing balls of napkins over dirty plates. I can hear the whole Van Darian team laughing at the hopeless Heathclef goalkeeper who got tricked into cleaning up their mess.

I get out of the car and open the passenger-side door. "Go get your own teammates and clean it. I didn't come here to taxi you anywhere."

Rosa sighs and stands next to me. I can smell lavender on her hair, and some kind of citrus on her breath. I take a step back.

Rosa looks me over carefully, sizing me up the way I sized her. She nods to herself.

"What?" I ask defensively.

Rosa raises an eyebrow. "Don't you think you're taking this whole thing way too seriously? It's only *field hockey*."

Her nose scrunches in slight disgust, as if she's talking about the least appetizing entrée on a menu.

My brain short-circuits.

Field hockey has made up nearly every part of my life. All of my friends have come from field hockey. Every award I've ever won has come from field hockey. My memories of Mom are all wrapped completely in images of us on the field. Any hope I have of a career is resting on how we perform this season. Field hockey is my whole existence. It's both my past and my future. And this girl—this absolute *bitch*—is treating it like some trivial game to make fun of. Like she'd much rather be doing anything else than kicking my ass and shattering my dreams.

Without a word, I push the passenger door closed behind Rosa. I stomp around the car and climb back into the driver's side.

She doesn't care, I think. Not only has she completely ruined the thing I love most, but she doesn't even care about it.

Rosa leans toward the window as I start the ignition. She taps on the glass.

"I need my stuff," she calls from outside.

"I don't give a shit about your stuff," I mutter.

My tires squeal as I turn out of the parking lot. I barely take my foot off the gas, rushing to throw as much space between me and Rosa as possible. All the playfulness, the winking, the barging straight for the ball, those weren't genius playing techniques at all, I realize. They were signs that Rosa was just goofing around.

Katie and the girls are gathered at the center of the soccer field when I pull back into Heathclef. They're sitting in a circle and talking, their sticks piled up on the sidelines. I watch their somber faces through the windshield and shake my head. I promised Katie I would deal with Van Darian. I said I would do something.

I toss my keys to one side. They bounce off the passenger seat and land on Rosa's things. Her library books fan across the floorboard, with her jacket draped over the top. The *Alvarez* in black stitching practically glows against the green fabric.

I pause. If Rosa wants to leave her name on our campus so badly, maybe it should be on our terms instead of hers.

Katie checks over her shoulder and stands as she sees me. She raises both arms, as if asking, *Well? Did you take care of it?*

I owe them all an answer.

I reach for the jacket.

CHAPTER EIGHT

"All right, Evie!" Dad calls. "Let's see if you can block this one!"

We're standing in the backyard a week later, on the wall-to-wall lawn I've officially claimed as my personal "No-Goal Zone." A game-sized net sits behind me, and Dad stands just inside the shooting circle I drew over the perimeter in white chalk. Seth likes to complain and say that if he had his way, the yard would be his own private badminton court, but I know that's a bald-faced lie. That boy has never liked sports in his life.

Dad raises my hockey stick way over his shoulder.

"Lower!" I yell out. "Or you'll hit the window instead of the net."

"Oh. Right." He drops the stick down by his side, then lines it up carefully behind the field hockey ball. I ready my stance.

The stick half connects, sending the ball limping across the green. With one leg still planted, I gently kick it away from the goal box.

"All right! Great job, kiddo!" Dad pumps his fist in the air. I sigh. "Thanks, Dad."

Obviously Dad didn't grow up playing field hockey, so he's more of a cheerleader than a coach. I know it's unfair to wish he was better at it, especially since he's never asked me to bone up on football spiral throws or whatever. But I miss working hard in the backyard. This used to be my main training ground—where Mom and I threw everything we had into getting better. Mom would have me out here for hours, perfecting my stance, working on drills. Now the yard functions more as a show-and-tell stage to impress Dad with whatever new skills I've picked up from Gloria.

I toss the hockey ball back across our lawn.

"Go again," I say. "Maybe this time a little harder."

Heathclef's next game is less than a week away, and while I'm pretty confident there won't be another Alvarez situation, I decide it's a safe bet to spend all my free time out here practicing.

Dad hits the ball over and over. Each time, I give a little more direction, like how to angle his swing, and maybe not to aim the ball directly at me. The point is to make me *work* for a save.

"All right," Dad pants less than an hour later. "I'm beat, and the game's on in ten. Let's head inside."

I throw my face cage up. "What? We just got started!"

Dad shrugs. "It's the Eagles, kid! If I don't make a sandwich and turn on the TV to cheer them on, all will be lost."

I roll my eyes. "Seriously? Two more saves. Come on."

"Compromise. One more save." He barely knocks the ball

toward me. It stops rolling halfway across the yard. I'm about to say that one totally doesn't count when Dad dramatically throws my hockey stick to the side in mock defeat. He marches toward the back door, yelling over his shoulder in his "sports commentator" voice.

"And Feltzer completely boxes Feltzer out! It's a no-goal game! Wooooooo! The crowd goes wild!"

He heads inside and right to the refrigerator.

I grumble and loosen my chin strap. Even if Seth were home, I couldn't pay him enough money to be out here. And my teammates are never down for extra practices. Katie lovingly tells me I don't have boundaries when it comes to playing field hockey versus "having a normal life." As if playing field hockey isn't a perfectly normal way to spend afternoons . . . and evenings . . . and, okay, maybe some mornings too.

Instead of ricocheting the ball to myself for saves, I give up on practice entirely and head inside after Dad. He's left the cold cuts and mayonnaise out on the counter. I slap together a quick sandwich and settle on the couch armrest just as kickoff begins.

For a while it's just Dad and me, silently chewing and watching the screen, then throwing crumbs into the air whenever the Eagles gain more yards. Between my dad and Caleb, I know the ins and outs of football almost too well at this point. Honestly, it's a little weird to me that football is about the only sport out there without a real women's equivalent. I've played against enough field hockey teams to know there are a ton of women who could *dominate* in tackle football. The NFL loves to say they care about women in sports—but come on. It's easy to see where they put all their resources.

I get bored in the second quarter and pull out my phone.

Me: *Wanna make out?*

Caleb: *Game's on. Come by later tonight.*

Me: *OR you come here now and I lose my shirt immediately.*

Caleb's icon blinks as he types a response. I can always count on him to prioritize boobs over almost anything else. I tap my nails over the keypad, waiting.

Caleb: . . .

Caleb: *OR I come by right after the game ends.*

Dammit, Caleb. I tuck my phone away.

"Touchdown!" Dad suddenly yells from his armchair. He looks over at me. "Where are you going, Evie?"

"Out," I say. "Homework. Robbing a bank. Something."

Dad's eyes are already back on the TV. "Okey-dokey. Have fun. Be safe."

"Uh-huh." I grab my keys from the kitchen counter and head out the front door.

When Mom was still here, she and Dad felt like the ultimate power-athlete couple. Dad's the football guy, sure, but Mom never let us forget for a second how good she was at field hockey. One of the best on Duke's team.

"And I was *this* close to going pro," she would say, her fingers pinching a centimeter of air between them. "I didn't make it through the door, but I know I opened it for someone behind me."

She'd always wink right after saying it, sometimes at Seth, but mostly just at me. As if we already had our own little spyglass into a future of me going professional. That was Mom's and my dream from day one. I just used to think she'd be around to see it happen.

Now that she's not around, so much of the time I feel completely smothered by the whole football-mania thing. The neighborhood seems too quiet as I creep over to my car. I can imagine everyone else in their houses, being honorable Pennsylvanians glued to the Eagles game. Skipping out in the first half seems near equivalent to a kid breaking curfew.

I crank up the stereo and root around the center console for a granola bar or bag of trail mix or something. Rosa's library books peek out at me from the footwell. I glare at them over a snack bag of Doritos.

On Monday night I had to sneak back onto campus and clean up every damn inch of Rosa's party all by myself. Somewhere between tripping over streamers and having to reach into an actual gopher hole for a wad of napkins, I decided stealing a measly field hockey jacket was *not* enough by way of revenge. As soon as I was done yanking the red Solo cups from our fence, I would go back to my car and rip every single page out of Rosa's books. Then I'd crumple the pages and scatter them all over Van Darian's field. I could just picture their team showing up to practice the next day and discovering a ball pit of trash in front of them. Rosa would bend down and grab one of the pages. Her long eyelashes would flutter in panic as she smoothed it out.

Just the thought of her face made me feel all warm and tingly inside.

But by the time I dragged my feet back into the parking

lot, I was too tired to crack a single book open, let alone rip every page out. So I went home and decided I would trash Van Darian the next day.

But then it was Taco Tuesday and Katie and I went out after practice.

And then Wednesday I had a dentist appointment.

And Thursday Gloria had us doing extra drills until dark.

And by Friday I hadn't seen Caleb the whole week, so we met up at our usual spot to fool around.

And that's basically how I went from master schemer to library book cabbie. The books are practically a staple of The Mermaid now. They make me look a lot smarter than I actually am, at least. I've never checked out any books from Heathclef's library. They're way too intimidating, books. How am I supposed to commit to reading an entire book when I can't even finish a ten-minute-plus YouTube video? And here's Rosa, walking around with eleven whole-ass books at once.

Deep down, I think I always knew I was never going to touch them. It's not the library's fault that their school's field hockey team is a bunch of vandalizing little shits.

I sigh and start the car. I might be the first person in history to turn in more library books than she's ever checked out.

The drive to Van Darian is easier than the first time, even if the gate still jumps out at the last second. I pull through security and coast along the same road as before, curving around the clusters of academic buildings and students walking along the paths.

One girl squints at me and I roll down my passenger window.

"Hey," I say. "Where's the library?"

The girl tilts her head, like she cannot believe we are however many weeks into the school year and I'm only *now* asking where the library is. She points behind her to a large stone building at the far end of the quad.

The full stack of books feels surprisingly heavy in my arms. I bump the car door closed with my hip and stumble across the lot toward the double doors at the front of the library.

Outside the building is a humongous, maybe ten-foot-tall, statue of a woman. She smiles serenely with her hands held out in front of her, palms face up. Her fingers curl in slightly, as if inviting little birds and chipmunks to perch on her like a Disney princess.

Lady Van Darian, an inscription reads at the woman's feet.

I roll my eyes and walk on past, confronting the thick double-door panels to the building. Luckily, another student is coming out, and she keeps the door open wide enough for me to squeeze in past her.

"Thanks," I say, though my face is half-hidden behind the book spines.

The main room of the library stretches back and back. Rows of long study tables dotted with low green lamps make the vast space feel intimate. Portraits of old white ladies line the walls. I turn to my right and am grateful to see a main circulation desk. At least I can unload Rosa's books off on them.

I set the books down as gently as I can over the counter. The stack blocks my view of the librarian.

"I'm, uh, returning these."

"Oh, thank God," the librarian says. Their voice is uncannily familiar.

I twist around the tower. "Rosa?"

Rosa pulls the books over, her scanner gun at the ready. She holds each one under the red light, glancing at the computer monitor with every small *beep!* from the scanner.

"These were so close to getting fined," she murmurs to herself. She shakes her head and wipes her brow, then looks up at me like she forgot I was standing there. "I figured you tossed them."

I shrug. "I thought about it."

"Well, thank you for bringing them back. Seriously."

"Yeah, whatever," I say. I hate how adorable her relieved face is. She doesn't deserve to look cute after everything she did to me and my team. But at least we're done now. I walk back through the foyer. The sun is already on my face when I hear Rosa again.

"Wait."

Rosa brushes against me as she slips through the doors. She pulls me by the wrist under a nearby tree.

"What now?" I ask, jerking my arm away.

Rosa does a full 360 scan before she turns back to me.

"I didn't throw the party," she says, her voice low. She looks down at her shoes. "My teammates threw it for me."

"If you think I'm stupid enough to believe that your WASPy teammates threw *you* a quinceañera—"

"They did," Rosa says. She clenches her jaw a moment,

then lets it go again. "They were chanting about fifteen goals on the way home from the game, and I told them what a quince was. Like, as a joke."

She folds her arms across her chest. "I thought they were going to clean it up after. They told me they were. I left early."

I turn on my heels. "It's clean now. Don't worry about it."

But Rosa runs ahead of me again.

"I can help you," she says breathlessly.

"I told you, it's already cleaned up."

"No." She grabs my shoulder. Her hand feels strangely warm, even over my shirt. "I mean I can pay you back. Make things even."

I raise an eyebrow. "Yeah? How?"

"You miss slap shots," Rosa says. "You look great when you're extending up, or when you have a leg out for a sweep shot. But it's like you let your hips take over in close shots, and you have to use your arms if you're going to make any of those saves."

My mouth gapes open. I'm pretty sure this is the *exact* definition of adding insult to injury.

"Are you serious? This is your idea of paying me back?"

Rosa blinks. "Yeah. If you want to know the truth, this is, like, the one trick I have in field hockey. It just also happens to be the thing most goalkeepers miss. Our own goalkeeper is total shit at blocking slap shots."

She steps closer and takes hold of both of my arms. All the little hairs on my skin stand straight up. This might be what it's like to get electrocuted in slow motion. I should step away and scream at her. I should run to my car without looking back. But under the painfully insulting situation of a soccer player teaching me how to block in field hockey, I realize: Rosa's right. I don't cover this zone. Most field hockey players take wide sweep shots, and the ones who do try slap or squeeze shots always end up popping the ball high.

"Let your arms go looser. Bend your elbows," Rosa says gently. She opens my palms and twists me so my wrists are facing her. "Like you're standing in airport security. Now lower it a little. You want your hands to get used to the space between your waist and hips."

As Rosa shifts me around like a doll, I forget how to breathe, let alone move on my own. My body goes numb from neck to fingertips. Somehow, being touched lightly like this is a million times more overwhelming than getting pummeled with an actual field hockey ball.

Finally, Rosa steps back and looks me over.

"Good," she says. "That's much better."

I stare at her, still frozen. She meets my gaze and holds it. The birds stop chirping in the trees. The electricity buzzing on my skin crackles and grows into a force field between us.

"Well," she says. "Okay. We're even."

She turns and runs back into the library.

CHAPTER NINE

By the time we walk off the field at our next game, Heath-clef has won by so many points, and I've blocked so many attempts, that it almost feels like we never lost our winning streak at all. Even Gloria calls me No-Goalie when she takes roll on the bus. Not a single shot gets by me from start to finish. Not even the tricky slap shot aimed in the final few minutes.

"Hell yeah, Feltzer!" Katie calls out for the hundredth time on the ride home.

"Hell yeah!" the others chant, waving their sticks in the air.

Gloria stands from the front row and swats one of the sticks away. "Calm down, all of you! You're going to poke each other's eyes out."

We're all completely slaphappy, and Gloria's frustration only makes us dissolve into giggles.

Katie turns to Gloria. "Coach! Did you even *see* Feltzer's knee slide on that last save?"

"I saw it," Gloria says gruffly.

Katie throws her arms up. "She looked like she had just smashed a guitar on stage at a concert! Like a rock star! Gloria, tell her she was a rock star!"

My cheeks go deep scarlet as I beam at Katie. She is the only person on the planet who compliments the way a comedian roasts. Once she gets going, there's no stopping her. The ultimate hype woman.

Gloria sets her clipboard aside. "No one is a rock star here," she says. She points her pencil at Katie. "You can be a rock star's arm."

Katie cocks her head. "Why would I want to be a sentient arm?"

I barely swallow my laugh, but luckily Gloria doesn't notice. She turns and points at our teammates, one after another. "You, the other arm. You, a foot. You can be an ear."

She looks squarely at me. "Sometimes one of us gets to be the knees sliding across the stage. But no one is a rock star alone. We function together. Yes?"

"Yes," everyone mumbles.

Gloria sits down and faces forward. Melanie turns and winks at me before she sits. Natalia throws me a thumbs-up. Katie digs her shoulder into my side.

"Don't let her take away your steam," Katie whispers. "You carried us today, and she knows it."

I smile. "Thanks."

We swarm back into our locker room and volley for the showers. I settle onto the bench and wait for the first wave of players to finish, as usual. As I sit and stare off into the corner of the room, something keeps niggling in the back of my mind. I was the one who made all those saves this morning. I jumped and slid and leapt and punted. So why does it feel like I owe the win to someone else?

I open my right arm again, palm and wrist out. Just remembering Rosa shaping the bend in my elbow gives me shivers.

"Dammit," I say to myself.

"What was that?"

Katie comes strutting out of the shower with a towel wrapped over her head. She opens her locker and starts rummaging for her clothes. She holds out a shirt I haven't seen before. It's hot neon orange with a lace bodice and back zipper. I have *never* seen Katie rock a look like this.

"Does Bryce like orange?"

I squint. "Bryce? As in 'football idiot Bryce'?"

Katie glares at me. "No, as in 'Caleb's hot friend Bryce.' And what the hell? I thought you said you liked dating someone on the football team."

"I mean . . . I like Caleb," I say.

I can see traces of hurt building in Katie's eyes.

"The football team is cool," I add quickly. "They're like a slightly less-cool version of our team. And we're astronomically cool, so—yeah. They're not too far behind. And I don't know if Bryce likes orange. But I'm sure he likes strong, beautiful women no matter what they're wearing. Or at least he should."

Katie sighs and gives me a half smile. She stuffs the hot top back in her bag and pulls on a normal T-shirt. I watch her shrug on our Heathclef field hockey jacket over the top.

My breath catches. I know how I can stop feeling guilty about every save I make from now until the end of the season. I clear my throat and saunter next to Katie.

"Hey. Do you still have Rosa's jacket?"

Katie looks at me. "Whose?"

"The Van Darian girl. Her field hockey jacket."

"Oh!" Katie's eyebrows rise. "You're giving it back to her already?"

"Well, I—"

I pause. How did Katie know that was my plan? And why would she want me to return Rosa's jacket? She doesn't know Rosa helped me with slap shot saves. No one knows.

"I was thinking about it," I say coolly. "Why?"

Katie dips around the corner and reaches into Melanie's gym bag. She comes back to me holding a tight wad of green fabric. At the sight of the jacket in Katie's hands, the rest of the room goes quiet. All our teammates are watching, their eyes darting between me and Katie. Something's up.

"So here's the thing," Katie says. "At first, we were just going to keep the jacket all season. You know, like a capture-the-flag sort of thing."

I nod. This had been my intention as well.

"But," Katie goes on, "Natalia stayed on campus late that day, and she saw you cleaning the field all by yourself. After Alvarez completely trashed it. That wasn't right."

She didn't trash it on her own, I think. But I say nothing.

"So then we decided to change things up. That if Alvarez wanted to embarrass you and leave her name on your stuff, we would do the same to her. So she knows that *no one* messes with Heathclef, or our captain."

Katie unfolds the jacket in front of me. Right under Rosa's embroidered last name is a line scrawled out in thick, black Sharpie.

𝒜lvarez
EATS FELTZER'S SHIT

"Wow," I murmur. I look up and see everyone waiting on my reaction. "Um . . . thank you?"

Jade touches my shoulder. "We got you, Feltzer."

A strange mix of pride and shame circles around and around inside me, spiraling like water down a drain. I ball the jacket right back up so I don't have to look at the writing again.

After showers and change-out, I toss Rosa's jacket into the back of my car and slump against the seat. My idea for paying her back is completely out the window. I drum my fingers on the steering wheel, thinking. Rosa helped me with slap shots. But she's not a perfect field hockey player either. There were definitely weaknesses in her strategy on the field.

"That's it!" I say.

I hop right back out of the car and raid the storage room in our gym. Thirty minutes later, I pull up to the Van Darian gate for the third time in less than two weeks. I even wave to the security guard as I pass through.

I have no idea where exactly Rosa is inside this gargantuan, preppy-ass campus. But I do have a pretty good idea of where to start looking for her.

I breeze past the princess statue of Lady Van Darian and press my way inside the library. One of the two field hockey sticks under my arm immediately knocks into a stone wall and echoes across the entire foyer. Everyone in the main study room looks up from their laptops and sends me a collective hard glare. I shudder and turn to the circulation desk.

"Um. Hi," I say, half whispering, half not.

The girl behind the desk looks up from her own book at me. She seems as annoyed as the others in the study room, which doesn't seem exactly fair, seeing as how she's actually supposed to expect interruptions.

"Yes?" the girl asks. Her lips look bruised from half-rubbed-off purple lipstick.

I scan the shelves and offices behind her. "Is Rosa here?"

"Nope." The girl immediately returns to her book.

"Is she . . . in class?"

"It's Saturday."

"What about field hockey practice?"

Purple Lips raises an eyebrow. "Why do you want her so badly?"

"I don't!" I take a giant step backward. "I just have some-thing to give her."

I hold up one of the sticks as evidence.

"Uh-huh." The girl looks at me like she was done talking to me five minutes before I even came through the door. She slowly turns a page in her book.

"Dorm room," she says without looking up.

I immediately turn for the door. "Thank you! And the dorm building is . . ."

Pause. Page turn. Pause. "Third building on your left heading out. I think she's in two-fourteen."

"Got it. Thanks again."

I bound back out of the building before anyone else has time to glare at me for hauling around sports equipment, or tracking in mud, or breathing too loud, or whatever else they consider a crime in the library judicial system.

Thanks to Purple Lips, I find the dorm building easily enough and slip inside behind another student. As I turn the corner down Rosa's hallway, I hear music pouring out from underneath one of the doors. It's some kind of hip-hop song, with the lyrics all in Spanish. I'm not really a good dancer, but even I can't help walking along with the beat. My feet hit each hard note. My hips sway to the melody. My head bobs along. The music grows louder the closer I get to 214. By the time I'm standing in front of Rosa's room, I know this is the source of the music.

Rosa answers on the second knock.

"Fine! Fine! I'm turning it off," I hear her yell behind the door. It swings open and Rosa steps right into my face, her brow firmly creased.

"Quiet hours don't even start until—" She stops when she realizes it's me. "Oh. Hi."

"Hi," I say. I look over my shoulder. "Were you expecting someone else?"

"Not exactly," Rosa says. "Just warding off people who hate music."

She leans against her doorway and folds her arms. "Saturdays are strictly for silence, didn't you know?"

"Does that mean you at least get Sundays to scream into the abyss?" I ask.

She laughs. We smile at each other, then remember ourselves.

Rosa presses her mouth into a flat line. "So, what do you want?"

I pass the sticks back and forth between my hands. "Do you know of any secret fields around here?"

"I'm sorry," Rosa says. "Did you seriously use the phrase *secret fields*?"

"Or an abandoned lot," I add. "Even a short grass meadow could be okay. We won't be running around too much."

"*We* won't be running around at all unless you tell me what you're talking about," Rosa says. "And what you're doing here."

"I'm here to make it up to you."

"Make what up to me?" she asks.

I bite my lip and look at Rosa. There's no way I can admit what happened to her jacket. I picture the balled-up wad of green nylon fabric in my car. I think of what's written over the fabric and wince. At this point, it would be better if she thought I threw it away, full stop.

"Your advice about slap shots was good. It gave me an unfair advantage," I explain. "And it's important to me, for official record purposes, to not feel like I'm cheating. So I'm here to help you with slide passes."

"Ah."

A smile pokes its way right back onto Rosa's face. Out of all the people I've come across on this campus, she seems to be the only one who doesn't make me feel like I've rudely barged in and interrupted her life. She looks amused as she eyes the field hockey sticks in my hands. If I didn't know better, I might even think she was happy to see me.

Rosa grabs her gym bag and locks her room behind her. She leads me across the quad and over two different fields before we step into a small, grassy area partially hidden by the tree line.

Rosa walks to the middle of the makeshift field and opens her arms.

"Well. Here we are. What now?"

I lean the sticks against a thick tree trunk and look around. "And you're sure no one comes this way?"

"Positive."

"Not even people coming here to make out?"

Rosa reaches into her gym bag. She takes out a field hockey ball and throws it in the air, catching it on her palm. "No one hooks up out in the woods," she says. "We have dorm rooms for that, Evelyn."

My cheeks go hot, but Rosa just laughs. She tosses me a ball and I catch it with one hand.

Rosa and I spend the next two hours practicing in the secret field. I help her with slide passes. She makes me dive after a bunch of slap shots. I caution her about running too impulsively during gameplay. She calls me a viejito and asks how often I yell at kids to get off my lawn.

As we pass the ball in turn, Rosa tells me about New Mexico and her old school. I get to hear about her old neighborhood, and the block parties they held every weekend. Rosa tells me about playing fútbol in the street with her abuela and little cousins. She tells me about her uncles slow-roasting peppers at dusk. She tells me how the stars would come out in droves, chasing the sun right off the edge of the sky.

Once or twice I think about mentioning the No-Goal Zone in my backyard, and how sometimes, when my mom and I used to practice at night, it would get so dark that the field hockey ball almost seemed to glow. A tiny moon that orbited only the two of us.

But if I bring up the Zone, I'd probably have to bring up the fact that no one goes out with me after dark anymore and my dad doesn't understand shit about field hockey and my mom's dead now. So I just listen to Rosa's stories instead. They're way better than mine. Plus, I remind myself, it's not like we're friends. You only talk about your dead mom with really, really good friends. Or, better yet, with no one at all.

"I think you're pretty much an expert with slap shots now," Rosa says after I make another save.

"You too," I say, throwing her the ball. "With slide passes, I mean. You learn fast."

Rosa picks up the field hockey ball and studies it. "So I guess now we're really even."

"Yeah." I clutch the top of my stick. "I guess we are."

We stand there a minute. A soft breeze tousles the long grass around us. Without a word, Rosa drops the ball and knocks it over to me again. I stop it at my feet and make a slide pass back to her.

We go on playing until the sun runs from the stars, until the night swells so deeply that at one point, it's like we're passing a little moon back and forth between us.

CHAPTER TEN

I pull off my shirt in one fluid motion and close my eyes. Nimble fingers slip their way inside my waistband, unbuttoning my jeans and tugging them down to my knees. I lean back against the pillows. My breath is hot and uneven. Her lips touch mine, melting me inch by inch until I'm just a puddle.

"God, you're sexy," Caleb says.

My eyes pop back open.

Caleb stands by the edge of my bed. His cheeks have bypassed their normal pinkish tinge and are now full-on ruddy. His hair stands up in all directions. He kind of goes into animal mode whenever we have sex, which I don't necessarily hate. But it's not really a turn-on, either.

I prop myself up on my elbows as Caleb crawls into the bed. The full weight of his body crashes over mine. His hands shove my bra to the side without bothering to unfasten it. As his fingers rake over my skin, I can feel my mind start to leave my body. I used to think that's just what people did during sex. Go somewhere else. But lately I'm wondering if that's not how it's supposed to work at all.

"Wait," I whisper.

Caleb pauses and looks up at me. "What's wrong?"

I stare back at him. I wish I had an answer. But I have no idea why I can't seem to make myself like the things I'm supposed to like. I don't know why, these days, it feels impossible to close my eyes when we kiss and picture him there on the other side.

My phone buzzes on the nightstand.

I duck under Caleb's arm and swipe it open.

Fútbolhead: *VIEJITO! Come chase some kids off your lawn. PS bring your backpack this time.*

My heart catches with a strange kind of relief.

"Oh. Damn," I mutter. I stand up and hoist my jeans over my hips. "I have practice."

Caleb shakes his head. "On a Sunday?"

"No rest for the wicked," I say, half smiling. "Don't worry, I'll make it up to you."

It's not a whole lie, I tell myself, not really. I do have extra practice. So what does it matter if Gloria's the one running the practice or not?

I pull my shirt off the floor. Caleb stands and reaches for his own jeans and shirt. As I pack my gym bag, he grabs my field hockey stick leaning against the wall.

"Maybe I should come with you," Caleb says. He rolls a field hockey ball off my desk and putts it across the floor. "Take some shots."

I eye him warily. Normally, I love seeing Caleb's big hands

grip the field hockey stick—almost making it disappear under his fingers. But the way he clumsily knocks the ball from side to side starts to make my stomach turn. Something feels off about having Caleb mess with my stuff. Suddenly, I don't want him to touch my gear at all. I want to get him as far away from that world as possible.

I stride across the room and toss the stick aside. Before he can react, I press my body between Caleb's hands as a replacement.

"Go ahead," I murmur, rising on my tiptoes until I can feel his breath on my cheek. "Take a shot."

Caleb grins down at me. He mashes his mouth right onto mine. His tongue slides across my teeth. I let myself go into the kiss, leaning into his wildness, hoping that this will be enough to make up for me leaving.

"Mmm," Caleb moans as I pull away. "I can't wait until our seasons are over."

He links his fingers through mine and squeezes my hand.

"Three more weeks," he says. "Then it'll be nothing but time."

My response gets caught in my throat.

Three weeks is when *football* season ends. Field hockey always goes on longer. When the team's good, we make it all the way to nationals, which doesn't end until the first week of December. And Caleb knows I need to be good. He knows I'm basing my entire college plan on field hockey. So why does he constantly have to act like this sport is no big deal? Who the hell decided that if women were playing a sport, it just wasn't important?

"Hey." Caleb wiggles my hand. "You okay?"

"Yeah. Oh yeah." I shake my head. Caleb and I always keep things easy. That's how the magic works. We don't fight. We don't get in each other's space enough to fight. I lean up and kiss him again.

Barely a half hour later, I pull into my usual space in the visitor parking lot. I heave my padding out of the back seat and fasten it as I walk across the quad. Rosa's already waiting in our secret field.

"You don't have your backpack," she says as soon as she sees me.

"And you don't have gear," I shoot back. "What gives?"

Rosa rolls her eyes, but I know she's not upset. Giving me grief seems to bring her a special kind of joy.

"What gives is I have homework. Is your stuff in the car?"

I blow a piece of hair away from my face. "I mean, yeah, but—"

"Great!" Rosa runs to me and throws her hands around my waist. My breath hitches until I hear the small *click* behind my back and she yanks my chest protector off. "Let's go to the library."

I want to protest immediately. Doing homework over the weekend isn't really my thing. My thing is racing through math problems and readings and essays during study hall and, the second that time is up, I let every assignment go and never think about it again. My thing isn't homework at all. It's field hockey practice. You would think after secretly meeting every single day over the last week, Rosa would get that.

She leads me back to the car and unceremoniously shoves my pads inside, then reaches into the passenger seat and hoists my backpack over her shoulder. I grumble as I follow her through the heavy panel doors of the library. Rosa shimmies behind the circulation desk and grabs a tall stack of books.

"Can you take these?" she asks.

I hold the pile, tilting my head to read the spines. They're different books from before, I notice. Books on philosophy, Latin poetry, epic sagas, and collections of Eastern folktales. I wish I would have looked at the books she left in my car last month.

We leave the grand study room behind and ascend two flights, where the stairway spits us out into rows of books that seem to go on forever.

"I think you already have enough books," I say.

"Hush," Rosa whispers. She heads down the main aisle, parting the rows of shelves like the Red Sea.

I follow Rosa back and back, and for a minute or two I'm pretty sure the only place we could possibly end up is in some sort of library dungeon for people who don't see the outside world, ever. But as we approach the final few rows of books, I suddenly catch glints of sunlight spattered across the thin carpet. I look up and see that Rosa's leading us to a wall of windows facing a lake.

Rosa sets our backpacks down and sits, not at a desk or long study table, but on a fat armchair facing the windows. She pats the chair next to her.

"What is this?" I ask. "Are you messing with me?"

"No." Rosa kicks her feet up on an ottoman. "I just felt like doing something different today. Don't you ever get tired of standing out in the field?"

"Not really," I answer. I set the books down on a side table. "I don't spend a lot of extra time on homework."

"Okay . . . Well, what about other stuff? Don't you like reading books? Or looking at art? Or watching movies?"

"Who the hell do you think I am? Michelangelo?" I perch on the chair next to Rosa. "If I were some great artist, I'd be doing art. If I was any good at watching those super deep, super boring movies, then maybe I'd do that. I'm good at field hockey. I thought that was obvious."

Rosa studies me. "I didn't say you had to be good at those things," she says quietly. "I just wanted to know something else you liked to do. Nobody has just the one thing."

I cross my arms tight over my chest. "Maybe I do."

Rosa leans forward in her chair. "What's with you and field hockey? Seriously."

My arms remain folded.

"Nothing! I just like it, that's all. What about *you* and field hockey?"

"What about it?" Rosa asks.

"Well, you basically showed up out of nowhere and made the rest of us look like little league. Did you come from some underground training world?"

Rosa laughs dryly. "No."

"What then?"

She presses her lips tight, considering. "There wasn't room

for me on the soccer team here," she says finally. "So I got pushed into field hockey instead."

Huh.

"But you like it, right?" I cock my head. "You look so happy on the field."

Rosa shrugs. "I'm always happy when I'm playing sports. Plus, my teammates are okay, I guess. Not like Van Darian's fucking soccer team."

The anger in Rosa's voice surprises me. It's strange enough to imagine someone being so ambivalent about field hockey, let alone someone so freaking good at it. But then I think about what it would be like if I moved to a new school and got shoved out of field hockey and into some other sport. I nod, understanding exactly why there's resentment under all the glory of Rosa's new superstardom.

"Why didn't they let you play soccer?" I ask.

"They said their starting lineup was already locked in." Rosa takes a deep breath. She gazes out the window. "But that was bullshit. Really, it was a bunch of Wonder Bread legacy assholes who didn't want to look bad next to the Chicana new girl."

I swallow. I hate that I know exactly what Rosa's talking about. There are so many student athletes who think they can claim a sport for themselves, excluding anyone who doesn't fit their model of what a player should look like. It's gross and more about them being insecure than anything else and . . . oh God, I suddenly realize that's exactly what I was doing before in hating Rosa just for being new, and being good. I'm literally the definition of a Wonder Bread legacy asshole.

I touch Rosa's knee. "To be fair, you sort of have a knack for making us assholes look bad in whatever sport you're playing."

This draws a smile from her. "You're stalling," she says. "Now you know my shit with field hockey. Tell me your shit."

I pull my hand back.

"Mine's not . . . easy to explain," I say, sinking into the chair.

"Try me." Rosa cradles her chin in her palm. She raises her eyebrows and gives me one of those "I've got all day" looks.

I sigh. "Okay, fine. I love field hockey. Like, probably an unhealthy amount. But I also don't know how not to love it, if that makes sense. It's tangled up with too many other things I love. And I don't know how to tell them apart."

"Like a brain association," Rosa offers. "Pavlovian response?"

"Pav what?"

"Pavlov. It's this psychology experiment," she explains. "Where dogs were given little treats after hearing a bell ring over and over, until at some point the bell made them salivate, all on its own. Even after they stopped getting the treats."

I think about this for a while.

"I guess it's like Pavlov," I say. "Field hockey's the bell ringing. And when I play it . . . I think about my mom. Even though she's not part of it anymore."

"She used to play?"

"Yeah." I clear my throat. "She was really good. She taught me everything about goalkeeping."

I hesitate a moment. I'm okay with talking about Mom in the past. I can talk in circles about the moves she made up on the field, the records she set, the way she totally would have been in an athlete hall of fame if she had kept going.

But Mom in the present tense is way harder.

"She, um . . . she died. When I was twelve."

Rosa reaches for my knee. "I'm so sorry."

I shrug and look away, but Rosa's hand stays in place.

"So she's connected to field hockey?"

"Yeah." I nod. "She and field hockey have sort of, like, melded in my brain. There's this scholarship at Duke I have to get, because if I don't go to Duke and keep doing field hockey the way she did, I don't know how else to feel close to her. I don't know how to love her unless I do all the rest, too."

My breath catches. I've never been able to explain all this so clearly. Not even to myself.

"That sounds really hard," Rosa says.

If the sentiment were coming from anyone else, I would probably jump to defend the whole Mom-field-hockey package deal. I don't want anyone feeling sorry for me. I don't want anyone thinking I don't have my shit together.

But somehow, there's such an ease in Rosa's voice. I don't feel like she's judging me or seeing me in a different way. It's more like we're just understanding one another.

I nod. "Sometimes it *is* really hard."

Rosa squeezes my knee.

"Well." She leans back into the chair. "You don't have to be Michelangelo to like more than field hockey, you know. But you also don't have to like anything else if you don't want to. It's your life. You get to decide what to do with it."

"Yeah. Right." I laugh a little.

Rosa raises an eyebrow at me, and I suddenly realize I haven't told her about The Promise. But this moment is too good to spoil. I've already said enough weird things about me. I hit the quota, at least for today.

Rosa picks up a book from the top of her stack.

"We don't have to do homework. I just want to hang out here. With you."

"Okay," I say. I smile at her. "Me too."

And I really mean it.

We sit side by side as the afternoon slides by, looking out at the water and cradling books on our laps. And even though homework isn't my thing, and I am going to win nationals and get to Duke through that scholarship, I decide to pull out my laptop and take a second look at all the assignments I have that are due the day *after* tomorrow. Just because.

And what do you know, some of them actually seem half-interesting.

CHAPTER ELEVEN

Melanie pounds the table.

"Who are we? Who are we?"

"Heathclef!" I yell out with the others.

We lift our pizza slices in toast, then take a collective first bite. The cheese is too hot and immediately burns the roof of my mouth. It's absolute perfection.

"We're the damn top is what we are!" Melanie yells out.

And she's right. We're starting November with a 10–1 ranking, giving us the top spot in our region. Well, nearly the top spot. We're sharing the title with Van Darian, who's also at 10–1. I don't mention this to any of my teammates, but the only reason we're tied for first is because Rosa was sick last Saturday and missed the Van Darian game. Poor girl got food poisoning from the day-old grocery-store sushi I warned her not to eat. I had to basically inject her with IVs of Gatorade and *Golden Girls* reruns the rest of the weekend before she felt even the teensiest bit better.

I cozy up at the table next to Katie, who's busy scrolling through her phone. As I peek over her shoulder, I see image after image of mostly blond, white girls wearing matching T-shirts.

"Is this from a Halloween party?" I ask, squinting.

Katie spent all of Halloween night at my house watching scary movies. I *miiiight* have made her abstain from any form of partying since we had a huge game early the next morning—the same game we absolutely crushed and we're now celebrating today, so, worth it. But maybe she has some cooler circle of friends who did group costumes for Halloween. Or something.

"No, they're sororities," Katie says. She points at one set of girls in burgundy shirts with disturbingly wide smiles. "I'm trying to figure out which colors would look best on me."

I pause before taking another bite. "Since when have you wanted to join a sorority?"

Katie shrugs. "Sororities are cool. And last week Bryce mentioned wanting to date someone in a sorority."

"Of course he did," I say, rolling my eyes.

"It's a sisterhood." Katie finally sets down her phone. "Like our field hockey team. Except, you know, no field hockey."

"But field hockey's the best part," I point out.

She stares at me a moment, and a strange thought worms its way into my head. Katie is my person. She's the one who's spent countless hours next to me on my couch watching stupid movies and then crying laughing about the same stale jokes in the middle of the night when we're delirious. She's the one who always carries an extra tampon in her bag even when it's not her cycle in case I need it. She's my best friend. But for that one second, it's like I'm looking at a complete stranger. We blink and each pick up our pizza slices. I notice Katie shift her hips slightly away from me as she looks across at the rest of the team.

I take another few bites before my phone buzzes under my ass.

Fútbolhead: *I feel like you definitely dressed as the guy from Up, though.*

I wipe my hands and hunch over the screen.

Me: *I told you, I didn't wear a costume.*

Fútbolhead: *You don't need an old man costume! You already own his exact sweater. I saw it in your holiday post from last year.*

Me: *I'm sorry, did you just admit to stalking me?*

Fútbolhead: *Says the girl who literally tracked me down at my school.*

Me: *That's not an answer.*

Fútbolhead: *Keep your friends close and your enemies closer, bb! ;)*

I bite my lip to keep from smiling.

"Ooh, what's Caleb saying now?" August asks.

"Huh?" I shake my head. "Oh, nothing."

"Riiiight," August says, smirking. "I know that look."

Jade suddenly lunges across the table and snatches my unlocked phone. My heart immediately plummets into my butt.

This is bad, this is bad, this is probably the worst, most awful thing that could possibly happen to a captain of a competitive team with an archnemesis who's also stupidly cute and hilarious and way too fun to text with. I am officially the Icarus of high-stakes field hockey.

Jade and August lean together over the screen and my entire body pulses, heartbeat pounding in each limb. Do I admit everything right up front? Do I blame it on Rosa? *I didn't mean to! She half-nelsoned me into being her friend!* Maybe I can pass this off as my own little scheme. Like I'm spying on the other side. As my brain flips through the cards of anything that could possibly get me out of this mess, the phone slides back next to my plate.

"That's so cute." August folds her hands under her chin. "Football Head. You guys are seriously goals."

I look across the table, brow stupidly scrunched as I try to figure out just what the hell is going on. Are they . . . *cool* with this? Do they think I'm with Rosa?

And then the answer hits me. *Fútbolhead.* I don't have Rosa's contact saved under her name. I want to laugh and give myself the biggest internal high five for being so clever way back when I added her number to my phone. I'm safe. Everything is just as it should be. Rosa's still a secret, and I'm still with—

"So, what nickname did he give you?" Jade asks. "Goalie Head?"

"Ha," I say dryly. I stare down at my pizza. "No."

Caleb doesn't really refer to field hockey at all when we're together, except as the annoying thing I have to leave to do instead of taking off my shirt or showing up to his games. My stomach starts to turn. I pocket my phone.

Melanie's voice floats over from Katie's other side.

"I dunno, Kay. . . . If you join one of those groups, you know you're basically committing to living the straight-and-narrow life forever, right?"

"What do you mean?" Katie asks.

Melanie draws herself up. "Well, as your friendly neighborhood lesbian, it's my solemn duty to encourage every hot, straight girl I know to consider the endless benefits of lugging and bugging."

The other scattered conversations around the table find a pause.

Natalia leans toward Melanie. "What's lugging and bugging?"

"Only the most fabulous way to go through college," Melanie says, clearly pleased to be drawing the general attention of the team.

"It's not lugging and bugging," Jade says, exasperated. "It's LUG and BUG. Lesbian—or bisexual—until graduation."

"Exactly! Thank you, high school LUG!" Melanie winks at Jade.

Jade scowls back, but I notice her exchange a quick glance with August before staring down into her lap.

I pretend to be super interested in moving an artichoke heart to the other side of my pizza slice.

"Why is that even a thing?" I ask, as though I wouldn't care about the answer either way. "Like . . . why would someone only be a lesbian for a little while?"

"It's more like being fake gay," Melanie says airily. "But in a fun way! Well, fun for me, at least. I'm going to call it right now: at least eighty percent of the sex I have in college will be with LUGs and BUGs. And then, when I'm doing my hot, older lesbian thing and sipping chai lattes in Paris with gray hair and camel-colored slacks that expose my scandalous ankles . . . I'll come across one of my former conquests, arm hooked over some idiot wearing a parka and a baseball cap, and she'll look over at me across the café and remember the best three nights of her life and think: *damn*. That's the BUG life."

Katie blows a raspberry. "That doesn't sound fun at all," she says. She picks up her phone and goes back to scrolling through sorority photos.

A few people laugh uncomfortably. One group at the far end of the banquet table shake their heads.

Melanie rolls her eyes and grabs another slice. "Oh, don't act so scandalized, like you're all not two hops and a skip away from some gay tourism. You're already on the freaking field hockey team."

"What is that supposed to mean?" I ask, suddenly bristling. "Field hockey doesn't have anything to do with being gay."

Melanie lets out a single, bullfrog laugh. "Um, yes, it does."

The familiar tendrils of panic begin to wrap across my chest. My fingers go white gripping the edge of the table.

"No, it does not," I say, each word brittle. "My mom played field hockey in high school, and in college, and she was straight the whole time. She married her high school sweetheart."

"That's so sweet!" August says.

"Do you think you might marry Caleb?" Natalia asks.

My shoulders go stiff.

"Maybe." My voice rings in a weird falsetto. Katie shoots some kind of look in my periphery, but I don't turn and catch it.

"Anyway," I say, feeling the full weight of the conversation as I try to drag it somewhere else. "This all smells highly of bullshit. I hate to break it to you, Mel, but there's no such thing as LUGs or BUGs. That's just a crappy way to put down bisexual people."

"Thank you," Jade and August say in unison. Both their cheeks turn red, and they quickly reach for more food.

"Jinx," Melanie says softly, smiling. She looks over at me, an odd smugness radiating from her. "Okay, Captain. Why do you think so many baby gays spring up in college and then go running back to their old 'high school sweethearts' after graduation?"

I carefully ignore Melanie's use of air quotes as I consider an answer.

"Maybe . . . they didn't feel comfortable coming out in high school. Maybe they just don't end up finding the right person. Maybe it takes a while to figure out what they want in a relationship."

"Hmmm." Melanie smiles a strange, sad smile. "Or maybe . . . they're not really gay. Maybe they're just unhappy living in a misogynistic world, and they want to escape any way they can. So they try out being gay for a little while. But then graduation comes, and reality hits, and they realize that they're caught between two shitty worlds: a world where men pull them around, or a world where men hate them. And they decide being hated is worse. So they drop the gay bit and leave us real dykes to fend for ourselves."

The room goes silent. Several teammates shift and look at me, waiting to see if I have a counterargument. But any hope of continuing a real debate on the validity of the sapphic spectrum has died completely. Instead, I'm frozen, bracing as hard as I can while wave after wave of overwhelming nausea hits me.

I know Melanie is talking about a whole population here. There are hundreds, probably thousands, of people who experiment in college. She's upset because they don't share the same queer experience, the same hardships, as lesbians. This conversation is about a *type* of person, not an actual person.

But also.

Whether it's the way Melanie's eyeing me right now, or the way my phone seems to be burning a hole in my pocket . . . I feel like—I *know*—that she must be talking about me. About all the stupid, hungry wants I've had crumpled up inside me for years, like back-seat trash that just won't go away. Wanting to be bigger than my partner, wanting delicate lips to put mine over, hands to envelop in mine, long hair to tease and twirl with my fingers.

I should be madly in love with Caleb, the way Mom was with Dad. I shouldn't wince at the thought of marrying him. Something is seriously wrong with me. I'm like a little kid pushing away a plate of perfectly good food, and for what? For a few silly fantasies? What if Melanie's right, and I'm fake gay? What if *I'm* that coward who just wants to cut and jump away from my life without realizing there's nowhere for me to land on the other side?

Katie's face bobs directly in front of mine. "Eve. Are you okay?"

"I must be cold," I say absently. I reach for the jacket hanging on my chair, then realize there is no jacket. Then I realize I'm already wearing the jacket. It feels like I am wearing fifty jackets.

"Or maybe I'm hot."

Katie grabs my cheeks and twists me so I'm facing her full-on. "What's going on, crazyface?"

"*Machicsure.*"

"What?"

I pull her hands down. "I said, 'My cheeks hurt.' I'm fine, Kay. Really. Maybe I had a bad slice of pizza."

I trace my finger along the wood grain. "I just don't want to be talking about this anymore," I say under my breath.

Katie nods at me once, as if I've given a clear order. She bangs her fist on the table.

"Okay, people!" she calls out. "Only topics that are allowed are field hockey and how awesome we are. Get it together."

I nestle my head on Katie's shoulder in gratitude. She always has my back when it comes to wrangling the team.

For a few blissful minutes, the only sounds in our event room are clanking, chewing, and the occasional deep moan of pleasure that only good pizza can provide. Then, all too soon, Melanie picks up her salad fork and points the end at Katie.

"Oh, okay, but this is absolutely on topic. You want to know a great example of some high school BUGs? Look no further than Van Darian's field hockey team."

I jerk my head up. "What are you talking about?"

Katie nods slowly. "Oh yeah. . . . E, remember how Alvarez was flirting with you on the field? Is that the kind of thing you're talking about, Mel?"

"She was not flirting." I cut off Melanie before she can answer. "She was just being . . . goofy, or something. Maybe that's her personality."

But even August and Jade shake their heads.

"No," Jade says. "We saw everything play out, Captain. She was definitely pulling strings."

"Maybe we should've put something different on her jacket," Natalia offers. "About being a BUG."

"Or BUG *bait*," Melanie adds. She keeps looking at me in that way that makes my head want to explode. I stand up too fast from the table and bound out of the room.

"Evelyn!" Katie calls. "Hold up!"

But I'm already gone. Outside our event room, the pizza place is overflowing with little kids toppling chairs and hiding under tables as their parents tune out the world on their phones. My hands shake as I get out my own phone and open my Favorites list in the Contacts tab. My thumb hovers over the first name.

I want to call the number, just to see what would happen. Even though I know it doesn't lead to her voicemail anymore. Even though I know she would never, ever pick up.

So I hit the third contact instead.

Seth picks up on the fourth ring. "What?"

He sounds annoyed.

"Seth! You answered!"

"I'm in the middle of rehearsal here."

I hear someone scream bloody murder in the background. "What was that?"

"Don't worry about it," he says. "We're doing *Arsenic and Old Lace*. Listen, Evie, I have to call you later. We're going up in three weeks and no one fucking knows their lines. Maybe this weekend we can video chat or something."

I can hear the phone drop down from his ear, can hear him fiddling with the screen to hang up.

"Do you think people can be fake gay?"

The fiddling stops.

"Seth? Are you still there?"

"Bathroom break!" Seth's voice yells from far away. "I'll be back in five!"

Hurried footsteps echo in the background. I can hear Seth's breathing speed up, then eventually settle.

"Okay, I'm alone," he says, his voice much clearer. "You think you're gay?"

"No," I say quickly. "That's not why I called. I just want to know what you think about people experimenting and stuff. Like, if they can be with men and women and have both things be real."

"Um . . . Eve. You have heard of the bisexuals, yes?"

I groan. "Obviously."

"Then why the hell are you calling me like I'm Encyclopedia Brown?" Seth sighs. I can picture him rubbing his chin and shaking his head, the way he does every time he's annoyed with me. "Just Google that shit next time. There's a whole spectrum of sexuality! Unless, of course, you're a bigoted white senator from a red state. In that case, sexuality doesn't exist at all. Especially not in the hidden folder on your desktop labeled *Kinky Porn*."

"Eww. Thanks for that."

"So why do you think you're bi?"

"I didn't say I was."

"You have a crush on Katie?"

"What? No!" I hold the phone away from me and glare at the screen.

"Someone on my team was talking about LUGs and BUGs and being fake gay, or doing gay tourism, or whatever. I just . . . didn't know if that was a thing."

"Interesting." Seth's voice lilts like he's hiding a secret. "Do you want it to be a thing?"

"No," I say steadily. "It seems offensive."

"To you?"

I splay one hand out, like Seth is right in front of me. "To everyone!"

"But maybe especially to you. Because you have a crush on Katie."

"I do NOT have a crush on Katie!"

"Who, then?" Seth asks.

I grind my teeth back and forth. "No one. I was just feeling like—"

Something crashes in the background.

"One sec." Seth's hand presses down on the phone speaker. His voice goes muffled. "I have to get back to rehearsal," he says a second later. "Apparently the actors are staging a mutiny against my AD. Anyway, call me later if you want to talk about your being-bi crisis. Your bisis!"

"Wait—" I say.

"Bye, sis!" Seth laughs. "Get it? *Bisis*."

He ends the call before I can respond.

CHAPTER TWELVE

The irony isn't lost on me that I'm essentially turning to the lion's den as a sanctuary from my own team.

The guard waves as I pass through the towering Gothic gate. We're sort of buds at this point. As much as any security guard and frequent student visitor could be.

I rush down the path from the visitors' lot toward the library. I'm already up the front steps and past the statue of Lady Van Darian when I pause, my hand on one door handle. I don't know what exactly I'm doing here, I realize. I have no idea what I'm going to say to Rosa, how I would even begin to unfold myself in that way. Maybe she'll respond exactly like Seth. She'll think I'm really here about a crush.

"This was a mistake," I say out loud.

I let go of the door handle.

I should go home and sort this out myself. Or better yet, I should go home and practice saves until my body's completely spent and way too tired to house any thoughts about being gay or straight or whatever the hell exists in the world. I should just turn around and go.

I take one step back from the library when the door opens, slamming directly into my face.

"Mother—!" I grab my nose and hunch over.

A collection of books drops onto the pavement next to me. "Oh my God, I'm so sorry! Do you think it's broken?" The girl squats on her haunches.

She tilts her head to look at the damage. Both our eyes widen.

"Evelyn," Rosa says. She touches my cheek in a way that makes me want to both explode and disappear. Her brows knit in tight concern. "What's wrong?"

My nose, I want to say. Obviously my nose is wrong. But then, it can't be obvious, because why else would Rosa be asking? And why is she talking so softly, and looking at me that way, and holding my face in her hand like I'm a porcelain doll cracking down the middle?

I don't want Rosa to think I'm broken. I want her to see me the way everyone else sees me. I want to be the steady one, the dependable one. I want to be a wall.

But as Rosa strokes my cheek again, I choke on a sob and completely fall apart.

My legs buckle under my weight and give out. My knees land hard on the sidewalk. Rosa throws both arms around my middle, trying to cushion the fall.

"Careful," she says. "You can break a kneecap like that. And I refuse to be liable for Heathclef losing their MVP just in time for regionals."

She smiles at me, but this only makes me cry harder.

"I don't know who I am," I wail through tears.

"Eve—it just means Most Valuable Player."

"No, no. Not that." I press the heels of my palms into my eyes. My chest trembles as I take a deep breath in, then out. "I mean, I'm afraid I don't exist. Like I'm a total anomaly on the spectrum of everything."

"Ah." Rosa sits on the ground next to me. She pulls her stack of books closer. "Join the club."

"It's not the same," I tell her. "You're the type of girl who thinks she's different, but in the story version of your life, everyone relates to you or wants to be you."

Rosa raises an eyebrow. "Is that so?"

"Yeah. Girl moves away from her cozy, vibrant home to a cold, pretentious boarding school that keeps her at arm's length because secretly they know she's better than them. Even though she's kind, and friendly, and ridiculously humble, they still see her as a threat. Because she's too beautiful. Too smart. Too crazy-talented. So they push her out and make her feel like an outsider. But in the story version, every reader loves you. Every single person is saying, 'That girl— I want to be like her.' You exude main character energy."

Rosa tucks her hair behind one ear. She bites down a smile, but I still see it form at the corners of her eyes. Her cheeks turn slightly pink and—oh my God—this is her being bashful. How can every expression look good on her.

She looks back up at me.

"I wish I could see myself that way," she says quietly. "But I'm glad you do."

116

The silence expands between us like a sponge. The air fills with static. I get the sudden, intense need to either move closer or get far, far away.

Luckily, Rosa makes the decision for me. She scoots back and hops up to standing.

"Come on," she says. She picks up the stack of books. "I'll go put these in my locker at the library. Then we can take a walk."

I stand next to her, still blotting at my face with my sleeves. "Where?"

"There's a dock that way that curls around the private lake."

"Okay, now that's fucking pretentious," I say, laughing.

Rosa laughs and nods. "Yeah," she agrees. "It is. But it's also fucking pretty, so let's go look at it."

I wait for her outside the library, hiding myself halfway behind Lady Van Darian in case any other members of the field hockey team happen to walk by. Rosa reemerges and points us down a narrow path. We break off from the rolling Van Darian hills and meadows and walk out toward the water. The sun scatters into pebbles between the leaves, turning thick and golden as it sinks into the horizon.

My breathing slows with every step. The panic tears dry away, leaving me with the deliciously sleepy sensation of deep calm. Rosa looks back at me and smiles in the sunlight. I don't even know when it happened, but somehow this girl went from being the person who completely wrecked my life to now being the only one who seems to understand it.

The dirt path eventually shifts into wooden planks twisting over the water like a fanned-out deck of cards. Inch-wide gaps peek out between the planks, which moan with every step. I rise to the balls of my feet.

Rosa checks over her shoulder and laughs. "You're not going to fall in."

"I might," I argue. "This dock is ancient. It's like walking on a bunch of glued-together toothpicks."

Without a word, Rosa suddenly throws her elbows on the dock railing and hoists one foot up, centering her shoe on maybe five inches of splintering wood.

"Rosa!"

She plants her feet carefully, then stands until she's at full height. Rosa spreads her arms wide like a tightrope walker and smiles. "This is *much* more like walking on a bunch of glued-together toothpicks."

"Great. You win," I say, teeth clenched. "Now get down!"

"I can't hear you," Rosa sings.

She goose-steps, one foot in front of the other, along the railing. I watch her take two more steps then trip over a knot in the wood.

I gasp and lunge toward her. Rosa grabs onto my hand and jumps back down on the dock. My fingers go numb from the tightness of her grasp.

"Shit," Rosa murmurs. She looks up at me sheepishly. "Thanks for that."

I smile. "Hey, being a viejito has its perks. Who else would keep you grounded?"

The reference seems to throw Rosa off. She blinks a moment, then turns and gazes at me like a hole just tore in the universe.

"What's the spectrum?" she asks suddenly.

I cock my head. "What?"

"You said you were an anomaly on the spectrum. What spectrum?"

"I *said* 'spectrum of everything.' "

"But you *meant* 'spectrum of . . .' "

I sigh and lean against the rail. "Multiple spectrums, I guess. Whatever people use to define themselves. Life just always seems easier when I fit into a specific label. Like being a goalkeeper. I like knowing exactly what that role means. I'll always know how to define that part of me."

"Unless you stop being a goalkeeper someday," Rosa adds.

I pause and squint at her. "Of course I'm never going to stop being a goalkeeper. Not until I'm, like, eighty."

Rosa shrugs. "Or if you don't want to do it anymore."

I shake my head. Sometimes I forget that Rosa's a field hockey transplant. She wasn't built on this sport the way I was. Her future doesn't hinge on it the way mine does.

"The point is, not everything is as easily defined as sports positions," I say. "I hate this idea that if I like someone one day, I'm straight, and if I like someone else the next day, I'm gay, or even worse, *fake* gay, and I don't even like the idea of being bi anyway because that feels like you're supposed to like guys and girls the same way, and my brain is messed up, like, really messed up, and it doesn't fit any of that."

I look down into the water, watching the eddying waves as if the emotional vomit I just expelled were a real thing, floating on the surface beneath us.

Off the reflection of the lake, I see the last pale traces of daylight drain down the horizon. Frogs poke their heads out of the reeds and bellow the deep, aching sobs that only frogs seem to have mastered. The dark blue of the evening moves in and makes my head feel heavy. I want to hide away here and not deal with myself anymore.

Rosa's arm brushes mine as she stands next to me. She stares across the lake.

"Labels can be great," she says slowly, "if you think they're great. I love being Chicana. I love being from New Mexico. But sometimes labels aren't great. Sometimes they're shit. And when that happens, just throw them out."

I look at her. "What do you mean, throw them out?"

Rosa smiles. Her skin is soft and blue under the shadows.

"You don't need to be straight or gay or bi, or even pan. I just say I'm queer, because I see it as a catchall term. But you don't have to say anything. You don't have to *be* anything, because you already are. If the labels are failing you, that's on them."

I chew on this thought. "So, I don't have to know what I am."

"Nope," Rosa says. "Just follow your heart and be open to whatever."

"Huh." I prop my elbows on the railing. "That's . . . that's different advice than I've ever heard before."

I think about how when I was a kid, Mom would comfort me whenever I felt lost or confused by telling me exactly what I was going to be like when I was older. I would be a great field hockey player, just like she was. I'd meet someone wonderful, like how she met Dad. Someday, I would even have kids of my own who Mom could take out on the field and work with on passes and saves. Near the end, that last part went away. But it was more important than ever that I stick to the plan, that I follow things step by step, because that was how to take Mom with me. If I open myself up to whatever . . . what if she ends up getting left behind?

"Hey there." Rosa touches my arm. "What's on your mind?"

I blink and turn to her. "Nothing. Stuff from when I was younger."

Rosa's brows furrow. She's looking at me with more concern than I really deserve. Probably more concern than anyone has ever looked at me with before.

"I'm not trying to make things harder on you," she says. "Throw out whatever I said that doesn't feel right."

"It's not that," I say quickly. "Everything feels right."

I pause. The words float away from me, from the entire context of the conversation, and hang between us. They go heavy in the middle, like bubbles with too much soap.

Everything feels right.

The streaks of light tug on Rosa's cheekbones. They slide down the ridge of her nose and curve over her deep brown eyes.

This is the most beautiful human I've ever seen, I realize. And here I am, up close to her. I get to look down at her eyelashes, and smell the overwhelming pulls of lavender in her dark curly hair. I can feel her energy crackling and snapping in the night. It's that tension again, the one telling me to get lost or come closer. But now all I want to do is get so close that the space between us disappears into nothing.

I have no idea what Rosa's thinking, if she's panicking

about taking me here, wishing she never would have been my friend. But she doesn't move either. She plants herself in front of me and looks up, her chin sharp and defiant. It feels like a dare. It feels like an invitation.

I take one step closer.

Eeerrrrrrrrrrrrr.

A loud moan from the planks echoes around the corner.

"Shoot," Rosa says. "No one ever comes out this way."

She ducks to look behind us and all the space whooshes back. The feeling of the world turning on its side goes away. Balance restored.

"Should we go back?" I ask.

Rosa doesn't answer. She squints down the dock.

Suddenly her eyes go wide. "Oh no."

"What is it?"

"ROSITAAAAAAA!" a voice echoes in the distance.

Rosa turns to me. "It's Galen."

"Who?"

The planks begin jolting with the weight of someone bounding toward us.

"My *teammate*," Rosa hisses.

The planks vibrate harder. My stomach clenches. I consider diving right off the side of the dock into the water. But they'd notice the splashing anyway. There's only one way out of this.

Rosa rubs her chin. "I'll see if I can go explain to her— Evelyn? Evelyn!"

She turns and tries to catch me, but it's too late. I plunge farther into the trail of the dock, pounding the wood with my heels and praying it won't come to a dead end in the middle of nowhere.

The landscape of the lake blurs into a fever dream. Sloshing water tangles with sharp, jutting branches. As I run, I lose track of what's real and what's in my head. People don't actually turn blue in the twilight. No one looks that beautiful in real life, or sounds that caring, or smells that good. Maybe I just wanted Rosa to be all those things. I wanted her to be a safe place.

But as the dock spits me out into the woods surrounding Van Darian, the magic drifts away. There is no safety here. I wade through the trees back to campus, feeling once again like I'm lost in enemy territory.

Rosa's my rival, I remind myself. She's playing for a team that wants to see me lose everything.

Seeing her isn't a sanctuary.

It's a dangerous game of risk.

CHAPTER THIRTEEN

Later that week, I'm face-to-face with a creepy cardboard cutout of an anthropomorphic golf ball. It's an early Friday evening, filled with a symphony of chirping crickets, the sting of November air, and the stomach-churning feeling that one way or another, this night is probably going to turn into a huge mistake.

Katie threads her arm through mine, hoedown-style, and pulls me in close.

"He's so cute, though, right?"

I blink at Gordon the Golf Ball. "Uh, who?"

"Who do you think?" Katie says. "My date! Bryce!"

I give her a side glance. "Katie, you've seen Bryce a million times."

Katie rolls her eyes. "Duh, fool. *I* know he's cute. I'm trying to get hyped up by my best friend here. Has he said anything to Caleb about me? Is he excited? Was this his idea or Caleb's—tell the truth."

We're standing outside Gordy's, the miniature golf venue

of choice for little kids, old men, and, for some reason, basically everyone from our high school. I feel like most of us claim we're only swinging balls at blue dragons and spinning windmills ironically, but the truth is, we're probably even more giddy about it than the kids are.

"It was both of their idea," I say. "Caleb wanted to hang here. Bryce wanted to come. Caleb said I might bring you. Then Bryce *really* wanted to come."

Katie shoots me a cheesy grin and tightens her hold on my arm. "There's my hype woman. Okay, breathe in. Breathe out. Oh shit, here they come."

She nods toward the parking lot. I look up just as Caleb and Bryce slam the doors of Caleb's pickup truck and saunter over, hands half-dug into pockets.

"Hey there," Caleb murmurs as he leans in to kiss me.

For a moment time stops, or does that thing in movies where the seconds downshift into slow motion. The lights of the mini-golf building catch on Caleb's hair, and even his eyes sort of twinkle, and I realize: Holy shit, this is how the rest of the world sees him. This is how I'm supposed to see him all the time. Caleb's the literal embodiment of tall, blond, and handsome. He's the quintessential all-American jock. And if I could just want to burrow under one of his massive arms instead of wanting someone to burrow under mine . . . then things would work. We would be the couple everyone else thinks we are.

But then time catches up and like an optical illusion, the shiny parts vanish.

Oh, I think as our lips touch.

We aren't a dream team at all.

I glance over at Katie, who's currently sharing an incredibly awkward side hug with Bryce.

"Are you sure this was a good idea?" Caleb says in my ear.

I pull away fast to cut him off, before Katie can overhear. I don't want her to even think this was all my doing—that I asked Caleb to turn a romantic dinner into a double date at Gordy's and blamed it on Katie's burning crush on Bryce.

Instead of answering, I sweep my hair back and grab hold of Katie.

"Let's mini golf!" I say cheerily.

I march Katie ahead of the guys, up to the front booth where we carefully select hot pink and lime green golf balls with matching clubs. Our group winds its way through the fixed labyrinth of holes.

Things begin easily enough. There's an army of old-school Troll dolls that are supposed to look like an obstacle, but really they make an easy bumper to send the ball right back on its path. I guess everyone deserves to feel good about at least one hole. Bryce mostly talks to Caleb, although I do see him steal glances at Katie's ass as she lines up her shots. I make a mental note to tell Katie all about this later.

Then, as we round the corner after the first set of holes, the evening of fun and games comes to a dead halt.

"Oh my God," Katie says. "Is that Alvarez?"

"Nope," I say quickly without even looking. Because it can't be. Because the laws of the universe do not allow collisions between rival field hockey teams at a miniature golf course.

But then I steal a glance where Katie's pointing and—*dammit, universe!*—it's her.

At hole seven, barely two holes ahead of us, Rosa and another girl I recognize from Van Darian's field hockey team are holding matching golf clubs with bright purple handles. Rosa is hunched over laughing while the girl watches in horror as her ball slowly rolls down a sand hill and into a pond. Some deep muscle twinges in my chest. I didn't think Rosa really connected with her teammates outside of practice.

I face back toward the guys.

"Anyone want some snacks? I'm going to get some snacks."

"But it's your turn," Caleb says.

I throw him my club. "You take it for me!"

"Want me to come?" Katie calls.

I shake my head and sweep the air with one hand, motioning her closer to Bryce. Katie squints at me a minute, then looks over at Bryce, realization taking on slowly.

"Ohhhhh," she mouths. She nods and smiles, then takes the tiniest step ever to the bench Bryce is currently collapsed onto.

The second her back is turned, I rush off in the opposite direction of the Snack Shack.

Rosa's golfing partner is still trying to fish her ball out of the water with the end of her club. I can hear the splashing and cursing as I peer through the nearest hedge. Rosa's standing at the top of the hill, eyes turned to the first few stars winking in the night sky. I wish I were standing next to her, totally normal, asking what she was thinking about.

Instead, I throw a small rock at her through the bush.

"Psst!"

The rock sails right past Rosa, unnoticed.

I squat over the cold ground to find another one. There is a serious pebble shortage in this establishment. After grabbing a handful of nothing, I settle for shaking the bush as hard as I can.

"Rosa! Psst! Rosa!"

Rosa looks back from the sky. I thrust one arm through the bush and beckon her over.

"It's me!" I stage-whisper.

She stares at the hedge, head to one side. "Evelyn?" With each step, a small smile grows on Rosa's face until she's full-on grinning by the time she's within reaching distance. She bends down, her nose nearly brushing mine. "Practicing your camouflage techniques?"

I scowl at her, though I hardly think she'd be able to tell my eyebrows apart from the crisscrossing branches in front of me. "You have to leave," I say.

Rosa pulls back. "What? Why?"

I hitch my thumb. "My teammate's here."

"Yeah, so is mine. So what?"

"So, they can't see us together."

"You mean the way you just slunk over here like the world's clumsiest Double-O-Seven to be next to me?"

I click my tongue. "That is so *not* the reason I came over here. Listen, our group is going to catch up to you soon, and I know Katie: she is scary-fierce when she's being protective, so it would probably be better if—"

Something pulls my other arm and yanks me backward.

"Eve! Are you okay?" Katie brushes a twig off my shoulder.

"Oh. Yeah. I just . . . tripped."

The moment I stand up next to Katie, it becomes excruciatingly obvious that the hedges between us and Rosa only reach up to chin height. Katie glares over the top of the brush.

"What do you want?"

Rosa raises her golf club. "You came over to my hole!"

Katie strides past me. "Gordy's is a certified Heathclef hangout. You and your little friend came to *our* holes!"

"Okay, no one was going to anyone else's hole!" I yell out. "We were . . . getting snacks. I was getting a snack. And got lost."

"Uh-huh," Rosa says, rolling her eyes.

I can tell immediately that this sets Katie off. She narrows her eyes at Rosa and sets her jaw. For an incredibly tense four seconds, no one says anything. Then Katie turns and pulls me with her.

"Not worth it," she says under her breath, which, actually, is incredible progress for someone as loyal and hot-tempered as Katie.

We find Caleb and Bryce only a few yards away, already teeing up at hole six. Caleb drops my lime green ball onto the Astroturf and extends my club out.

"Your turn again," he says.

I reach for the club, but notice that Caleb doesn't let go. Instead, he parks himself directly behind me. His hands grasp over mine.

"Make sure to hit the ball nice and slow," he says. I can feel his groin pressing into my ass. "Nice and slow."

A small *"harrumph"* comes from the next course. Rosa's cheeks are flushed as she stares over the hedge at me and Caleb together. I try to tamp down the little feeling of glee that rises in my stomach. She almost looks . . . jealous.

"Are y'all on a date too?" Bryce asks Rosa. He points down the hill toward the other girl. "Like, a lesbian date?"

"No," Rosa responds primly. "Is it really necessary to sexualize every pair of femme-presenting people you see?"

"Only the lesbian ones," Bryce says, and laughs like this is the most clever line ever thought up by anyone.

Caleb still hasn't let go of my arms. I can barely breathe as his chest pushes down over my shoulders. Every instinct is yelling at me to shimmy away, to catch my breath and just stand on my own. But I can't do that here.

"You want to take a shot?" Caleb whispers. He says it the way I did in my room weeks ago, and I can feel from his body pressed against mine that he's turned on.

"You do know your girlfriend plays field hockey, right?"

Caleb finally breaks away from me and looks up. "Excuse me?"

Rosa has a death grip on the handle of her club. "She knows how to hit a ball. Probably better than you. Stop treating her like a child."

She turns away abruptly and tromps down the sand hill.

"What was her problem?" Caleb mutters as he not-so-subtly adjusts his pants.

I shrug, relief flooding into every corner of my body. "Who knows. Forget her."

I knock the ball, and we all watch as it makes a perfect hole in one. I say nothing as I jot my score on the group score-pad. Rosa would be so ridiculously pleased if she could see the look on Caleb's face.

"My turn," Katie announces.

She steps out from the group and places her ball at the mark. We watch her reposition herself over and over, moving one foot slightly in an inch, then back out. She sways her club like a pendulum. I know Katie well enough to recognize this as textbook "I'm-with-a-cute-guy-and-I'm-nervous" behavior.

"Sometime today, maybe?" Caleb asks.

Katie gives him the finger and pulls back to swing.

WHACK.

Before the club can even connect, a purple ball suddenly rains down from the sky and pops Katie on the head. She yelps and drops her club.

I throw mine to the side and jog over. "Kay! Are you okay?"

"I think so," she says, wincing. She touches her hair. "Am I bleeding?"

I look closely at her hand. "No, it's just . . . wet."

We pause, then look over at hole seven, where Rosa and her friend are staring up at us from the edge of the pond. Rosa's frozen, her own club still raised.

"Oh *fuck*," I murmur.

Katie quickly pushes off me and storms down the hill. She reaches Rosa and jabs her hard in the chest.

"What the hell was that?" Katie roars.

"I was trying to help get the ball out," Rosa says, palms raised. "It was an accident."

"All right, lady fight!" Bryce calls behind me. He looks around, as if he thinks an excited crowd is going to form and start chanting like schoolkids. Caleb sighs and shakes his head.

The other Van Darian girl steps next to Rosa.

Rosa touches the girl's arm. "It's fine, Galen."

Galen, I think, remembering the name.

I picture Galen and Rosa standing together on the dock, in the same place I had been standing when reality forgot to function and Rosa's skin turned blue and soft and perfect under the moonlight. Suddenly I wonder what Galen was doing that night, creeping out to find Rosa after dark. Do teammates just hang out on docks under the stars? Is that even a normal friend thing to do?

"It's definitely *not* fine," Katie says. The edge in her voice snaps me right back into the moment. "Don't act like you're going to hit me with a ball and then walk away like cowards."

"Does it look like we're walking anywhere?" Galen gets up in Katie's face. "If you want to do something, then do something."

Katie cocks her arm back. "That's it."

Rosa's eyes go wide. She looks up at me, and I can see in an instant how scared she is.

"Stop!" I scream.

I rush down the sand hill, running to protect Rosa. But just as I wedge myself between Katie and Galen, I suddenly remember where I am, remember who I am. I turn my back against the Van Darian girls and face Katie head-on.

"Don't do anything stupid," I say, trying to sound calm. I place my palms over Katie's shoulders. "Alvarez is right. It was an accident."

Katie's mouth drops open. She points at Rosa accusingly. "Eve! You *know* this asshole knows how to hit a ball."

"Yeah, in field hockey," I say. "She's a field hockey asshole, not a professional mini golfer. She was an idiot and overswung. Let's go. She's not worth it."

I hear a sharp inhalation behind me. I pretend not to notice.

My hands stay firmly on Katie's shoulders as she glares ahead, nostrils flared. Katie's breath is rapid and heavy. Her teeth and hands are tightly clenched. I don't know how to push Pause on this, how to stop the wave of anger building up inside her.

"Everything okay over here?" Caleb asks from the top of the hill.

Of course not, I think.

Everything is a complete and total clusterfuck. My life feels like I put it on backward. I'm defending my rival against my best friend. I'm pulling away from the perfect boyfriend. I have a whole circle of people around me and all I want is the one person I should be staying away from. Everything is messed up because of me.

I press Katie toward the guys.

"This place sucks," I say. "Let's go drive somewhere and make out."

The suggestion has its immediate intended effect as Katie's eyes suddenly bulge wide and the tension drains from her hands.

Bryce shrugs. "I'm down."

"Great!" I say. I gather our scattered clubs at hole six. Caleb practically tosses them onto the return shelf as we leave. I huddle under his arm, leaning into his chest like a bird with its head in the sand.

I don't look back at Rosa.

I absolutely cannot allow myself to look back at Rosa.

CHAPTER FOURTEEN

Rosa leaves me on read the next day.

Saturday

Me: *Je-SUS that was intense.*

Me: *Katie's all bark, don't worry about her.*

Me: *What's the deal with Galen, btw?*

Me: *Hello?*

Me: *. . . Ro?*

Thunder rumbles across the lake as I march down the sidewalk to Rosa's dormitory on Sunday evening. The wind swoops down from the trees, lifting my hair off my shoulders and tossing it from side to side. I can tell the sky's about to split open and drench everything. I don't care. I didn't even bring my field hockey gear with me. If Rosa's going to suddenly ghost and never hang out with me again, then I at least want to know why.

I brace against the high wind as gusts start to slam into my shoulders. The first drops begin to fall just as I approach the dorm building. I duck in behind a group of girls using their backpacks as umbrellas.

My knuckles rap hard against room 214.

"Rosa?"

No one answers.

"Come on, Rosa. I . . . I miss you."

I lean against the frame and let my fingers brush against the door.

"Even if you don't want to be friends anymore, please say it to me. Please talk to me. I have no idea what's going on."

"Really? No idea?"

I turn to see Rosa standing in another doorway across the hall. She's wearing an apron tied tight around her waist and donning two oversized oven mitts. I rush down the hall, then stop myself before I reach her.

"You shit, you were just listening to me sob outside your door?"

"I didn't hear any sobbing," Rosa says airily. "I was listening for an apology. You might have been getting there, maybe. But there definitely wasn't any sobbing."

She disappears back into the room and I poke my head inside. It's a communal kitchen, complete with a fridge, a microwave, a few cupboards, and an oven that looks like it should have broken down about ten years ago. Hip-hop music glides through the air and I trace it back to Rosa's phone on the countertop. She hums softly as she bends down and checks through the grimy window on the oven door.

"Not yet," she says to herself.

"I didn't know you cook," I tell her.

Rosa straightens. "I don't," she says. "My stepdad does all the cooking at home. But the food in the dining hall is garbage, so here I am."

I fold my arms. "Really? The food at Van Darian is garbage?"

Rosa clicks her tongue. "It's bland, okay? I don't want dry chicken and white rice every night. Sometimes I need a little bit of spice."

The oven beeps and Rosa leans to look through the grimy window again. "Ah, yes!"

She pulls the door open and the room floods with the smells of chili powder, garlic, cumin, and tomato. Rosa carefully emerges with a ceramic dish of bubbling cheese and corn tortillas. My mouth instantly begins to salivate. But Rosa tuts.

"It would be a million times better with green chile," she says, more to herself than me.

"Yeah, right," I say, staring at the dish. "How could any one thing possibly make that much of a difference?"

Rosa looks at me like I just slapped a kitten. "Excuse me, green chile is *life*," she says seriously. "Every good New Mexican knows the answer to 'red or green' is always green. You can eat green chile cold and diced, or warm and roasted, or part of a salsa, or just by itself. Green chile is the most magical vegetable to ever exist."

"Well, okay then." I nod. "Good to know."

Rosa chuckles, then remembers it's me standing in front of her and instantly gives me a deep scowl. I sigh.

Rain pelts the outside window over the table in the corner. The drops are practically flying sideways. I'm not in a particular hurry to get back out there. Rosa hasn't invited me in, and I know it was rude to burst into her dorm in the first place without asking. But I have to know where things between us stand.

I look down the hallway. "So, is Galen coming, or whatever?" Rosa squints at me. "No. Why?"

"No reason." I sit down at the tiny, beat-up table and interlace my fingers. "I just thought maybe she was a really good friend. Or more than a good friend. Not that I'm trying to sexualize every pair of femme-presenting people out there."

This line earns the faintest smile from Rosa. "That's exactly what it sounds like you're trying to do."

She sighs and grabs two plates and forks from the cupboard. I watch her load three rolled tortillas covered in cheese onto each plate. She hands me one of the plates and sits with hers across the table.

"Enchiladas," she says.

"I know what enchiladas are."

"Good for you. Now, eat."

I section off a slice with tortillas, cheese, and a thick, red sauce. The sharp, spicy flavor hits me instantly. A rush of sweetness from the tomatoes follows. Despite eating more than my body weight in Mexican food with Katie over the years, I've never had this combination of spices before. Somehow, the arrangement makes every familiar ingredient taste new and different. The cheese and sauce fold together perfectly, and it takes everything in me not to inhale the entire plate in five seconds flat.

"My God," I say, wiping my mouth. "You're a freaking chef."

"Huh." Rosa twirls a string of melted cheese around and around her fork. "I thought I was an asshole."

"What?"

"Or, wait, I'm an asshole *and* the idiot who overswung."

"Rosa . . ."

She shakes her head. "And I'm not worth it. We can't forget that one. I'm a field hockey asshole and a golfing idiot and either way I'm not worth the energy."

We stare hard at each other.

"You know that's not what I meant," I say.

"Well, it's what you said."

I set my fork to the side. The enchiladas in front of me are ridiculously good, but I need to gather my full focus for this. I draw my hands under my chin and try to come up with the right words to make Rosa understand the bigger situation going on.

"Rosa, look, I'm sorry. But our teammates cannot know that we're friends. We're right in the middle of field hockey season, and your team trashed my team's field, like, two months ago. Everyone is still pissed over that. I don't want there to be issues for either of us down the line, especially if both our teams keep doing well. But I do care about you. I like being your friend. Katie went off the deep end at the golf course, and if I thought she really was going to punch you, I would have tackled her down. She was just blowing off steam. I mean, you smacked a ball right into her. . . ."

Rosa holds up a hand.

"Okay, stop. First, this apology sucks. You're not supposed to make excuses or blame shit on me. An apology is just an 'I messed up and I'm owning it' moment. That's it. You can apologize for calling me those things without pulling in context to absolve yourself of blame."

I swallow.

"Second," Rosa goes on, "I did not hit that ball at your friend. I would never, *ever* do something like that. The party was stupid, and you already know it wasn't my idea to throw it at Heathclef. But even then, that was just trash. It wasn't targeting anyone or hurting anything. I would never do something hurtful on purpose."

My mind instantly thinks of Rosa's field hockey jacket balled up in my car.

It's not the same, I tell myself. I didn't write those words on Rosa's jacket. And I called her those things at Gordy's to protect her from Katie. I wasn't hurting her. I was *protecting* her. Wasn't I?

Rosa looks at me expectantly.

"I was . . . trying to protect you," I mumble.

Rosa pushes her plate away.

"I don't want to do this," she says.

I stand up from the table. "I can leave. You enjoy your food."

"No." Rosa stands after me. "I mean, I don't want to deal with this side of you."

I lower my brows. "What side of me?"

She waves her arms toward me like I'm an exhibit at a science fair.

"The side that curls into yourself, that makes bullshit excuses that even you know are bullshit."

Rosa slumps back down into her chair. "I'm not mad you didn't want to be my friend in front of your people. I'm just . . . disappointed, I guess. I know that's a worse thing to say. You're usually so strong and passionate and in the moment. But you disappeared into yourself on the golf course the second your group caught up to you. And you're doing it again right now. I want the real Evelyn. Just crawl the fuck out of your weird little hiding place."

I sit across from her again, staring down at the table.

I'm always hiding, I think. Rosa might be the only person I don't have to hide with. But I don't want her to know that.

"You were different out there," Rosa goes on. She lingers on the next thought. "You weren't the person I know."

She looks up at me earnestly, like she's hoping I'll say the magic words and this whole fight can just disappear. I want to say the right words so badly. The wanting to make her smile, to be close to her again, is so strong that it physically hurts. But I also can't ignore the truth. The version of me that Rosa sees, the one that she wants . . . that's only a tiny sliver of who I am. It might not even be the real me at all.

I *have* to be someone else around my family and teachers and teammates. I've worked so hard to be that person, to line up everything exactly right. There's a reason I'm captain of our team, and I'm dating the football quarterback, and I'm browsing Duke sweatshirts online. It's all prescribed. I can't wake up one day and decide to drop my whole life.

I clear my throat.

"Maybe . . . maybe I'm not the person you know," I say carefully.

Rosa's shoulders deflate. Her chin tips down. If there was an exact opposite of the magic words, I've definitely said them.

We finish our food in silence. I resist getting seconds, especially since I know Rosa will probably be eating this for the rest of the week. I wash the chipped plates and bent forks in the scratched-up kitchen sink. Rosa dries them with paper towels and sets them back into the cupboards.

"Thanks for dinner," I mumble. "I gotta go."

Rosa doesn't turn or wave as I walk out of the kitchen and down the hall. I don't know how to feel as I push the dormitory door open. We might be done. I might never see this person again, and it's all my fault.

I walk out into a storm with the acoustics of a heavy-metal concert. Rain beats down over the eaves with pounding ferocity. The noise crowds out the sadness in my head, forcing me to duck and run so I can make it to my car without looking completely like a drowned rat. But after a few steps I hear someone shouting over the rain. I turn around.

"Why?" Rosa shouts again. She's standing just inside the doorframe.

"Why what?"

"Why *him*?"

I wipe a layer of rain from my forehead and jog back under the awning. I don't have to ask who she's talking about.

"Because," I start. "We . . . don't fight. We don't take work the way other people do. I don't have time for a relationship that takes work."

Rosa bores her eyes into mine. Her gaze almost knocks me senseless. There's a nakedness to it, an expression of every emotion she's feeling, without holding back. She's angry. She's sad. But above all that, she's hungry. She craves so much that it's terrifying.

I want to press my hand into the side of her face, see how much of her cheekbone would hide under my palm. I want to sweep my thumb across her brow and tuck the rest of her hair away. But she's not mine, I tell myself. She can't be mine. I'm with Caleb because he fits into the world I've already built for myself. If I were with Rosa . . . there wouldn't be a big enough place to fit her. I'd have to turn my whole life inside out, shifting piece by piece around her. Nothing would be the same.

"You don't like him, though" Rosa says, breaking me from the trance. I realize I've raised my hand halfway between us.

I draw my hand back. "What?"

She furrows her brow. "I said, you don't like him. He doesn't understand you, and I wouldn't have to know anything else about you to know that. I can see it on your face when you're with him."

"You saw us for two minutes," I mutter. "You can't look at anyone for two minutes and know their story. Do you know how presumptuous that is?"

Rosa leans against the doorframe. "Well, do you like him or not?"

"Of course I do," I say. "If I didn't like him then why would he be my boyfriend?"

"I don't know," Rosa says coldly. "Why would he?"

I only glare back at her.

Rosa shakes her head. "I don't know why you split yourself into so many pieces. You cuddle up to your boyfriend. You prop up your team. You come here and open up to me. Maybe your whole thing is only giving away little glimpses of you. You don't want anyone to have too much. That way you can keep yourself safe."

"Safe from what?" I ask.

Rosa steps out of the doorframe and under the awning. I take a step back, giving her space, but she keeps coming toward me. We move together, inches between us, until we're both standing unguarded in the downpour. Rosa steps in again. My shoulders and head sting from the rain. I can feel the soft heat of Rosa's breath on my collarbone. Her eyes trail up my skin, lingering on my neck, my jawline, my mouth. I can barely exhale.

Rosa tilts her head back. Rainwater sluices down her cheeks.

"You tell me," she whispers.

The air pops and crackles. I can feel a line being drawn from my mouth to Rosa's. But I don't part my lips. I don't say anything at all. Everything I've built feels like it could crumble in an instant, with a single word. I draw myself higher, trying to pull every thread of my life taut.

I have never felt less like a wall.

After the longest minute in existence, Rosa takes a rattled breath and steps back under the awning. A cold wind cuts though the sudden gap between us.

"Right," she says, droplets rolling off her hair. "So that's how it is."

My heart splinters as I watch Rosa go through the door. I want to go after her. I want to forget everything I owe the rest of the world and pull Rosa right back into the rain.

But I know what I have to do instead.

CHAPTER FIFTEEN

The next morning feels like an emotional hangover.

My head is thick and heavy as I drag my feet down the hall. I don't share any classes with Caleb, and while I never particularly minded that before, today I'm extra thankful I don't have to see him.

Katie does have Spanish with me, and I catch her side glances the entire time we practice asking directions to the flea market, haggling over prices for sweaters, and then smugly informing our friends of our purchases. I notice our teacher, Señora Esquivel, is rocking a new colorful patchwork cardigan as she walks around the room and listens in on our conversations. I wonder if this entire activity is just a daylong validation for her choices last weekend.

After class I hang back for a minute to ask Señora Esquivel some questions. Katie's waiting for me in the hall when I come out.

"¿Qué compraste?" Katie asks.

I fold the note from Señora Esquivel and stick it into my pocket. "What did I buy? At the pretend market, you mean?"

"Yeah," Katie says. "I ditched the sweater thing and went with motorcycle boots. I feel like I could really pull off motorcycle boots. Not that Bryce would like them."

"Why would that matter?" I ask. I pause as Katie's smile cracks into a full-on grin. "Wait. Are you guys . . . together?"

Katie throws her arms up and spins in the hallway. "Thanks, matchmaker!"

I watch as she unabashedly gets in everyone's way at once and does a spontaneous jig from wall to wall.

"Someone's happy," I say, smiling.

Katie wraps both her arms around one of mine and tilts her head onto my shoulder. "Well thank God you got us out of that hellhole with Alvarez and suggested driving somewhere to make out."

I shake my head. "Yeah, I'm so sorry about that. I really should have asked you in private first. What an awful situation to suggest—"

"It was perfect!" Katie yells. "We just got to let go of all our nervousness, and he's such a good kisser, and then he DMed me on Saturday! I can't believe I'm dating a tight end. Hells yes for me!"

I laugh as Katie tugs my arm like a small child and bounces up and down on the balls of her feet.

"I thought you hated the football team," I say, teasing her. "Getting all the fall sports glory and taking it away from us."

147

Katie raises her eyebrows. "Mmm, maybe they're not taking *all* the glory away from us," she says mischievously.

"What is that supposed to mean?"

"Oh, you'll see. Later," she adds, and then winks, just because Katie has never been known for her subtlety.

We're at the part of the building where she heads downstairs and I go left for next period. Just as she lets go of my one arm, Katie gives me a last full-body squeeze, this time pinning both my arms to my sides.

"I'm so excited our boyfriends are besties too," she says breathlessly, her voice muffled in my hair. "Okay, see you!"

I watch as she dips down the staircase, still bouncing step by step.

"See you," I echo, waving stupidly until she's out of sight. "Shit," I say under my breath.

Nothing is going to be easy today.

I rehearse the words in my head in the shower post-practice. Caleb is so great. He's an amazing person: athletic, funny, kind. There are millions of people out there who would be so lucky, who would pass out cold, if he asked them on a date. He deserves the best of the best. He deserves the perfect girlfriend. But—

But.

And there the imaginary speech stops. Because I can't figure out how to switch gears from telling Caleb all the nice things about him to telling him that, actually, I'm not that perfect girlfriend. He's always wanted me to be someone I'm just not. And I want . . .

I want impossible things.

My hair's still dripping as I hurriedly cram my head back through my sweatshirt.

"Whoa, there." Katie pulls up next to me and hands me a hairbrush from her locker. "Here. Try this fancy new gadget."

"Gross," I say. "I'm not sharing a hairbrush with you."

"Oh, right, because we haven't shared a million other things worse than that."

I roll my eyes. "Fine. Fair." I take the brush and do two strokes on either side of my hair part. It clatters as I toss it back into Katie's locker.

"Okay, thanks! Bye!"

"Wait up. You're always rushing out of here right away. Where are you going?"

I turn and see that almost half of my teammates are staring at me along with Katie. Their brows are furrowed. Arms crossed. If I didn't know any better, it would feel like I had just walked into my own intervention.

"I'm going to see Caleb," I say slowly, looking over the team. "Is that, uh, *okay* with everyone?"

Katie grabs her own sweater. "Oh, good! I'll come with you and see Bryce!"

No! I want to yell. I need to do this myself. But I have the shaky feeling that I might be on thin ice with Katie, and maybe even the rest of the team. So instead, I wait by the door, impatiently bouncing on my feet as Katie meticulously brushes her hair and finishes putting on makeup.

We head out of the gym together. Caleb's practice is on the other end of campus. The football team has their own locker room connected directly to the main stadium.

"If you get bored, feel free to jet," I say to Katie. "They might be a while."

"Or not," Katie says, grinning. She nods her chin to two figures walking our way. It's Caleb and Bryce. I look at Katie.

"Were they already on their way here?" I ask.

She shrugs and grins even wider. I shake my head slightly, realizing that the surprise Katie winked about earlier is probably about to happen, right now.

Athletic, kind, funny, I remind myself. Stick to the script. *Athletic, kind, funny. Deserves so much better than me.* He'll have to agree with that, at the very least.

"Ladies," Bryce says as the guys get closer. He opens one arm for Katie, and without a word she skips over and slips right next to him.

That used to be Caleb's move on me. I hated the strong, musky smell while standing under his arm, but I never said anything, would never not go immediately into his side. I look at him now, hoping, pleading that he won't pull the same gesture.

He doesn't.

"Hey," Caleb says. His cheeks look particularly rosy. "Got a surprise for you."

"Huh," I say, trying to laugh a little. "Cool."

My entire body twists like a washrag. Why are breakups so hard? Why are they this impossible thing to bring up while everyone else wants to carry on as normal? What I need is to get Caleb alone. Once it's just him and me, I can rip off the Band-Aid.

"How about you show me in my car?" I ask. I reach out for his hand.

Caleb bites his lip and looks down at my open palm. The possibility of making out seems to have wiped whatever he was going to say completely out of his head. Then Bryce elbows Caleb's side.

"Right," Caleb says. He resets. "The surprise is I'm finally making the guys come cheer for you!"

I blink at him. "What?"

"For your last away game in two weeks. The football team's off the schedule, and Coach was going to have us running drills through November. Then Bryce and I realized the perfect way to get out of it. We'll all come to see you! Tell Coach we're doing important team bonding or whatever."

"Isn't that great?" Katie says, squirming like a puppy against Bryce.

I want to cry. Why does Caleb have to be doing something nice? Maybe I should just wait this out another two weeks, or two months, or two years, or, hell, even the rest of my life. Maybe I should just make everyone around me happy and keep things easy.

I close my eyes. There's Rosa again, rain catching on her eyelashes outside the dorm. My hands hurt from wanting to hold her. My chest feels like it's never going to get warm again until I can lean against her. It's not fair, I suddenly realize, for me to feel this way about someone else. It doesn't matter whether I can have Rosa or not. Caleb deserves better than being a placeholder.

I look at him, abandoning the script entirely. "We have to break up."

Katie releases a soft gasp under Bryce's arm.

Caleb stares at me. "Are you serious right now?"

"Yeah," I say. "I just don't know if we're right for each other. I feel like you see me as this specific type of girl who cares about specific things. But then in real life I care about completely different things and people and—"

"People?" Caleb's voice seems to bump mine out of the way with his intensity. "Is this about someone else?"

My breath catches. I don't know how to answer that at first. If I think about it, deep down, I know this isn't really about a person I want to be with. This is about the person I want to *be* in a relationship. I want to be the protector, the way I am with my team. I want to be someone who I cannot be when I'm with Caleb.

The pause between us stretches on for too long.

Caleb narrows his eyes. "Who the hell is the guy, Evelyn?"

The edge in his voice makes me want to cower. I've seen him get angry at his friends a few times. But not at me. Never at me. I picture the way Caleb looked at Rosa back at Gordy's. My insides turn.

"There is no guy," I say, nearly a whisper.

Caleb shakes his head. "I fucking bet."

He shoves his hands into his pockets. His mouth is pressed so tight that his lips turn pale. Nobody in the group speaks. Bryce's eyebrows seem permanently fixed halfway up his forehead. Katie laser-focuses her bewilderment on me, and I can tell she's asking me a million questions in her head. Even if I was a mind reader, I wouldn't know how to answer them.

"I shouldn't have told you like this," I say quietly.

Caleb's jaw hardens. "No, no, no. It's cool. I love getting dumped in front of other people. Especially after I do something really nice for my girlfriend. Especially after I pull a bunch of strings to get our *varsity football* team out at a freaking *girls' field hockey* game."

"What is that supposed to mean?" I ask, looking up.

I've heard the subtle digs from Caleb about field hockey so many times. And every time I've told myself that I'm imagining it, that he doesn't really mean it, that the problem is on a much bigger level than one boyfriend not caring enough about my sport. But the disdain is now practically dripping off him. It couldn't get any more obvious.

"It means whatever you want it to mean," Caleb mutters. "Have a nice life, Evelyn."

Caleb does an about-face and marches back up the main walkway he and Bryce just came from. Bryce immediately turns after him. Katie pauses a moment, eyes ping-ponging between Bryce and me before she makes up her mind. She sends me one last inscrutable look as she runs to catch up with the guys.

Their footsteps echo under the trees, fading into the distance until it's just me standing there. I take a deep breath in.

The Band-Aid is officially ripped off. No more Caleb. No more being the perfect girlfriend of the football quarterback.

The funny thing is, of course Mom never asked me to date a football player. Neither of us even knew Caleb when she died. But somehow, stepping away from him seems like stepping away from her too. It was easy to see my future if I followed in Mom's footsteps exactly. Play goalkeeper. Date the quarterback. Get into Duke. Check, check, check.

So what happens when I deviate, even just a little, from our plan? Is everything else going to unravel?

I turn away from Caleb and Bryce and Katie, stepping down the winding side path toward my car. I've taken this route after practice a million times. But today, for the first time, it feels like I'm going somewhere completely new.

CHAPTER SIXTEEN

The rest of the week turns out to be exactly as quiet and lonely as one would expect after a sudden, apocalyptic-level breakup.

Outside of field hockey passes and mandatory Spanish class exchanges, Katie says absolutely nothing to me all week. Caleb becomes ridiculously good at making me *feel* his silence every time we pass each other in the halls. And Rosa still hasn't said a word to me since Sunday. Although, to be fair, I haven't exactly reached out to her, either.

Every time I think about seeing Rosa, my mind goes in eight different directions all at once. Part of me wants to yell at her, to tell her I broke up with Caleb and everybody hates me now and I hope she's happy. Part of me doesn't want her to have the satisfaction of knowing about the breakup at all. Part of me just misses seeing her. We haven't played together on the field in over a week. We haven't whispered over the tops of books, or laughed about how stupid and pretentious each of our prep schools are. I miss hanging out with Rosa. I miss having her as my friend.

And then there's the part—the really, really scared part—that knows exactly how I feel about Rosa on top of all that. It's the part of me that secretly wants to explode into her arms and stay there forever.

When I was with Caleb, I could dream about Rosa and think about her in this distant way, and it was safe because she was completely outside the realm of possibility. And really, she should still be outside the realm of possibility. I'm still at Heathclef and she's still at Van Darian, and both our teams are kicking ass and clawing our respective ways to nationals. I have no business trying anything with this girl.

But what if . . . ?

The question catches in my head all week. Just when I think I'm handling everything okay, that I'm too busy with school and practice to worry about anything else, her face pops right back up. It's like the image of her from home-coming, haunting me everywhere I look, every time I close my eyes. Except this time, it's not just some hot girl scoring against my team. This time, the image is Rosa. *Rosa.* The transplant from New Mexico who plays loud, bouncy music and shakes her hips when she cooks. The girl who carries towers of books that soar above her head. The girl who taught me how to block slap shots for no good reason, just because she wanted to help. The girl with long, dark hair and chestnut eyes and a smile that lights up the sky better than the sun.

Jesus Christ.

I'm not supposed to want her this way, I tell myself. *I'm supposed to want one thing right now, and that's Duke.*

Caleb or no Caleb, Rosa's still off-limits.

Even so, by Thursday evening, I'm so tired of existing in a vacuum where no one wants to even acknowledge me. I don't know what I would say to Caleb, and I know there's probably nothing in the world I could say to Katie to get her to stop hating me right now. But I do have some unfinished business across town.

"It's just payback," I tell myself as I climb into my car after practice. No other motives. I'm only returning a favor.

I try not to think about how this entire thing with Rosa started in exactly the same way.

I pull out the note Señora Esquivel gave me on Monday and squint until her red pen squiggles turn into actual words.

Hatch green chile.

El Mercado.

Señora Esquivel's directions to El Mercado—the best Mexican supermarket in town, apparently—are easy enough, and after twenty minutes of driving I find the tiny bodega squished between a barber shop and a florist.

Navigating through the market itself, however, turns out to be a completely different story.

I'm pretty sure I've stepped into a bigger version of a Mary Poppins bag, as the inside of the bodega seems to be at least four times bigger than the outside. The right wall is completely stuffed with wooden crates of fresh vegetables, and the ceiling has hanging baskets of fruit so plump and vibrant that I can't stop my mouth from watering at the sight of them. Past the produce, the aisles on the left hold hundreds of cans and bags and jars filled with every food imaginable.

I feel like I've only stopped for a second to take it all in, but from the stares of the few other customers, I might as well have a giant *I'M LOST* sign around my neck.

The woman behind the counter props herself forward on her elbows. "¿Qué busca?"

"Oh." I walk over and show her Señora Esquivel's handwriting. "Estoy buscando Hatch green chile," I say. "De Nuevo México."

I might not be a total pro at Spanish, but I at least know enough to ask for help.

The woman nods and takes me down an aisle, then hands me a slim can with a bright yellow label. I look at the picture on the front showing crisp, diced squares of a green pepper.

I don't text Rosa until I'm sitting in the visitors' parking lot at Van Darian.

Where are you? I type.

She answers right away.

Fútbolhead: *Why do you care?*

I sigh and roll my eyes. The lengths I have to go to do something nice for this girl.

Me: *I'm already on campus. Just dropping something off. If you're busy, I'll leave it outside your room.*

The message goes on read. I get out of the car and tuck the

brown paper sack under my arm. I've only taken a few steps toward the dorms when my phone goes off again.

Fútbolhead: *Behind the library.*

I change directions and make my way toward the pale stone building I know almost too well at this point. The area behind it is thick with forest vegetation. Slivers of the lake peek out between the branches. As I get to the very back, the vegetation unexpectedly thins and reveals Rosa perched on an old bench, whittling away on a stick. Dappled light falls over her hair as she scrapes a small, blunted chisel against the wood.

At first, I nearly crack a joke about how she's also a viejo at heart. But as I get closer, I see that she's not just carving on any stick. It's her field hockey stick.

"The engraving," I whisper.

Rosa looks up at me.

"Hey," she murmurs. She goes back to whittling. "I thought that was you."

I forget everything I came here to say or do. Instead, I crouch next to her, watching.

The first time I noticed the engravings on Rosa's field hockey stick, I wanted to use them to get her thrown out of the game. I only saw the stick for how it was different from everyone else's—how it needed to change to be more like the rest of ours.

But now I can't stop staring at the wavy lines and hook shapes and eyes dotting the wood. I love it for every way that it's different. I love how Rosa's taken something I've seen a million times before and yet somehow, magically, she's made it new and exciting. The images remind me of hieroglyphs. They're not words, like I had first thought, but they're definitely not just random pictures, either. I don't know exactly what Rosa's making, but it looks a lot like a journey. And right away, just from seeing her like this, I know I at least have to tell her how I feel. That I'll regret it forever if I don't even try to come along on the journey too.

I nudge the bag closer to Rosa.

"I'm really sorry I called you those things at Gordy's," I say. "There's no excuse for it—I'm just sorry. And I'm sorry I ate part of your enchiladas. Here."

Rosa pauses. She sets the chisel and field hockey stick aside and eyes the bag. "What is it?"

"Look inside."

She reaches in tentatively and grabs the small can of diced green chiles.

"It's Hatch green," I explain. "Which my Spanish teacher says is the best. And it's from New Mexico, so. Yeah. For your next home-cooked meal."

I stand up and lean against a small, smooth tree. I want to give her plenty of space for what comes next.

"I like you," I say softly. "I don't know why. . . ."

I laugh a little. "Okay, I know a million reasons why I like you. But I also know the reasons why we shouldn't. And if things between us need to be done, now . . . if we can't meet up anymore, I totally understand. I just wanted you to know how I felt. How I *feel*."

Rosa furrows her brows. She looks from me to the green chiles, then back at me again.

She's not saying anything, I realize. Even with me taking the step away, her face looks flushed and nervous. She probably feels like I'm too close. Like she doesn't know how to say no.

"That wasn't meant to sway you," I say quickly, pointing to the can. "It's just an apology thing. For, you know, eating the enchiladas. And being an asshole."

I give the tree trunk a small tap with my knuckle, then head back around the building.

Rosa remains silent in the distance as I leave. I try to keep my heart from turning into a lead weight and sinking into my heels. I try to tell myself this is a good thing. I probably wasn't going to see Rosa again anyway. At least now she knows the real reason why.

I'm halfway around the library when I feel a hand come over my wrist.

"I like you too," Rosa says, her voice fluttery and breathless.

I twist over my shoulder to see her.

"But you're right," she goes on. "There are real reasons why we shouldn't."

I nod. "Yeah. I know."

"I . . . shouldn't have judged you. Last weekend." Rosa lets go of me and stares down at her feet. "Relationships look different from different angles. You're right: I don't know Caleb."

I shrug. "Well, to be fair, I don't think I knew him very well either."

Rosa's head jerks up. "What?"

"We broke up," I say. "I broke up with him. So actually, you were right."

Rosa widens her eyes at me.

The shivers take over fast, spreading from my fingertips to toes. At first, I think I'm careening headfirst into another one of my signature panic attacks. Except this time, I don't feel numb. I feel the complete opposite. Every hair on my body buzzes with the sensation of being deliciously alive. It takes me a moment to register Rosa's hand on my cheek. She cradles my chin in her palm.

"Can I . . . can I kiss you?" she asks.

I swallow. I know I probably shouldn't step into this too fast. I know I should give myself time, should probably be alone for a while. But in so many ways it feels like I've been alone for years. I've spent enough time wanting things and not letting myself have them. I don't want to run away. This time, I want to reach back.

My hands answer for me.

I touch either side of Rosa's hips and pull her in. My arms come under hers, wrapping around her back and floating to the nape of her neck. No one has ever fit this perfectly into my body. Our noses touch, our cheeks brush, and then my mouth is on hers and the entire world dissolves around us.

We drink each other like water. Our lips part open, then come down again and again, lingering over the other's. I feel Rosa's teeth on my lower lip and I can't stop the low moan it draws from me. I don't know how to hold her any closer, but I need to. I need the cells in our bodies to break open and meld together.

Rosa presses me into the wall. My lips leave hers and trail over her cheek, onto her earlobe, down her neck. Rosa rolls her head back and smiles. She looks flushed and breathless and so, so ridiculously beautiful. She takes hold of both my hands.

"Eve," she murmurs.

I have never loved the sound of my own name so much.

"If we're going to do this," Rosa says, "I want to do this for real."

"What does that mean?" I ask.

"It means I don't want to be your secret friend anymore. I want to go on dates with you. I want to be with you. Can you do that, viejito?"

Rosa clasps her hands behind my neck and looks into my eyes. I don't know how she manages to switch from wickedly sexy to sweet and adorable in seconds. But I want it all. I want every part of her there is.

"Okay," I tell her. "Let's go on a date, for real. Tomorrow night."

"What about all your bloodthirsty Heathclef teammates?"

"Hey," I say, "your teammates are just as bloodthirsty. And it doesn't matter. This isn't about them. It's just you and me."

Rosa raises an eyebrow. "That sounds like work," she says teasingly. "I thought you liked it when relationships were easy."

I lean down and kiss her again. "For you, I can do a little work."

She grins, but we both know the truth: This is more than just a little work. This is going to be a demolition job in the making.

I'm about to rearrange my world for this girl.

CHAPTER SEVENTEEN

Phffft!

The shrillness of Gloria's whistle hits a new pitch in my brain, causing an instant headache. I turn off the water and step out of the shower, hoping I can at least get some pants on before she dives into our post-practice meeting. We're now down to our final week before Heathclef's last regional game out of town. After that, we'll find out whether we've performed well enough to spend our Thanksgiving break playing the first round of nationals.

"Round up!" Gloria barks. "I'm not waiting on anyone to finish their damn forty-step skincare routines this time."

Someone groans over by the mirrors.

The team warily finishes pulling sweaters over their heads and slamming their lockers shut. I yank my jeans on and join the circle at the center of the room. Katie stands across the way from me, conveniently focused on tightening her shoelaces.

I understand why Katie's upset. The moment she starts dating Bryce, I pull an awful friend move by dumping Caleb.

And worse, I didn't tell Katie about it beforehand. I can see how it looks like I did this all to spite her, or at least did it with zero regard for her feelings. But the weird thing is, Katie hasn't even asked me about the breakup. She's ignored me full stop all week long. She has no idea what's going on behind the scenes, or how I'm feeling. And that's sort of an awful friend move, too.

Gloria claps her hands twice and my focus goes back to her.

"Heathclef! You've been determined over the last two months. Relentless," she says, her voice hard and gritty. "I admit, we had a rough start to the season. I know you haven't forgotten it."

She flashes me a look, and the momentary shame from homecoming hits me so hard that I want to melt into the floor.

"But you came back from that," Gloria continues. "You learned from your mistakes, and you fought hard, and now you get to ride the high of sitting at the top."

We wait as Gloria pauses. Gloria's all about keeping her team on its toes. She doesn't do victory speeches. She does "prepare for death and gloom" speeches. She does "give me a hundred and fifty percent" speeches. She's not about to lavish us with praise over a great season, and we know it.

Gloria scans her clipboard one more time. She holds it to her side and looks around, making eye contact with every one of us in turn. "Thanks to your dedication and efforts over the last month, I have the honor of informing you that—no matter the outcome of next weekend's game—we are one of the ten teams qualified for the High School National Invitational."

The stillness in the room somehow feels even tinnier than the sound of Gloria's whistle. Someone shrieks without opening their mouth. Most of us stand, dumbfounded. We have never, not ever, known we were heading to nationals before our last game.

"We're a high-seed team," I say.

Gloria nods. "We are. That means the first two rounds of the tournament are on our home turf. May be a good time for a homecoming, part two, huh?"

We stare at Gloria another moment. The sound of rhythmic clacking disrupts the collective, stunned silence.

I look over and see Katie tapping her field hockey stick against the floor. I grab mine off the wall and do the same. Our teammates all scramble for their own sticks, and within seconds the room explodes in pounding energy.

Right, left, sweep it under!
Right, left, bring the thunder!
Right, left! Right, left!
Who are we?
"Heathclef!" I scream.

I catch Katie's eye, and like a magician snapping his fingers, suddenly we're back to the way we always are. We both grin and clack our sticks in the air like an epic high five. Even after the breakup, after the stony silence, we're teammates first and foremost. This is what field hockey does. It makes you forget whatever else is going on in the world. It makes the game feel like the whole point of life.

Gloria thumps her clipboard for attention. "All right, fatheads! All right! Calm down! You've got your ticket to nationals. But I don't want to be embarrassed next weekend no matter what. Do you hear me?"

"Yes!" we all say in unison.

Katie steps closer to Gloria and tries to peer down at the clipboard. "You said something about a homecoming, part two. Does this mean Van Darian's coming here again?"

I freeze. I hadn't considered that as a possibility.

"No," Gloria says. She tucks the board out of Katie's sight.

A few people around the room groan, but my lungs flood with relief. I don't know how to take Rosa on the field right now. She's helped me perfect my defense against slap shots, sure. But if a glimpse of half a tattoo swayed my focus before, then seeing Rosa run at me full speed now might kill me. I would probably abandon my post and tackle her right there on the field.

Gloria turns for the hall outside the locker room. She stops at the doorway, as if an afterthought has only just now caught up to her.

"Van Darian's high-seed too," Gloria tells us over her shoulder. "They'll also play host for the early rounds. If you knuckleheads manage to keep your cool in the first two games, you'll face off against them in the finals."

"Ooh," August says. She presses her fingers together menacingly. "Showdown of the century."

Jade laughs into the mirror as she applies some lip balm. "We are *so* going up against that bitch again."

Both my hands ball into tight fists, and I have to stop myself from turning and rushing my own teammate. They can't talk about Rosa like that. I won't *let* anyone talk about Rosa like that.

Gloria snaps and points at Jade. "Language!" she calls. Then she turns and waves me to her. "No-Goalie. Get over here."

My heart is still racing. Palms are still sweating. But I obediently follow Gloria's orders and head across the room to the hall. Only once the locker room door closes behind me does Gloria turn around and give me her full attention.

"Is that going to be a problem for you?"

I step back, surprised. "What?"

"Van Darian. Is that going to be a problem for you?" Gloria says again. She taps her red nails on her clipboard.

I have no idea how to answer Gloria's question. Not honestly, obviously. I decide my best strategy is to play dumb.

"Why would it be a problem?" I ask her. "Like you said, we learned from our mistakes, right?"

Gloria peers at me under the buzzing fluorescent lights. Her expression remains unmoved. "And what was your mistake on homecoming?"

I shrug. "I didn't know how to block slap shots."

"Before you told me it was about the girl. Alvarez."

I try to keep a careful poker face at the mention of Rosa's name. "I was making excuses before."

Gloria folds her arms. "That's true. And you know how I feel about excuses."

"Yes, definitely. I'm good now, Coach. No more excuses, I promise." I wring my hands, waiting for Gloria to dismiss me so I can go back inside.

But she doesn't. As I stand there, the hard look usually fixed to Gloria's face slides off. She tilts her head down at me. Her eyes are deep and open.

"You're so much like your mom that it's scary sometimes."

My mouth instantly goes dry. I thought Gloria and I had a mutual understanding not to bring her up randomly like this. Gloria and Mom played field hockey at Heathclef way back when. I've got the baton now. We don't talk about the pass-off. We *never* talk about the pass-off.

I squeeze the life out of my fingers. "Thank you."

Gloria shakes her head. "I don't know if that's always a compliment," she says softly. "You know I loved your mom. And I know you're doing amazing things on the field. But you're speeding down a highway at full force, kid. If something gets in your way, you're not going to be able to swerve at this rate. It will be a head-on collision."

I nod like I know exactly what Gloria is talking about. But she's got it completely wrong. I don't rush into things. I'm not careening down some open highway. I'm on a one-track, set path. I'm checking things off a list.

You can't move too fast down a road built just for you.

Gloria pats my shoulder and continues down the hall. I take the cue and gratefully disappear back into the locker room.

Inside, the team is still vibrating with energy. Katie's hopping from bench to bench, making up rhymes about the other top teams we might face at nationals.

"Broadneck can get *wrecked!*"

"Delmar won't go *far!*"

"We'll lay Palmyra out to *dry*-a!"

"And Van Darian will be *carrion!*" Natalia yells from the sinks.

Katie pauses and looks down at her.

"What?" Natalia asks. "Carrion? Like roadkill? You know that's clever as hell."

Katie nods slowly. "Okay . . . okay, yeah. I like it!"

Katie makes eye contact with me as she belts out the last line. "And Van Darian will be *carrionnnnnnnn.*"

The rest of the team breaks into applause. Katie bows to all sides of the room. I make a beeline for my locker.

"We have to keep this going," Katie says, hopping to the floor. "Let's all head out for pizza to celebrate. Or ice cream. Or hell, both! It's a Friday. Tell them, Feltzer."

"Oh." I open my locker and grab my phone. "Don't you think it's sort of last-minute? Like, most people probably already have plans."

"I don't have plans," Katie quips. "And even if I did, I'd break them for this. How many times are we going to find out we're high-seed at nationals?"

I nod weakly. She has a point.

My phone buzzes twice. I peek down and see a text lighting up the screen.

Fútbolhead: *Looking forward to seeing what viejitos wear when they're taking a hot lady out on a date.*

Fútbolhead: *See you in an hour ;)*

I turn my phone over and press my fist into my mouth. Rosa's texts have a way of making me smile so hard it hurts.

Katie jostles me. "Hello?"

I close my locker door hard. "Yeah, sorry. God, Katie, I'm so sorry, but I have something going on tonight."

She stares at me, and like an idiot I only just now remember that I broke up with my boyfriend *in front of her* on Monday. By high school conventions, I'm not allowed to have plans. I'm barely allowed to be happy over nationals.

"My dad," I explain, like this is a legitimate reason for ducking out. "He has some news, I think."

Katie stares at me. "So his news is more important than ours?"

"That's not fair. He doesn't know about ours," I say. "Let's come up with another time to hang out with the team. It's not that big of a deal."

Katie doesn't say anything, but I see her mouth tighten. She shares a look with Melanie across the room.

"Tomorrow?" I ask as I pick up my bag. "We can all meet up for doughnuts and coffee."

Katie folds her arms. She gives a stiff shrug. "Sure."

I sigh and shuffle past her. Obviously I don't want things to cool off again between us. But I did already have plans. And they could have easily been with Dad, or a classmate from school, or anyone socially acceptable for me to be seen with. The fact that I'm about to hang with our top nationals rival shouldn't make any difference, I tell myself.

No difference whatsoever.

I triple-check my rearview mirror the whole way to Van Darian anyway. Just to be safe.

CHAPTER EIGHTEEN

Rosa is already standing in the visitors' lot when I pull up. She slips into the car wearing black jeans rolled at the ankles, a tight-fitting auburn sweater, and fiery red lipstick. I lean across the center console.

"You look nice," I say.

I can feel Rosa's dimples pull into a broad smile as she kisses me. She presses my mouth open with hers and I let myself melt into her. God, I forgot how much I love the shape of her lips. I forgot how easy it is to fit into her like a puzzle piece. I clasp one hand over the back of her neck.

"Hmmm," Rosa moans.

She sits up straight in her seat. "Dinner first," she says. "Dinner first. Dinner first."

"You don't have to remind me."

"I'm reminding myself," she says, laughing.

I drive us north, slicing into the wooded outskirts of the suburbs. Rosa gazes out at the trees through her window. The evening sky slowly becomes speckled with stars.

"Secluded," Rosa murmurs. "I can't decide if that's either super romantic or super creepy."

I smile. "Let's go with the first one."

What neither of us is saying out loud, of course, is that seclusion is basically a necessity right now. It's the only real way to make things work without getting booted off both our teams. Obviously there are way better places I'd rather take Rosa than some highway diner out of town. But this isn't forever, I remind myself. We only have to stay low for a few more weeks, until the final nationals game is over and someone's declared champion.

One way or another.

I spot our exit and hit the blinker.

We turn down a small road and pull up to a tiny restaurant that's been built to look like a log cabin. Rosa leaps out of her side of the car and opens my door for me. I run ahead past a Smokey Bear–looking figure and open the restaurant door for her. She pulls my chair out at one of the three empty tables in the seating area. I have her order first from the laminated single-page menu. We trade teasing smiles as we punt roles back and forth, acting more like we're back on the field playing catch than two girls out on a date.

The server disappears into the kitchen with our order, and Rosa takes a long drink of water. She sets the nearly empty glass down.

"Okay," she says. "Is it out of our system now?"

"Is what out of our system?"

"The butterflies."

I reach for her hand over the table. "Nope. I still have some butterflies."

She squeezes my hand back. "Me too."

Our fingers stay interlocked as we wait for the food. Neither of us says very much, which is pretty weird, since we usually always have something to talk about. I can feel Rosa's heartbeat stretch across her palm.

"I heard you're going to nationals," I say, trying to lighten to mood. But the joke doesn't land, and I immediately regret it.

Rosa rubs her thumb over my knuckles. "You too."

She pauses. "I'm so proud of you. You worked so hard for this."

"So did you," I say. I squint at her. "Though you probably don't have to work nearly as hard as the rest of us. You weird little field hockey prodigy."

Rosa gives me the same flat smile she always does whenever we talk about how good she is at field hockey. I had always thought she was just humble, or maybe embarrassed by being complimented so much. I can't believe it's taken me this long to see what expression she's really making.

"You hate it," I say quietly.

Rosa looks down at our hands. She doesn't answer.

I feel like I'm in two different bodies. I'm the goalkeeper who would do absolutely anything to win that nationals title. The one who should be pissed that our top competition doesn't even care about field hockey, let alone the invitational. But then I'm also the girl who's holding Rosa's hand right now, catching her sadness in my fingers.

The food arrives at the table.

"Tell me more about soccer," I say. I let go of her hand and unfold my napkin. "If you want to."

Rosa's mood instantly changes at the question. She picks up her fork.

"What do you want to know? I could tell you about how soccer started three thousand years ago as tchatali with the Aztecs and cuju in China. Or I could tell you about how entire countries have staged uprisings and declared independence all because of who plays and who doesn't play in the World Cup. I could probably use soccer as a jumping point for talking about anything. Fútbol is the most amazing sport there is in the world. It encapsulates its own thread of our history as humans."

I sigh dreamily into my hand and smile at her.

"I would love to hear all about that sometime. But actually, I want to know about *you* and soccer."

"Me?" Rosa straightens and takes a bite. I can see her guard going right back up. "I don't play soccer anymore."

"But let's not talk about that," I say. "Tell me about when you did. Tell me about when you were a kid and loved the bejesus out of it. I want to see it the way you do. I want to imagine you in love with a sport."

Rosa smiles faintly at her plate. She cuts her eyes up at me.

"Don't you dare ruin this date, Feltzer. I have plans for you after."

My cheeks go red as I imagine what Rosa might have in mind. But I don't want to let go of this conversation. I want Rosa to see that she can be sad or disappointed around me,

that she doesn't have to be this superstar who's good at everything and cares about nothing. I want to be here for her the
way she's been here for me all season.

"Do you still watch fútbol games?" I ask.

"Of course," Rosa says without looking up. "Only in
Spanish, though. English commentators are so dry and boring. But in Spanish, the games are magically loud."

I laugh. "Magically loud?"

"Well, yeah." Rosa laughs a little. "You can turn on a game
and suddenly feel like you're in a giant room surrounded by
people you love. There's so much excitement there. It squeezes
out all the loneliness." She takes a deep breath. "Even if the
same loneliness comes back as soon as the game is over."

I grab her hand again.

"Well I'm going to watch the next game with you," I say.
"And then you won't be lonely, even after it ends."

Rosa brings my hand to her cheek. "Oh yeah? And will
you yell out things in Spanish?"

"I'll yell out everything in Spanish," I tell her. "And every
time you kiss me, I'll have someone across the hall shout
'GOOOOOAAAAL!'"

Rosa's signature megawatt smile returns, and finally I see
her relax back into the moment.

"Okay," she says, nodding. "I guess that would be pretty
magically loud, too."

We walk back to her dorm under a velvet sky. I can feel
Rosa's heartbeat in my palm. I can feel my own heart pounding in my chest. I can't stop thinking about what she said
earlier at the diner. I'm guessing she has a lot more experience

than I do when it comes to being with girls. I don't even know what else there is to do other than kissing.

"Nervous?" Rosa asks as she unlocks her door.

"Shut up," I say.

"I'll take that as a yes."

"Well, you're not helping by talking about it."

"Yeah, I am," Rosa says. She leads me inside her room and closes the door behind us. "When it comes to sex, there's nothing hotter than communicating. That's how you get what you want instead of just wishing your partner could read your mind."

I raise an eyebrow. "Have you had a lot of partners?"

"I've had enough partners. But that doesn't matter." Rosa braces herself against her desk and looks at me. Her arms are taut. "Tonight, right now, I want to be with *you*. Is that okay?"

I close the space between us and lock my hands over hers. If she wants to make this a game, she better well know that I can play too. "Yes, that's okay. I'd like to take that sweater off you right now. Is that okay?"

Rosa bites her lip and leans all the way in to me. I reach under the hem of her sweater and help sweep it off her head. She unbuttons her jeans and hoists herself onto the desk, letting me tug them down her legs inch by inch. I uncover the mysterious tattoo on her thigh, this time from the other side.

"Aha," I say, nodding appreciatively. "Frida."

Rosa looks down at the portrait and grins. "Yeah, Frida. I had to. She always did her own thing, you know? Even when life handed her shit ingredients, she made something new and wonderful and painful. I'm trying to do that too. In my own way."

"But why did you put her here?" I ask. I run my finger over the tattoo, outlining Frida's chin.

"Because most of the world doesn't get to see all of me, so they don't get to see all of her, either. Only a piece. Until I decide to let someone in." Rosa moves my hand slowly up her leg and along her hips. "Then they can see her."

My breath hitches. "Oh. That's . . . that's very sexy."

"Well," Rosa murmurs into my neck, "Frida was also very, very sexy. Not to mention queer as fuck."

I pull back in mock surprise. "Wait a second. You put a queer icon on your thigh that only partially shows under a field hockey uniform. Isn't that, like, the definition of queer baiting?"

"Ah, no." Rosa wags a finger. "It's only queer *baiting* if I don't follow through. But I always reel in my catches, viejito."

She swings her legs over my hips and hooks her ankles around my back. I slide my hands under her and lift her from the desk. We both stumble to the side for a moment, and Rosa giggles as she grips tight to me. I take two steps and fall backward onto the bed. Rosa's knees pin me down.

She takes one of my hands in hers, tracing a line from the top of each finger down to my wrist. I gasp every time her fingertip grazes over my palm.

"Can I show you where to touch me?" she whispers.

I can barely answer, can only nod, as she pulls my hand up and up, over Frida's head.

Before Rosa, I would have thought that sex only meant one thing, one kind of act. But with Rosa, sex is like a mindset. I feel warm and heavy as I sink into her, kissing her everywhere. We fold together over her bed, and whether it's leg pressing into leg or breast to stomach, for that moment we get to be part of each other. My lips grazing her hip bone feels as sacred as anything I've ever done with another person.

I cannot get enough of this girl, cannot stop finding new places on her body. Being with Rosa feels like finding a secret hiding place that only I get to escape to. I want to live here forever and never, ever leave.

Eventually I hear Rosa's breathing turn soft and steady over my chest. My head floats down from the clouds, slowly returning to my shoulders. Every nerve ending in my body is deliriously fried. Everything pulses, throbs, beats along to my heart as it comes down from the high.

I kiss Rosa's forehead.

She squints through the dark and smiles at me. "You know . . . I think my abuela told me about you."

I raise an eyebrow. "What? When?"

"When I was a little girl." Rosa stretches and props herself up over the pillow. "She told me about all the lovers I would meet in my life."

I prop myself up across from her like a mirror reflection.

"Oh yeah? Tell me about them."

"Most of them are boring," she says. "Random boyfriends and girlfriends. Novie."

Rosa pulls me closer with her free arm. "But she also told

me about the llama gemela and the media naranja. Those are the special ones."

"A llama twin and a middle orange?" I ask.

Rosa laughs. "No, *llama* as in *flame*. A llama gemela is someone who will change you forever. They share your deepest secrets and worst pain. They'll help you grow as a person like no one else ever will. Then, eventually, you both will move on."

I run my hand up and down her side. "Now tell me about the orange."

"Media naranja," Rosa says. "It's the other half of an orange. But it's not just any half. All oranges are slightly different. They have different bumps and textures and shapes, kind of like fingerprints. There's only supposed to be one true half to your orange."

Rosa pauses. We both blink in the dark.

"So which one am I?" I whisper.

"I don't know yet," she whispers back. "I guess we'll have to see."

She turns on her side and fits her hips into mine, a little spoon I get to keep for the night. My hand falls over her waist and I draw her close to me.

A twin flame or an orange half.

Obviously I don't know Spanish nearly as well as Rosa, but from everything she said, I can tell she's already been a llama gemela for me. I want that to be a good thing. It sounds like a good thing . . . except the part where it doesn't last.

I bury my head into Rosa's hair. Maybe I've just slept with

this person for the first time, have only kissed her for two days, but I cannot stand the idea of sending her on to find another orange half. I want to keep her for myself. I want to be her orange half too.

Can someone ever be both a llama gemela and a media naranja?

I fall asleep thinking over the question.

CHAPTER NINETEEN

The next Wednesday afternoon, I hunch over my spiral comp book in the corner of Square One Coffee. I'm pretending to take notes on twentieth century government politics while Rosa sits across from me, actually concentrating on whatever's in front of her on her laptop.

I study her hands as her fingers effortlessly flutter over the keyboard, clicking and clacking without pause. The sounds of her working hit me like a song. Her wrists almost seem to dance to their own beat. She finishes a section and reaches for her matcha tea latte, sipping it slowly as she reads over her work. The mint green foam leaves the tiniest smudge on her Cupid's bow, and I have to fight the overwhelming urge to lean over and taste it.

Rosa raises an eyebrow at me over her screen. "What?"

I shake my head. "What, what?"

"You've been staring at me nonstop for the last thirty minutes."

"I hardly have that long of an attention span," I say. I

scribble a random word down in my notebook. "Maybe you just *wish* I was staring at you."

I pretend to jot more notes when suddenly Rosa pushes off her chair and whisks the notebook out from under my arm.

"Hey!"

She runs a fingertip across the lines. "Matcha. Mustache. Kiss. Nose. Lips. Kiss. Kiss. Kiss." She looks up at me. "Wow. I would have brought an extra water bottle if I knew you were going to be this thirsty."

I yank the notebook back. "How dare you. Everyone knows rough drafts aren't meant to be read by anyone else."

Rosa sighs and leans in to her chair. "I thought we were going to work together."

"I don't know how I'm supposed to get any work done outside your room," I argue.

Rosa eyes me, amused. "Well, we sure as hell haven't been getting work done *inside* my room, so."

"True," I say, blushing, "but this place is so . . . public." I crane my head and check out the front window for the millionth time. "I'm too busy doing Rival Watch to be able to concentrate on homework."

"Rival Watch." Rosa blows a raspberry.

"What?"

She rolls her eyes and looks back at me. "I don't think a field hockey rivalry is the great war you think it is."

I lay my pen down along the center of the table. "Rosa, we're on two of just six high-seed teams heading to nationals. We're the only two nationally ranked field hockey teams in the area. And our schools were already rivals before all of that! I didn't start this war. But I'm not going to pretend it doesn't exist, either."

"Mmm. Okay." She flashes me a look and turns again to her computer.

I huff and do another scan around the café. So far, we're in the clear. It's just the two of us, an adorable older couple holding hands and sipping hot tea through their mustaches, and a small book club meeting across the room. I turn again to the couple and watch the two men gaze lovingly across the table at one another.

Media naranja, a voice inside my head murmurs.

I shake my head and turn again to Rosa as she takes another long sip of her latte.

"What are you working on?" I ask.

Rosa swivels her computer around. I can see a Word document shoved to the bottom of her screen filled up with text, but the main tab open is some article on women's colleges.

"I'm trying to see which schools have decent field hockey teams," she says. "Then I can tailor my personal statement for each one."

I furrow my brow. "Field hockey?"

"Uh, yeah. Did you forget I played?"

I force out an awkward laugh. "No . . . but I thought you wanted to play soccer."

"Yeah," Rosa says coldly, "two years ago. My last soccer records are from sophomore year. That's as good as ancient history on college applications."

I don't know how to respond to this. I knew that Rosa was

upset about being pushed out of soccer at Van Darian. But I didn't really think it would push her away from soccer for the rest of her life. I want to say something useful, or supportive, without messing up everything she's been typing over the last half hour, let alone cultivating over the last two years. But just as I open my mouth, I catch something red glinting outside the front window. I turn and look out into the parking lot.

"Dammit," I whisper.

Rosa seems too annoyed with me to ask what I'm freaking out over now. She's already back to typing.

I leap up from my chair and push the door open hard enough that the dangling bells from the handle clang loudly instead of doing their usual *clink clink*. Caleb's truck is parked right in front. I creep up to the driver's door, hoping to catch him before he comes inside. But the seat is empty.

"Caleb?" I cup my hands over my eyebrows like a visor and lean in to the glass. "Where are you?"

"You stomped right past me," Caleb says from over my shoulder. "I was at the front counter."

I whip around and see him holding a coffee to go and a small brown paper bag.

"Oh." I take a long step away from his car door. "Sorry."

Caleb's forehead wrinkles. "What did you want?"

"Nothing," I say quickly. "Just thought I recognized your car and I, uh . . . I wanted to say hi."

"Hi." He jabs the word back at me.

We both stand there.

"I'm not going to your game this weekend," he says finally.

"No! I didn't expect you to at all. I came out here be-cause . . . I wanted to make sure . . ."

I pause and look at him. Caleb inhales, his breath catching. He's trying to look angry, but I can see the hurt in his eyes. I see the little rosebuds of pink blooming on his cheeks. I see the gentle way his hair falls across his forehead. I've known this person for a long time—spent so much time hanging out with him, kissing him, tucking myself under his arm. And it never felt totally right, not the way it does with Rosa. But even so, Caleb's a good guy. He deserves better than the ending I gave us.

"I wanted to say I was sorry." I bow my head a little. "That sucked, the way I went off in front of Bryce and Katie. I just didn't know how to even start that conversation. It seemed so impossible. We've been together so long and—"

"I know," Caleb murmurs. "It would have sucked no mat-ter which way it happened."

I tilt my chin up. "But I made it the worst possible situa-tion. You've always been really good to me. And there wasn't another guy."

Caleb squints at me skeptically. "Are you seriously trying to get out of that on a technicality?" He nudges his elbow toward Square One. "I saw who you were with in there."

Fuuuuuck. My jaw goes slack. My cheeks get so hot that I'm certain at least one of them is in the process of catching on fire.

"I recognize her," Caleb continues. "From Gordy's. Were you two seeing each other then?"

"Of course not!" I say quickly. I pause. "I . . . did have feelings for her, though. I tried so hard not to, but—" I shrug helplessly. "I'm so sorry, Caleb."

"Ah." Caleb stares down into his coffee cup. He seems to be rolling his next words around on his tongue, considering them carefully. "Does this mean you—did you ever like guys?"

There's so much sincerity in the question, so much worry that I didn't have real feelings for him, that my heart breaks a little.

"I think so," I say honestly. "I think I still do."

Rosa's speech from the dock floats into my brain.

"I don't know if I'm bi, or pan, or queer. I don't know what label I am. But I know that for a while, I really liked you. And right now, I really like her. It's a person thing, if that makes sense."

Caleb nods slowly. I hear the bells tinkle as more people filter inside the coffee shop. I suddenly remember why I jumped out here in the first place.

"Please don't say anything," I add.

Caleb raises his eyebrows.

"It's not about it being a girl. It's about who she is. She's . . . she goes to Van Darian. We play field hockey against each other. And both our teams are going to nationals."

"Congrats," Caleb says. He sighs and glances through the shop window. "I'm not going to expose you or whatever, if that's what you're worried about."

"Thank you." I sigh with relief. I want to squeeze Caleb's arm, or reach for his hand, but any sort of physical affection feels almost cruel at this point. I fold my arms tight around myself and give him a nod. "Thank you."

As I step back into the coffee shop, I immediately notice that the table where Rosa and I had been sitting is now surrounded by Van Darian field hockey players.

Of course.

I suck my teeth and dart toward the bathroom. One of the girls has slipped right into my chair, as if it had been unoccupied from the start. Two more lean over the table, hunched on their elbows. The fourth, who I now recognize as Galen, is perched on Rosa's lap.

"The hell?" I murmur.

I hide out in the side hall while the girls laugh and talk. Someone from the book club meeting gets up and heads my way. I squeeze against the wall, pretending to take a call on my phone as she passes me by.

The woman squints at me as she slips into the bathroom. I shove my phone back in my pocket and watch our table, waiting for Rosa to shoo the other girls away. Instead, Rosa spots me across the café and waves me over.

"There you are, Eve! Come here!"

I freeze in the doorway for a moment, shaking my head. She cannot be serious. But Rosa keeps waving. I sigh and walk across the floor stilt-legged, like a Barbie doll who's just come to life. I stop short of the group.

"Uhh . . . hi."

"Ah, Heathclef." Galen at least has the decency to stand as I approach the table.

"I remember you," the player in my chair says. "You were supposed to be the really good goalie."

"She is!" Rosa says quickly. "She's amazing."

The other two players whisper into each other's ears. One of them laughs and leans in close to me.

"Your digs weren't bad," she says. "I mean, it wasn't Party City. But we had a nice time."

I grimace.

"Good for you," I manage to spit out.

"So, what are you doing bothering our girl?" Galen asks.

Rosa widens her eyes at me. She extends her arm across the table and opens her palm, like I'm supposed to just hold her hand in front of everyone like it's totally normal. I reach down and grab my notebook instead, pulling it close to my chest.

"Rosa's tutoring me," I mutter. "Our teachers are making us meet up."

Rosa blinks at me for a few moments. She turns and smiles at her teammates. "We should probably get back to the lesson."

"Okay, Miss Teacher," Galen says. "See you tomorrow."

She leans down and ruffles Rosa's hair. I want to overturn the entire table, but I keep my arms stiff and wrapped around my notebook.

I glare at Rosa until all four girls saunter back across the shop and head out the front door, drinks in hand.

"What was that?" I ask.

Rosa narrows her eyes. "I could literally ask you the same thing."

I throw out my hands. "You just bombarded me! And they were assholes! Especially Galen—with that lap-sitting and hair-teasing nonsense. What, is she your other girlfriend? Am I the other girlfriend?"

"I'm not even going to dignify that asinine question with an answer," Rosa says.

She opens her laptop and gets back to typing. Her fingers are no longer fluttering over the keys, but mashing each letter like she's poking it square in the chest. She huffs and sighs while she types, then stops suddenly and looks across the table at me.

"You know what your problem is?" Rosa says. "You pretend to be strong, but really, you're a coward."

I choke on my latte. "Excuse me?"

Rose pushes her computer away. "I'm tired of all the rules you've made up around field hockey that somehow trump everything else. *I have to get these extra practices in, Rosa. I need you to learn this tricky shot so I can figure out how to block it. See me every day, Rosa. Practice with me every day. But then put up with me while I treat you like absolute shit just because our teammates are around.* You think your connection to your mom gives you a free pass to put everything else second, including *us.* Especially us. But that's the easy way out of dealing with real life. You're hiding out in a fantasyland and losing what's happening right in front of you."

Suddenly I'm right back in that stupid banquet room at the pizza place again. Melanie's words wash over me, intertwined with Rosa's.

You're a coward.

You're hiding in a fantasyland.

My heart beats faster.

"And all for something ridiculously trivial," Rosa goes on. "It's field hockey, Evelyn. It's just a game."

I wring my hands over my lap until they start to lose circulation. This isn't fair.

"You wouldn't say that about soccer," I say.

Rosa shrugs. "Yes, I would."

"No, you wouldn't," I say, this time sharper. "You're acting like a coward too. You're judging me for taking something seriously, because you got burned in the sport you took seriously. You think this shit is stupid, that it's just a game, because it's only a game to *you*. But I am allowed to care."

Rosa says nothing.

I gesture out the doors. "Maybe for you it's not a big deal who knows and who doesn't know about us. But you're not close to your teammates the way I am to mine. I doubt those people on your team know anything about your life in New Mexico. They don't know about all your old friends down there, or your family. They don't know how much you really want to play soccer."

"*Wanted* to play soccer."

"That's part of my point!" I thump my palm down on the table. "I know you want to play soccer. I know you don't love field hockey. So what are you doing, writing essays about playing field hockey in college? Are you too scared to jump out of the box Van Darian put you in?"

Rosa takes a rattled breath and lowers her chin.

I should stop, I realize. Maybe the box thing was too much. I open my mouth to apologize, but then Rosa's head snaps right back up and instantly I can tell it's too late—she's about to lash out, hard.

"Look," Rosa says through gritted teeth. "We can't all have a legacy status scholarship awaiting us at Duke. I got pushed out of soccer by a bunch of shitty, racist white girls. You don't think those same girls are going to college? You think I can just forge my own path without running into roadblocks and walls? You think I *want* to be pivoting into a different sport?"

I swallow. "No, I—"

"And I'm allowed to be close to my teammates in my own way, without having to tell them every single thing about me. You told me stuff about your mom that you can't tell anyone else, right?"

My throat feels thick and froggy. "Right."

"Well, maybe you're that person for me. Did you ever think of that? That maybe I'm not freaking perfect. That sometimes I need an outlet for all of my shit too?"

Rosa's voice cracks, and I immediately spring up from my chair and kneel by her side.

"I'm sorry," I murmur into her leg. I touch the frayed edge along the rip in her jeans. "I'm so sorry. I want to be your outlet. I want you to tell me the things you can't tell anyone else, especially your team."

Rosa brings her hand under my chin and tips it toward her.

"Don't be selfish," she says gently. But the anger's already melting.

I rise up and kiss her. She lets me in, and for a moment we

get to leave the coffee shop and high school drama and the state of Pennsylvania and the entire world. It all goes behind us. The universe spins around the axis of her mouth on mine.

She pulls away, breathless. I lean in for another, but Rosa keeps her head back.

"I have a lot of work to do," she murmurs.

"Oh. Okay." I sit across the table.

Rosa centers the laptop in front of her. She strums her nails over the side of the keyboard, considering.

"Want to read me your essay?" I offer.

She shakes her head and gives me a flat smile. "Not really. Thanks, though."

Something's on her mind. She clicks around the screen a few times, then slips back into her sequence of typing, then reading, then typing, then reading. Except this time, I notice, she's glaring at the screen like it cut her off in traffic.

I silently open my notebook and start taking actual notes.

CHAPTER TWENTY

The coach bus bounces and sways, wheels going round and round like a nursery school rhyme about twenty sweaty, triumphant players on their way back from their latest big win of the season.

It turns out Heathclef didn't need an entire football team of support to get us through the game after all—my dad and one very pissed-off-looking Bryce were plenty. Our opponents didn't have the best ranking, which was probably why Gloria got the news early that we were heading to the invitational. Still, I'll take the win. Anything to help boost us to the top of the competition and secure my chances for Duke.

Katie and the others break into an old camp song while I curl into a seat in the back and stare at my cell phone. I know I'll eventually get carsick from it, but Rosa's blowing up my screen with texts and I have to read them all.

Fútbolhead: *Knew you'd sweep it!*

Fútbolhead: *You badass*

Fútbolhead: *No-Goalie #goals*

I grin at the texts. According to Gloria, now that all's said and done for our regionals season, Heathclef has earned one of the highest ranks in the entire National Invitational.

So has Van Darian.

Me: *Should you really be texting during your own half-time?*

Rosa starts typing back right away.

Fútbolhead: *Meh. It's boring in here. Gotta pass the time while the others catch their breath.*

I laugh out loud at Rosa's feigned arrogance. I know she has to be tired too. Forwards never stop zipping around the field. But that's part of Rosa's magic when she's in the game. She acts like she could do this all day, every day, 24/7.

"Hey."

Katie slides onto my bench and presses in to me so close that I have to jam my shoulder against the window.

I tuck the phone into my lap. "Um, hi."

"Texting a new man?" Katie asks. I can tell she's trying to be light, but we both know it's a sore subject. The words, the motions, still feel awkward between us.

I shrug and shake my head. "Ah, no. Just talking about the win."

Katie clasps her hands. "It's pretty awesome," she says. "Going to nationals. Getting that much closer to Duke!"

She elbows me and I laugh.

Katie nods ahead at the bus. "Thing is, though, you should be celebrating with *us*. You're the captain. You should be leading all these songs!"

"I don't know," I say. "I'm just really tired."

"Not too tired for your mystery guy." Katie raises her hand to point to my phone, and on instinct I fold myself around it.

Katie stares at me. "Huh," she says to herself.

"What?" I ask defensively.

She gives a subtle shake of the head, then looks up, her eyes suddenly a bit brighter. They know something. She knows something.

"Nothing," Katie says. "Have fun with your . . . person."

My palm lays flat on the screen. I feel like Katie can see right through me. But no one on the team knows that Fútbolhead is Rosa. None of my teammates have tailed me after practice or monitored my calls. No one has followed me into the shower and seen the soft bite marks between my collarbone and shoulder. I'm just being paranoid.

She doesn't know, I reassure myself. *No one other than Caleb knows, and he promised not to say anything. No one else has seen us.*

Katie's being salty over the breakup, that's all.

"Okay," I say, resting my head against the window and closing my eyes. "Have fun singing."

Through my squint, I watch Katie move to the far side of the bench and stand up. She pauses, then leans toward me again.

"Maybe tell her to go easy on her shots during our nationals rematch," Katie says softly. "If you can fit that in between your flirting."

My eyes widen into saucers.

Katie shakes her head. "Damn. So it *is* true."

I sit up, my chest suddenly impossibly tight. I pull Katie by the wrist until she's huddled next to me on the bench again. I might've even pulled her closer than she was the first time. My pleading comes out like hiccups.

"You can't—please—I wasn't—"

I pause.

"Wait a second. *What* is true?"

Katie folds her arms. "Bryce said you were hooking up with the hot Van Darian chick from mini golf. I didn't want to believe it at first. But now everything makes so much more sense."

Bryce? Why the hell would Bryce know shit?

Ooofffff coooourse.

My right hand curls into a fist. "Dammit, Caleb."

"He didn't tell everyone," Katie says, rushing to his defense for God knows why. "Just his best friend. Which is more than I can say for you."

I exhale through my nose, equal parts fuming at my ex, and reeling from the guilt of keeping such a huge secret from my own best friend.

Katie faces me full-on—her back blocking off the rest of the bus.

"So tell me exactly what's going on. You've left me in the lurch for freaking weeks. You think I don't notice things?"

I bow my head. "I know you notice."

And I do. Maybe I don't tell Katie my worst stuff, about Mom or the panic attacks or having a bi-crisis-bisis-whatever . . . but she's still my ride-or-die. I know she cares about me.

I shouldn't have put her on hold just because I got close to Rosa.

"We . . . we started off helping each other practice," I explain. "Rosa showed me some of my weak points, so I did the same for her."

Katie's eyebrows shoot up.

"Why the hell would you want to help her get better? I thought you wanted to win nationals."

"I did," I argue. "I do! It was a payback thing. She helped me first."

"So what, then?" Katie asks. She crosses her arms. "Did she randomly kiss you one day?"

"No." I think about this for a moment. "Well, sort of, yeah. But it wasn't random. I had just broken up with Caleb."

"Because of her," Katie finishes.

"Because it wasn't good anymore," I say. "Rosa and I had gotten into this fight about why I was still with him, and I just realized it wasn't right. I needed to get out."

Katie holds out one hand. "Hold it. You're telling me this girl gets pissed off because you have a boyfriend, makes you break up with him, then she pounces on you and kisses you?"

I go quiet.

"That's not it at all," I say. "I broke up with Caleb because I want to be with Rosa. And I didn't want to cheat on anyone. I would never do that."

"Hmm."

Katie stares off to the side. Her brow is creased.

"Well, you've sort of been cheating on the team," she murmurs.

The statement pierces me right between the ribs. I had convinced myself that hanging out with Rosa was okay. It's not like I swiped Gloria's clipboard and gave away Heathclef's gameplays. Rosa and I just talked, and hung out, and played some field hockey. If anything, being with her helped me learn how to be a better goalie. Wasn't it a good thing, to get us all those wins during the season? Wasn't it good to qualify, *high-seed,* for nationals? I don't understand how the math between me and Rosa and the team works out so wrong. But as I look at Katie, it's clear how much I've royally messed up.

Katie takes a deep breath.

"I'm not trying to offend you, E, but that girl is straight-up bad news. I've been super worried about you. I'm afraid you're going to get hurt by all this, and then we'll really be fucked, just in time for nationals."

I nod. "You mean if the rest of the team found out?"

Katie cocks her head at me. "What? No. I mean by being with that womaneater."

Womaneater? Now I'm the one cocking my head back at Katie.

"What are you talking about?"

"Eve . . . come on. Everyone knows Alvarez gets around. Weren't you paying attention to what Melanie said at House of Pizza? I heard Rosa's slept with every remotely queer person on Van Darian's field hockey team. Probably all the straight ones too. Don't you think it's weird that she comes around and seduces you just in time for the invitational? This is way worse than throwing some party on our field. It's, like, psychological warfare or something."

I shake my head at Katie. "No. You're wrong. Rosa didn't seduce me. Things just happened. We got to know each other, and it happened."

Katie pats the back of my hand like I'm a small child. She glances over my head, out the bus window.

"That's Main Street. We're almost back." Katie looks down at me. "If you're so sure about her, then come with me."

"To where?"

"Shipley."

"The high school?" Van Darian's last game is against Shipley. That's where Rosa is playing now. My eyes narrow. "What are you going to do to her?"

"Nothing," Katie says. "I just want to show you something."

I sigh. I don't want to go see Rosa with Katie. I don't want to bring Katie and Rosa near each other ever again. But I've also been caught sneaking around behind my team's back and lying to my best friend. If Katie says she wants me to see something, I sort of owe it to her to follow along, just this once.

As the rest of the team filters off the bus and into our locker room for showers, Katie and I quietly head to her car in the parking lot. Katie plugs Shipley's address into her phone. She peels out of the lot before my seat belt even clicks.

We park on the far side of Shipley's field. As I get out, I can see that the game is nearly over. According to the scoreboard, Van Darian's creamed the hell out of Shipley. They'll head into nationals with one of the top rankings in the country, just like us. I start to make my way over to the sidelines, but Katie holds my arm and stops me.

"Don't get too close. Like I said, I just want you to see something." She points to a nearby crop of trees. "Come over here."

"Are we playing botanists?"

"Sure," Katie says. "Whatever you want our cover to be."

We weave between the trunks of thick oak trees. Katie leans against one of the low branches and peers through the last of the golden yellow leaves. She scans the field from left to right. I watch the scoreboard as it counts down to zero.

BEEEEEEEP, the final buzzer sounds.

"There she is," Katie says, pointing to a figure at the center of the pitch. "Watch."

I stand close to Katie and squint at the tiny form of Rosa racing across the green, hoisting her stick up and down in celebration. She's so adorable-looking that I want to burst from the trees and scoop her up into a hug. I wonder if she's going to sprint to her phone right away and tell me everything.

But Rosa doesn't run off the field. She runs across the green, right into the arms of . . .

I squint harder. *Galen?*

Galen lifts Rosa up and spins her around. The sight of the

two of them makes me taste something horribly bitter, but I swallow it back down.

"That's her friend," I say to Katie. "You and I do that kind of thing all the time."

Katie doesn't answer. She keeps watching. I sigh and turn again to Rosa.

Rosa shimmies out of Galen's hold, but then pulls her right back in for an embrace. She places either hand on Galen's cheeks and kisses—*kisses*—next to her mouth. I inhale sharply. This can't be what I'm seeing.

I retrace all my memories of Galen with Rosa. She found Rosa on the docks as I left. They were playing mini golf together. Galen was sitting on Rosa's lap at Square One, for Christ's sake.

My mouth begins to fill with bile.

I want to explain everything away. I want to pretend like this is all normal, that it's not romantic at all. I want Rosa to just be messing around and teasing her teammates. But Rosa was the one who told me she doesn't queer bait.

She always reels in her catches.

"Apparently she's been like this since she first got to Van Darian," Katie explains. "And she knows what a badass you are on the field. I bet she thought you were hot and then decided to have some fun with you and help out Van Darian in the same go. It's a dick move for sure. But, it's not your fault, Eve."

"No," I whisper.

Rosa wouldn't do this to me. I'm supposed to be one of

the special ones. I'm her flame, or her orange. I'm not just some girl. She said her abuela told her about *me*.

Katie's hand comes over my shoulder and I realize I'm shaking.

"Let's go." Katie pulls me in close and turns us both toward the parking lot. She sets me into my seat and closes the door, then comes around through the driver's side.

The phone finally goes off in my lap.

Fútbolhead: *We won too!* :)

Fútbolhead: *Eleven points!!!!!!!!!!!*

Fútbolhead: *Practicing with a Wall sure has its upsides.* ;)

I blink and blink, but the words are still wet and blurry.

I can't do this. I don't know how to have a broken heart out in the open without coming completely unglued and disintegrating on the spot. Katie was right: this is all too close to nationals. I'm about to lose everything, all because I let my number one rival get closer than anyone else has ever been. Rosa shouldn't have this power over me. *No one* should. I'm the one who helps other people out with this kind of nonsense. I'm the one who drives my friends home when they get their hearts broken.

I'm not the girl who sobs in the passenger seat.

My phone buzzes again. Katie clicks her seat belt in and looks over.

"You can't let her mess this up," she says seriously. "Nationals isn't just about you, E. It's about the whole team."

"I know," I say. Of course I know that. I'm captain. It's my job to protect the team.

Even if I get hurt in the process.

I click on the "Fútbolhead" icon and hit a small button in the corner.

Block this contact? my phone asks.

Cancel. Confirm.

My finger hovers over the screen.

I make the right decision.

CHAPTER TWENTY-ONE

A week and a half later, I lie in bed, staring wide-eyed at the ceiling.

Usually, if I relax my eyes enough, the textured plaster begins to blur and I can turn a blank canvas into the backdrop of memories of Mom and me playing out on the field. I find her eyes in a smudge. I hear her laugh like an echo.

Tonight, I only see the plaster.

We've won the first two rounds of nationals. I feel like Mom should be everywhere. I should smell her in the grass. I should hear her coaching me with every blocked shot. She should be building me up, brick by brick, getting me ready to take the big title home.

Instead, she seems farther away than ever.

My goal box feels painfully empty every time I stand inside it. The two teams we've seen so far have been good—better than almost every other team we've encountered in our regional season. I can't be a perfect No-Goalie with competition like this. But I have managed to be good enough to help us secure the wins.

My cell phone buzzes next to me. I reach for it without turning away from the ceiling. I know it won't be a text from Rosa.

I don't get those anymore.

It turns out to be another late-night reply from Seth. We've been going back and forth ever since he left me high and dry over Thanksgiving break last week. I had to sit through not one, but *two* of Dad's failed attempts at slow cooking a turkey. If Seth had been here, he probably would have slipped out and had takeaway from Wawa before Dad even got the second turkey on the grill. Instead, Dad and I were stuck licking char off turkey legs all afternoon while watching the football game.

Seth: *YES I'll be home for winter break. Calm down, woman. Finals are just crazy this semester. They seriously up the game for seniors.*

Seth: *You hanging in there on the high school end?*

Mmmm. Barely, I type with a grimace. In truth, I haven't even started thinking about finals. My life is enough of a dumpster fire without throwing in schoolwork too.

I pause and glance up at the ceiling.

Me: *I wish Mom were here. She always knew what to do.*

Seth starts to type a response, then stops. I watch his cursor blink again and again. Finally, I get the text.

Seth: *Not always.*

I roll my eyes and exit out of the conversation. Seth can be weird when it comes to Mom. I don't know what sort of teen-age angsty shit he has against her. It's not like she's even here to have an ongoing fight with.

The phone buzzes again.

Kay: *We're outside.*

Right on schedule.

Two days ago, half of Heathclef's field hockey sticks mys-teriously went missing after our last game. The team found them an hour later piled near the dumpsters on campus, lit-tered with empty Red Solo cups. We all knew exactly who took them. Gloria told us to calm down, to stay focused, to not act like rage-filled morons. But Katie and I decided we're done taking the high road when it comes to Van Darian.

Maybe I don't know what Mom would do exactly in my situation, but I have a pretty good idea of what my next move should be.

I roll out of bed and grab the dark gray beanie from my desk. My window is already propped open. I kick one leg over, then straddle myself to the other side of the sill. My fingers cramp as I squeeze the bottom of the window ledge for dear life, waiting for my foot to catch on the awning. From there it's just an easy ladder-crawl down the trellis board, and I'm on the ground.

I stand up and see Katie, Melanie, Natalia, August, and Jade. Everyone has on dark clothes, just like we planned. I stuff my hair into the beanie while August passes around a small tub of forest-green face paint to dab under our eyes.

"I've never understood this shit," Melanie says as the tub

gets passed to her. "Seems like it would only give you away if you're trying to go undercover."

August shrugs. "My dad uses it for hunting all the time, and as far as I know he hasn't gotten eaten by any bears."

"How about any field hockey players?" I ask, receiving the tub. The others chuckle nervously.

We creep over to two cars parked down my street. Katie's manning one wheel, and I have the other. Everyone confers in a tight circle on the sidewalk.

"Remember," I whisper, "do *not* drive to the front gate. We're going to circle around and park behind the woods. I know how to get into campus from there."

The others nod and we wordlessly break into two groups, buckling ourselves in for the ride. Jade and August fold themselves into my car, while Melanie and Natalia ride with Katie.

The dark closes in around us, swathed across the car windows and making the outside world feel like one narrow tunnel. I keep my eyes focused on the skinny road unspooling ahead.

"There," I say. I pull over down a tiny side road.

We close our doors in unison, trying to be a random bump in the night. As the group heads into the woods, I look around and see how useful the clothes, hats, and—heck—even the face paint are. We slip into the dark and disappear. I get to the front of the line, whispering over my shoulder to keep everyone close.

"This way. Just a little farther."

Finally, I see the end of the dock I ran from weeks ago. We

keep wading through the tall grass and trees until we reach a group of eerie, empty picnic tables. I pull out a folded map and smooth it out on the table closest to the woods.

"Okay, we're currently right here. Our lady's over this way." I scroll to a photo on my phone and turn it to face the others. "This is what she looks like."

My teammates squint at the bright blue light.

"Oh damn," Melanie says. "She's sort of hot."

Natalia examines the photo. "Meh, she looks old."

"No, she doesn't," Melanie insists. "You're just saying that because her hair is gray."

I roll my eyes. "*All* of her is gray. She's a statue, for Christ's sake."

"Of Van Darian, right?" Katie asks.

I nod. "Yeah. It says *Lady Van Darian* on a plaque at the bottom. She's tall, so we might have to help each other up."

Jade looks at the photo over my shoulder. "What if her fingers are too hard to break off?"

"They won't be," I say. "I saw them in person. Super narrow. Remember, though, don't touch the two middle fingers."

"Duh," Katie says. "What's the point of this whole excursion otherwise? Needless destruction is tacky. But making Van Darian's founder give everyone the finger in time for the final round of nationals?" She does a chef's kiss.

We all smile uneasily. The truth is, none of us has ever done anything like this before. It was one of those ideas that seemed absolutely perfect after we found our hockey sticks in the trash. I told the others about the statue, and from there the plan seemed to shift right into place. We would sneak over and give a literal "fuck you" to Van Darian right before facing off against them in the final round. It would be so funny, we all said. No one could pin it on us, we reasoned.

Actually being on campus feels . . . different.

I fold the campus map away and tuck my phone back in my pocket. I have no idea what the others are thinking as we walk silently down the sidewalk. The only thing popping up again and again in my head as we tromp over to the library is that I hope to God we don't run into a certain star forward with an affinity for books. At least run-ins with anyone, even super nerdy book-lovers, seem highly unlikely at three in the morning.

The statue is exactly where I remember it from the first time I came to Van Darian's library. A nearby ground lantern bathes the woman in pale light. She still looks a lot like a Disney princess, and I'm grateful for how annoying the open-handed pose is. Maybe it will help me feel slightly less monstrous about what I came here to do.

The six of us form a semicircle around Lady Van Darian.

"Well," Natalia says.

Jade nods. "Here she is."

No one moves any closer.

Katie brings her hands together. "I can give someone a boost."

"No way." Melanie pokes Katie in the shoulder. "You're tiny. I'll give you a boost."

"I'll help someone up," August offers.

We all stay quiet.

"This is ridiculous," Katie says. "We're all here. We're all part of this. It doesn't matter who does the lifting and who breaks the fingers."

"Then you do it," August tells her.

Katie turns to me. "Feltzer should get the honor. It was your idea, E."

I look up at the statue and shake my head. Nothing about this moment feels like an honor. I look around the circle and see the expressions on my teammates' faces. Everyone seems completely scared shitless. We had just wanted to stick up for ourselves, to get back at the jerks who stole our field hockey sticks and trashed our campus. No one here actually wants to destroy anything.

"I can't do it," I say. I hug myself like a small child. "I don't want to break it. I just want to go home."

". . . Me too," Natalia says softly.

Katie sighs.

"Wait!" August pulls down her backpack and reaches inside. "I have an idea."

The rest of us lean forward over August's bag. The sudden intrusion from behind catches us completely off guard.

"What the fuck is this?"

I whip around. Rosa and a very drunk-looking Galen stumble toward us. Rosa pulls Galen along behind her.

She holds her phone out as a flashlight. "What are you doing here?"

I give a hard stare to Galen as she drapes herself over Rosa's shoulders.

"Another late night out on the docks?" I ask, bristling.

"That's my business," Rosa says icily. "I go to school here. Whereas the whole of you look completely lost. I'll ask one more time before calling security: what the fuck are you doing?"

I open my mouth and then close it, because I have no good answer. I can't tell Rosa we're here to destroy her school landmark. I can't say we're here for a random midnight stroll around the lake. And I especially can't say we're here because I wanted to feel close to her again, even just a little bit, one last time.

August yells out an answer from the back of the group.

"We're just doing some decorating!"

We all part and look back at her, opening a central aisle between us and a clear view of Lady Van Darian. There's now a short banner of fabric hanging between the lady's arms. As I step closer I realize two sleeves are tied to either wrist. It's—

"My jacket?" Rosa asks as she and Galen inch in behind us. "Where did you . . ."

"I found it in Captain's car," August says proudly, like Rosa was asking her the question.

The light hits the words scrawled over the fabric.

Alvarez
EATS FELTZER'S SHIT

"Ah." Rosa breathes. Her voice has the slightest rattle.

I turn toward her. She's standing close enough for me to touch. I could reach out right now, if I wanted, and explain everything. But there might as well be an entire field between us with all the reasons that keep me from moving.

Galen tilts her head to one side, looking up at the jacket dreamily. Her cheek has not left Rosa's body for one goddamned second.

"Hey. Didn't you lose that?" she asks, slurring every word.

"We wanted to return it," Katie says. She steps up to my side and throws her arm around my shoulders. "So you could wear it for the big game."

Katie and I stand hip to hip, now directly across from Rosa and Galen.

"How thoughtful." Rosa flicks her eyes to the jacket again, but she doesn't move toward it. Instead, she looks directly at me.

"Thanks for clearing things up," she says. Her words come out hard-formed and emotionless. "I was wondering what happened earlier, but now I get it."

I nod my chin to the human feather boa, who now appears to be snoring, wrapped around Rosa's side.

"Me too."

Rosa squints at me. She looks confused for a moment. Then she must put two and two together, must realize what I found out after the Shipley game, because she makes a show of sliding her arm around Galen's waist.

"Come with me," Rosa murmurs into her ear. "Let's get you home."

My skin is hot and itchy. I want to stomp after them. I want to push Galen to the side and press myself into Rosa deep enough that I get stuck there. I want to kiss her and trace her tattoo and disappear into our own world. But she ruined every chance of that—she freaking ruined it even though I went and broke my world open for her.

I cup my hands around my mouth. "See you at the game, then!" I yell.

"Shh!" Katie clamps down hard on my arm. "I thought we didn't want to get caught."

"Come on," Melanie says. "Time to go."

Everyone turns for the path back to the woods but me. I stare ahead at Rosa, but she never turns around. She just throws us a middle finger over her shoulder. A sidewalk lamp hits her hand so bright, the middle finger seems to glow.

CHAPTER TWENTY-TWO

The tingling starts in my fingers.

That's how it always begins.

Thankfully, I'm alone in my room this time. I don't have to contend with the obstacle course of the locker room, full of twists and turns in the form of my teammates. Gloria didn't call a final practice today.

"Rest up," she told us as we gathered after showers yesterday afternoon. "You've done all you can to prepare for the field. You're ready. Now, get some beauty sleep before Saturday."

She swept a finger over part of the room, looping me, Katie, and the handful of players we brought to Van Darian in her span. "Some of you really need it. Unless raccoon-chic is the new look we're going for these days."

Katie laughed a little, but all I could do was stare at the floor, ashamed.

Maybe that's where the feeling tonight comes from. I haven't been sick before games in a long time—not since the day Rosa chased me down outside the library and taught me how to block slap shots. The familiarity of the numb fingers, the sharpness traveling up my elbows, carries a strange sense of nostalgia.

This is what each week used to be like, I think.

This was my life.

I slump onto the floor of my bedroom, pulling my trash can toward me like an old friend. I'd rather stay here than crawl to the bathroom and hug the toilet again. Plus, this is bound to be the last hurrah. Tomorrow we face off against Van Darian in the final round of nationals. Whoever wins gets the big title. It's also my last-ever high school game. My last chance to prove to Coach Rampal and Duke that I belong there. My last chance to give Mom exactly what I promised her before she left us.

My arms and legs begin to shiver. I yank the quilt down from my bed and pull it over my shoulders. It was Mom's old quilt, the one that Grandma made her back in high school. My body feels a little less shaky under the blanket's weight. I look over by my desk and see the framed photo of Mom from her senior year at Heathclef. She's posed with her field hockey stick, wearing the same uniform as the other field players even though she was the team goalie. Her hair is plaited carefully into two French braids, both sleek and neat. That's how I know the photo is posed. That, and the lack of grass and dirt stains on her knees.

I crawl to my desk and grab the framed photo. Then I

reach for her old medals, for more photos, for her old hockey sweater. Everything crushes together in front of me, arranged on every side like I'm the center of a séance.

My breath quickens. In, out. In, out. Any second now.

Everything wells up inside me, fighting gravity until it's at the very edge. I pull Mom's picture to my chest, fold her in close to me. I let the churning in my stomach take hold, let the feelings slosh and grow stronger.

But then, right when I think I'm going to lose control and vomit everything I've consumed over the last twenty-four hours . . . there's Rosa's hand on my cheek. There are her eyes, staring deep into mine. I remember that there's another option: rather than letting the grief strip my insides raw. I can hone it. I can pull the feelings out of me, shifting them through the proper channels.

And that night, I don't get sick at all. Instead, surrounded by smiling pictures of Mom, I let myself cry and cry and cry.

"Knock-knock," Dad says at dawn, then presses my door open without knocking at all. "You decent?"

I pop up from the floor, my hair wild and sticking out in every direction.

"Yeah . . . ," I mumble.

Dad shakes his head. "I'm not so sure about that." He comes in and sits next to me, his back propped against the bed. All of Mom's stuff is still curled around us on the floor. Dad turns and studies my face.

"Actually, you look good," he says, smiling. "Your eyes look brighter."

I blink and smile back at him. The daylight hasn't even cracked yet. I can still hear crickets chirping outside. But the early morning feels sort of peaceful. My skin feels thick with the memory of Mom. Maybe I accidentally sucked her in through my pores, like osmosis. For the first time in weeks, she feels so clear. I'm standing at the final few yards, and Mom's the finish line. All I have to do is run to her.

Dad stands and helps me up beside him.

"It's the big day," he says.

I nod. "Yeah. I'm ready."

He laughs and looks me over. "Not quite. Get in the shower, kid. I've got breakfast to go and your duffel packed. Team bus for Maryland leaves at six-thirty, sharp."

The ride is long and slow as the entire Heathclef team stares, bleary-eyed, out of the bus windows. Gloria sits in the front, scribbling on her clipboard nonstop. No one asks her if she's changing her gameplay yet again. No one asks her anything.

Even Katie is unusually quiet as she stretches her hands, flexing and curling her fingers like a cat arching its back. No one wants to talk about this being the end. No one wants to even think about the idea of getting bested by Van Darian again. We're silent, meditative. I'm hoping we're all collecting the last bits of energy we have for the chant circle on the field, and, of course, for the game itself.

By the time we arrive at the University of Maryland, where the High School National Invitational has set their final round and ceremonies, the day has fully broken open. The sun is up, the last of the fall birds are singing, and nearly every inch of campus is crawling with people.

Even though we and Van Darian are the only schools playing today, every qualifying team has been invited to earn a final rank and take home a title. Hordes of field hockey players mill about, surrounded by friends and families. Small groups of college students dart on the outskirts of the crowd, probably wondering what in the world is happening at their school so early on a Saturday. There's a handful of journalists asking players questions, and even a few local news crews setting up professional video cameras. And of course, there's no missing the college recruiters. Everywhere I look I see representatives and coaches. They lurk by the refreshment stands, check scores at the information booth, and stride in front of the highest ranking teams wearing their college colors.

Gloria waves her arms at the lot of us.

"Come on, come on. You look like a group of tiny children stepping into kindergarten for the first time. Chins up! You know who you are. You know what you're here to do. Now follow me to our locker room and start acting like champions, for Pete's sake!"

She immediately snakes into the crowd, and Katie gapes behind her.

"We haven't even grabbed our stuff yet!" she says.

I smile. "I guess we'd better hurry, then."

We all scramble to pull our things out of the lower compartment of the bus and run after Gloria. My bag, the last one left, is shoved in the far corner. I sigh as I crawl into the space and slowly drag it out. By the time I've hoisted my gear over my shoulder, everyone else is gone. But I'm not worried. Gloria just wants the team to get some hustle before the game, that's all. We have plenty of time.

I make my way through the crowd, letting my bag do the work of parting people to the side so I can step through.

"Sorry. Excuse me," I mumble, ducking my head and pushing past.

Someone touches my arm. "Excuse *me*."

I look over and see Coach Rampal, who seems every bit as cool and composed as she did at our meeting over two months ago. I notice that unlike the other college reps, she's not sporting a bright blue Duke sweater. She almost looks like she's going incognito.

"Hi, Coach," I say, then immediately wince. "Not my coach, I mean. Not yet, at least. Or not ever? But maybe one day. Anyway, hi."

"Hi, Evelyn," Coach Rampal says, laughing. "It's good to see you here. I understand you've done extremely well this season."

I shrug and tilt my head down so she won't catch me blushing. "Oh. Thank you."

Coach Rampal leans closer to me. "I have to admit, I've checked in with Ms. Williams a few times in the last few weeks."

I look up. "You have?"

Coach nods. "Your season isn't the only impressive feat

lately. I heard your GPA is rising in several classes. And in the middle of your busiest season too. I don't think I would have very much trouble getting Duke on board with awarding you the nationals scholarship. If you qualify," she adds gently.

If we win, you mean, I want to say. But instead I just keep nodding, keep looking anywhere but right at her.

"Thank you," I say again. I point ahead. "I have to catch up with my, um—"

"Of course." Coach steps to the side, and now I am hurrying to find the others.

I can't let Coach Rampal's words sink in too much. I can't let the idea of Duke get in my head now. I can still feel Mom next to me, holding my hand from last night, taking on half the load of my gear as we haul it through the crowd. If she's here with me now, then it has to mean something. She wants me to keep going, I know it. I can get through this.

It's only one more game.

Heathclef wins the coin toss with heads, and I end up striding to the south goal box just before the game begins. I smile as I take in the field and stands. The day is perfect and clear. I catch my dad waving his arms like an air traffic controller from the highest row in the stadium, and I wave back. The rest of my team spreads across the field. Their sticks are tightly gripped, knees slightly bent. Everyone's out for blood and ready for battle. We've never looked better, never been more unified, than we are in this moment.

Van Darian breaks their starting huddle and finds their own positions. Rosa takes her place on the green, though she never once glances my way. I guess we'll have our staredown later, whenever she tries—unsuccessfully—to score.

"Protect the house," I say to myself, my voice sounding uncannily like Mom's.

Today, this field is my house. The championship is mine. It's already there, squished behind me against the net. All I have to do is protect it.

As the referee tosses the ball to the field, every still and solemn field hockey player jolts to life and converges with their opponents. Voices scream out plays. The ground trembles with running. Hockey sticks clack and clatter as they meet the ball. They do seem like swords, really. Maybe that portrait of Rosa in Van Darian's paper, the one of her holding her stick out like a knight, wasn't that stupid after all.

But I have to let go of this thought entirely as Rosa suddenly grabs possession of the ball, before we've even managed to score, and turns on her heels directly toward me.

Protect the house. Mom's voice echoes in my head.

"I know," I murmur. I'm guarding every precious thing in my life behind me. I'm going to protect it at all costs.

Rosa runs closer and closer.

My breathing quickens as the details on Rosa's body get clearer. There's the outline of Frida's chin tattooed on Rosa's thigh. There's Rosa's bright green ribbon looped through her braids. There's the dimple next to her mouth I've kissed so many times.

My eyes flick up and meet Rosa's. She looks more focused and determined than I've ever seen her on the field. All her playfulness is gone. Her mouth is pressed into a thin line. Her brows are furrowed.

This isn't the girl I remember from homecoming. That girl was wild and unfastened and straight-up joyful. She was the kid skipping over the viejito's lawn.

She played for fun, even when things weren't fun.

But Rosa doesn't look like she's having even an ounce of fun right now. As I watch her I suddenly realize Rosa's not focused—she's upset. She looks like a girl who just had her own heart stomped on.

Something flickers over by the sidelines, and I glance at the bench of Van Darian players waiting to get swapped in. There's Galen, sitting on some other girl's lap with her arms clasped around the girl's neck. They nuzzle into each other. Two other players sit next to them, twisting each other's hair into braids. One girl leans her head tenderly on another girl's shoulder.

"Oh my God," I whisper.

I see things now, exactly as they are. It's the goalie vision Mom talked about—the distance from the rest of the game that affords us clarity. Only now, the distance from Rosa and her teammates makes me see just how wrong I had gotten everything.

This is a team thing. The hugs. The affection. The friendliness. It's how they trade energy on the field.

Rosa wasn't hooking up with Galen.

Rosa only wanted me.

Rosa saw me for exactly who I was.

She might've even loved me.

And I might love her too.

My heart thumps hard in my chest.

Rosa is the precious thing I'm supposed to protect, I realize. Because being a goalie is, above everything else, about protecting what you love.

And I'm frozen now, completely unsure of what my next move should be. How do I protect the girl barreling at me with a stick? I open my arms wide, holding them ready for Rosa to run the rest of the way in—

—until Katie rams into Rosa's side with a sickening crack and sends her to the ground.

CHAPTER TWENTY-THREE

Rosa lets go of her stick and collapses right on the grass. She falls like a building in demolition, her legs completely giving out from under her.

"NO!"

My voice tears out of me, ragged and raw.

I throw my own hockey stick to the side and run as fast as my goalie pads will let me.

Katie stands there awkwardly, just looking down at Rosa's feet without making even the tiniest effort to move her own. I drop down to my knees.

"Rosa. Rosa, are you okay? Where does it hurt?"

Rosa moves both hands to her hip. I pull my hand protectors off and gently touch the fabric of her skort.

"Does it feel bruised? Broken?" I ask.

Rosa just moans.

I hear Katie snort from above me. "God, she really does have a background in soccer."

I spring up to my feet and thrust a finger to Katie's chest. "You fucking did that on purpose."

Katie's eyebrows shoot up. "What? I did not! We were both running for the ball! Maybe she bumped into me and went down."

"She already had the ball!" I scream.

Several Van Darian players stoop and gather at Rosa's side. A medic rushes onto the field. The head referee approaches Katie and me warily.

"All right, Heathclef," he says. "Back up from Van Darian."

"She's hurt," I say, and now I'm starting to cry. "She's really hurt." I glare at Katie, then turn to the referee. "It was a foul."

The referee shakes his head. "Van Darian already had possession."

"Exactly!" I say. "It's a flagrant foul by Heathclef. Rough and dangerous contact. Van Darian gets a free hit."

Katie steps back. "Are you freaking kidding me?" She looks to the referee. "If anything, Van Darian was obstructing. I was going for the ball. It's Alvarez's fault for shielding it with her body."

"Alvarez didn't do anything," I say defensively. I try to edge in between Katie and the ref. "It's a free hit, I know it is. I was watching."

The referee looks from me, to Katie, then at me again.

"Are you trying to tell me," he starts, "that I'm breaking up a dispute not between Van Darian and Heathclef, but between two Heathclefs, and the goalkeeper's asking me to call a foul against their own team?"

I nod. "It's what's fair."

Katie sucks the air in through her teeth.

The referee shrugs and turns away from us. He faces the stands and holds both hands out, palms down, making the signal for "dangerous play." He then places one hand behind his back and gestures the other toward the south goal—the one I've currently abandoned.

The announcer leans in to the microphone. "Free hit, Van Darian."

Half of the stands erupts in cheers, the other half in groans and booing. Gloria stands clear at the other end of the field's sidelines, but I can feel her glare even from here.

Katie turns to me. Her eyes are like ice. Her mouth a tiny stone. I've never seen her like this before. Though, to be fair, I can only imagine the way I look to her. I feel like a wild animal, ready to swipe at anyone who so much as looks at Rosa the wrong way. I'm sure Katie's never seen me like this, either.

"I hope you know what you just did," she mutters before tromping off.

I look down again where Rosa fell. The medic has her sitting up now. He has one of Rosa's legs bent at the knee, foot flat on the ground. The other leg is straight, toes pointed. I crouch next to the medic and look at Rosa.

"You have a free hit," I say. "Will you be able to take it?"

The medic pauses and turns to me, but Rosa doesn't shift her gaze from her leg.

"Rosa," I say. "Did you hear what I said?"

A Van Darian midfielder turns up over my shoulder. "Get

lost, Heathclef. She doesn't want you around. We're her team-mates. We'll help her take the hit."

I wave the midfielder off and lean closer to Rosa. "I won't get in your way," I whisper. "I'm so sorry. I thought you were cheating before. It was Katie, she told me— It doesn't matter what she told me. I'm such an idiot for believing it, and not even asking you. Rosa, can you hear me? Did you hit your head?"

Rosa doesn't move. She barely blinks. But then I hear the words, low and quiet, from her mouth.

"Go. Away."

I reach for Rosa's hand. She immediately pulls it back.

"I *said* go away."

The midfielder hovers next to me. "You heard her. Get back to your goal. We don't need any free shots from you."

Suddenly the atmosphere shifts, and I realize that out of the people surrounding Rosa—the medic she's never met be-fore, the teammates who don't come over for cheese enchila-das or know about her abuela or her life back in New Mexico, and me—I'm the outsider. I'm the one she wants the farthest away from her.

I stand up, shaky now, and collect the hand protectors I threw onto the field. The stands are eerily quiet. Everyone's eyes are on me.

They saw everything, I think. Everyone watched me reach for Rosa's hand. They saw me lean in close to her. They saw me jab my own teammate in the chest and report her to the referee.

Everything's out in the open now. I'm a traitor, a full-on traitor.

Rosa's teammates help her to standing. I return to my goal box, as instructed. The others back away and it's just her and me again, facing off.

"Look at me," I whisper.

But Rosa keeps her eyes turned down. She carefully shifts her weight to the unhurt hip and swings at the ball. I don't move as I watch it roll between me and one of the posts.

"Van Darian goal," the announcer says half-heartedly.

Everyone in the stands remains quiet. This isn't the game they were expecting from the top two teams in the country.

Rosa doesn't even bother to celebrate the point. She just turns away and shuffles off the field. I feel a part of myself limp across the green with her.

Once Rosa hobbles off and her replacement hits their spot, the game gets going again. Van Darian seems eager to jump on the lead I've handed them, and Heathclef seems even more eager to prove themselves now that I've shot us all in the foot. The ball swings into play and I watch as everyone races up and down the field. The movement around me swirls and blurs. I rub my eyes, wondering if it's starting to rain as the players all melt into running colors.

Then I realize I'm crying again.

The goalkeeper known as the Wall—the one who's supposed to lord above the game, distant and aloof—is crying.

The world inside me bleeds with the world outside until I can't tell anything apart anymore. I don't know Van Darian from Heathclef. I don't know a pass from a shot. I don't know if the empty space in my chest is for my mother, or for Rosa, or for no one at all. Everything around me becomes one muddled, wet mess.

We lose.

My dad will later insist the loss isn't my fault. He'll say Heathclef was all over the place. We were tripping on our feet in the offense, too slow in defense. He'll talk about the three goals I saved as proof I've done right. He'll say nothing of the four more I missed. He will tell me, over and over, how proud Mom is of me.

Dad is never any good at catching onto my lies. But I can always see right through his.

The final buzzer sounds and the crowd seems to collectively hang its head. I can only imagine the letdown of trekking out to see the most anticipated field hockey game in the country, and then having the outcome essentially decided in the first few minutes.

The other Heathclef players drag their feet into our designated locker room, with Gloria trailing at the end. She has to know I'm not ahead of the others. She has to know I'm behind her, watching. But she doesn't turn around. The gym door closes and I'm stuck outside, left to fend for myself.

I look around the field for Rosa. She never resumed play after the hit from Katie, though I did see her sitting on her team's bench. She's long gone from the field now, as is the rest of Van Darian. They're probably in their own changing room dumping celebratory buckets of water on each other and hoisting their coach up in the air. I think of Rosa laughing and cheering, and for a moment even that's enough to make me smile. Then I think of the way she looked at me today on the field. Even the biggest win can't possibly be enough to pull a smile from all the pain I saw. Pain I gave her in the first place.

"Evelyn."

I look over toward the stands and see Coach Rampal step slowly onto the field. I manage to take my helmet off, even though removing another layer is the absolute last thing I want to do right now.

"Hi, Coach."

"Tough game," Coach Rampal says. She looks truly disappointed, and I know, of course I know exactly what that means.

"Thank you," I manage to choke out. "Thank you for coming. I'm sorry I— I'm sorry."

My head drops down onto my chest. Coach Rampal steps to me and places her hand over one of my hand protectors.

"You know, our losses define us far more than our wins."

My lip starts to tremble. Jesus Christ, it would be less painful if she straight-out slapped me.

Coach Rampal shakes her head. "What I mean to say is, winning is easy. With wins, we get exactly what we want. The universe goes to plan. It's the losses that challenge us, that ask us what we're going to do next."

My chest is shaking as I try to catch my breath. Tears are quietly sliding down the sides of my nose and making me taste salt, but Coach doesn't seem to notice.

"You mean . . . like for college?" I ask.

Because I have no backup plan, I want to cry out. *This was it. This was fucking it.*

Everything that's happened this morning, and the last few weeks, and even the last couple of months, suddenly crashes down on me in wave after wave of brutal reality. I just made my team lose at nationals. I lost my own team. I lost my coach. I lost my best friend. I lost Rosa. I lost Duke.

I broke my last promise to Mom.

Coach Rampal tilts her head down to look at me. "I know college feels like such a big choice right now, as if everything hinges on where you'll be next year."

I absolutely cannot meet her eyes. There's nothing to protect me from falling apart. I'm a human-shaped exposed nerve in this moment. If I make a connection with one person I will implode on the spot.

The coach goes on. "But there are so many different paths that will ultimately take you where you want to go. And the best players, the one who love the game more than they love winning, will always find a next path after a loss. Always. I know you will too."

I stare at her hand. It looks almost comically small on my gear, like a small child holding a bear's paw.

"Thank you," I whisper. I don't know how many more beats pass by before I add: "Goodbye."

We both know all the things I'm saying goodbye to.

Coach Rampal nods. "Goodbye, Evelyn."

She gives my arm a final pat, then walks away.

CHAPTER TWENTY-FOUR

By the time Dad and I make the two-hour trip back home from the medals ceremony, it's already dark. I feel a strange sense of déjà vu, like I never left the house at all, like it could still be early morning and I have another chance to win the game and get the scholarship. But then Dad asks me what I want for dinner and I remember that every chance I had is already squandered.

"Nothing," I say.

He opens the refrigerator anyway. "You can't say 'nothing.' Win or lose, when you play, you burn calories, Evie. I don't care if you only eat ice cream, but it has to be something."

I sigh. "An apple, then."

Dad passes me an apple from the bowl on the countertop and I immediately take it into my room.

The evidence of my pseudo séance from last night is still scattered everywhere. I see the cocoon on the floor where I slept, surrounded by Mom's old field hockey photos and jerseys and medals. It's so tempting to step right back into that circle and lose myself in my mother. But all that is, is a temporary escape. It's a fantasyland, just like Rosa said. And I can't live in my mom's memories forever.

I can't spend the rest of my life trying to soak up the best parts of hers.

I carefully step over all the things from Mom's glory days. Instead of reaching for them, I reach far under my bed. I pull out a thin, light shoebox that once held some strawberry-printed sandals my mom bought me when I was eleven. I don't remember ever wearing the actual sandals. They were a decoy gift, a distraction gift. The day I got the sandals was the day Mom told Seth and me about her cancer.

I open the box.

Right on top are photos of Mom from her last year with us. I pick up the first photo and hold it out in front of me. Mom's hair was gone from the treatments by then. Her skin was just starting to lose its color. My stomach plummets as I see the darkened rings around her eyes. Her arms are around Seth and me, long before Seth came out. We're all grinning cheesy grins and smooshed at the center of the couch that's still in our living room. We look happy enough, like we're dealing well enough. But I remember Mom throwing up minutes after the photo was taken. She cried in the bathroom as my dad crouched over her.

"I don't want this," she sobbed, the words bloated and echoey as they seeped under the door and into the hall. "I don't want them to remember me like this."

"They won't," my dad cooed. "Everyone gets sick now and then. This is temporary. Temporary."

It turned out to be temporary in a way none of us was prepared for.

I lift the small stack of photos and set them to the side. I hold up the necklace with two gold hearts that my mom always used to wear. One heart for Seth, one for me. I read through the notes she would set out for me on the counter every time she left early in the morning for her weekly chemo sessions. I touch her favorite headscarf, already knowing it won't smell like her.

She didn't even smell like herself in the end.

In her final days, when Mom knew for sure that she wasn't getting better again, she made me promise to take her with me as I went to Duke, as I made it professionally, as I became everything she wanted to become in field hockey.

I read the last note at the bottom of the box.

Keep going, Evie. Love, Mom

The note wasn't supposed to mean anything special at the time. Mom had watched me practice some new move in the backyard the day before, and she wanted me to master it while she was at her chemo session. But then at the hospital her blood pressure unexpectedly plummeted, and things went to hell. When she came home the next day, it wasn't because she was finally better. It was because it was time to say goodbye.

Keep going, Evie.

The paper feels so fragile in my hands. As I read over the words again and again, I'm struck with the urge to tear them into a million tiny pieces. I want to scream at the writing and somehow have Mom hear me.

It was such a shitty promise.

Why did Mom think it was possible to stitch our lives together? That just because she made me, because she taught me how to play field hockey and love it the way she did, that I would want the exact same things she wanted? She didn't actually want me to go professional, not really. *She* wanted to be the one who made it.

Every major goal I've ever had for myself suddenly glares back at me as a placeholder for the things I wish my mom got to have. And where does that leave me? I'm like her sad little shadow. I'm a clone, a copycat.

I look around my room and immediately want to throw up. Seth was right: I made my entire life into a fucking shrine.

I kick the box away.

I do feel sorry for Mom. She was the one who went through hell at the end. She's the one who's not here now. But sometimes I'm so freaking envious of her, or at least of what she got to be like as a teenager. She didn't lose *her* mom two weeks after getting her first period. She didn't have to make an impossible promise and then fall down a rabbit hole of grief, clinging to anything just to keep herself from hitting the very bottom.

"I don't hear any chewing," my dad says in a singsong voice from the hall. He pokes his head inside. "Evie? What are you up—"

He stops as soon as he sees Mom's headscarf on the floor.

I look up at him, and him down at me. We're both deer frozen in the headlights.

Almost immediately after Mom died, we stuffed all the cancer things away. We stitched all the gaping holes in the house with stories of Mom on the field. We don't talk about that last year. In our household, there's a clear line between the Before and the After of Mom's diagnosis. We only talk about Before.

"Why . . ." Dad's voice cracks. He clears his throat. "Why did you want to see these things again?"

"I don't know," I say. I look down at the scarf. "Maybe because that year was so messy. And right now my life feels like one huge mess."

Dad nods. "That year was very . . . messy," he concedes.

I can see how uncomfortable he is, standing here. I know he wishes he'd never opened the door. It would have been less awkward if he had caught me dancing around to Elton John in my underwear, or making out with my pillow in the corner of the room. Unfortunately, both of those events have already happened in our personal father/daughter hall of shame. But I'm certain that he wouldn't mind a repeat cringe moment over seeing this. For him, anything is better than being reminded of the excruciatingly slow, excruciatingly painful way we lost Mom.

"Do you ever think about it?" I ask anyway.

Dad scrubs his chin. He looks so tired. "Of course I do."

"Then why don't you ever bring it up? Why don't you ask me how I'm doing, handling everything without her here? It's like you don't want me to get sad about her, ever. You won't let me."

"That's not true," Dad says. "I just don't want to bother you when I get sad, kid. And I'm sad all the goddamned time."

"Well, I am too!" I scream.

Dad and I stare at each other, wide-eyed. I've shattered the easiness between us.

"You should have been there," I tell him. "After she left, you should have stepped in."

Dad toes the carpet.

"I thought she had you," he murmurs. "The two of you were always . . . I thought you two had everything figured out."

I shake my head. "I was twelve, Dad. *Twelve*. The only thing I had figured out was to do exactly what Mom told me to do. You can't just leave someone with a list of instructions and call it parenting. I went from having two parents to being raised by a fucking ghost. What the hell."

Dad looks at me like I've sharpened my field hockey stick into a point and jabbed it into his side. I know I'm hurting him by talking about this. I don't think I've ever yelled at him in my entire life. But maybe I need him to feel some of the hurt that's constantly coursing through me. I need him to know I don't have my life together at all.

I take a deep breath.

"I'll be out for more food in a bit," I mutter. "I'm not hungry right now."

I wait to see if he's going to step through the doorway I've opened between us. But he only backs out of the other one, edging into the hall.

"Let me know if I can order you anything," he says, probably more to himself than to me. He closes the door tight behind him.

I glare at the space where he was standing.

I'm not going to put everything back just so Dad doesn't have to look at it. Somehow, the crappy photos and notes and phyllo-layered emotions of grief and anger and fear stuffed into an old sandals box make me feel more like myself than all the shiny sports mementos scattered around my room.

No matter how hard I've worked, I'm not some unstoppable, infallible field hockey star. I'm not a wall. I'm never going to be the girl playing for Duke, or the wife of the football quarterback.

I'll never be the person my mom was.

But I might relate to her outside of her highlights. I do know what it feels like to have a set future suddenly come crashing down. I know what it's like to be in denial, to be unsure and scared. I know what it's like to feel painfully fragile, painfully imperfect, painfully human.

I haul myself off the floor and crawl past all of Mom's things.

I grab my duffel bag from earlier today and dump out my gear. I yank my dresser open and grab several shirts and some handfuls of underwear. I stuff both into the bag, along with two pairs of jeans lying on the floor.

I can't talk to Dad about Mom, at least not about all the messy parts of Mom. I'm too beyond telling Katie. I can't face Gloria again. There's only one person I can run to right now, even if they don't particularly want to see me turning up at their door.

The light barely creeps over the hedges as I leave early the next morning. A note is out on the counter, where Mom used to leave all her notes for me.

Hi Dad,
    Had to get away for a few days. I hope you can understand. I'm safe and have my phone on me.
    Be back soon.
    Love,
    Evie

CHAPTER TWENTY-FIVE

Thanks to slow Sunday schedules, the train ride up to Boston takes nearly the entire day.

I step out of the T station on Davis Square by late afternoon. I've visited twice before, but on those occasions, I was ushered around from block to block, carefully guided by my older brother. I don't have anyone waiting for me this time.

I pull up his address on my phone and study the route from where I'm standing to his shared apartment house. The glaring purple line from me to him makes the trip seem easy, until I look away from the screen and see a hundred street names and buildings crowding over the sidewalk. I end up looking like a bobbleheaded tourist as I glance from phone to street, phone to street with every step.

I pass by ice cream shops and sushi restaurants . . . then basketball courts and parks . . . and then only quiet neighborhoods with old office furniture dumped on curbsides and potted-plant menageries arranged on porches.

Finally, I get to the end of the bright purple line, my destination on the left. I climb up the front steps and ring the buzzer for level three. The speaker crackles to life.

"Hello?"

"Hi," I say. "I'm looking for Seth."

The intercom goes static for a moment.

"Who is this?"

I take a deep breath, then look into the speaker like it's a peephole. "It's your sister."

The intercom turns completely silent. I pause, unsure of what to do next. I take out my phone to call Seth, just in case I got the wrong house altogether. But then I hear clomping down the stairs and the heavy front door swings into the house. Seth stares at me, wild-eyed.

"What happened?"

Nothing, I want to say casually. I came here to hang for a bit. I just wanted to see my brother—does that have to be such a big deal? But apparently even a question as simple as "What happened?" is enough to pop me like a water balloon, because instead of answering like a normal person, I throw myself onto him with one huge sob.

At first Seth freezes under my touch. Then his hands find my back.

"Oh . . . gosh. Okay. It's okay. Come on in, Evie. Come on. That's it."

He takes my bag and ushers us up the stairs. The staircase creaks and groans, and the dark wooden railing smells of mildew. We walk up and up together until he opens the door for apartment three and shows me inside.

There isn't much to look at besides an old TV, a video game console, a futon, and two ratty armchairs. I glance over the living room arrangement.

"This looks . . . nice."

"Yeah, it's a pile of shit," Seth says. "That's because no one wants to put their own stuff in the common rooms. Come on."

We wade down the hall, past a tiny, similarly sad-looking kitchen, and head into Seth's room. Seth's right: he clearly saved all his decorating for the space he gets to himself. A queen bed covered with a navy satin comforter sits nestled in one corner. A modest cherrywood desk and chair are pushed into another. In the third corner, opposite from his closet, is a mid-century leather armchair in front of a standing floor mirror with a gilded frame.

I point at the chair and mirror. "Where did you get those?"

Seth grins. "It's amazing what rich people throw to the curb on Saturday mornings," he says. He points to one corner of the mirror, where I see a tiny crack, and then to two deep scratches on one of the chair legs.

"Huh," I say. "Good finds."

Seth sets my bag on the floor and gestures for me to sit in the chair. He sits on the edge of his bed.

"I heard you lost the big game," he says quietly. "I'm sorry."

I stare into my lap.

Seth leans toward me. "But I don't think that's why you came here. So what else is going on? Really?"

I try to fake a laugh. "Jesus. You're not even going to hang out with me first?"

"We'll hang out," Seth says. "After." He nods at me. I have

always hated how he never lets me wriggle out of his stupid questions. But that might be exactly what I need right now.

I sigh. "I'm here because I don't know how to get over Mom and . . . I hate that you do. I hate that you got over it such a long time ago and I'm still spinning in circles from when I was freaking twelve. And Dad is awful about this kind of thing. He doesn't want to talk about Mom."

"Dad loves talking about Mom," Seth murmurs, staring off into the distance. "He just hates talking about when she had cancer."

"Right. And maybe that's where I sort of went wrong, you know? Like, you just seemed to absorb everything when it happened, how it happened. And then later you came out, and you freaking blossomed and got so cool and had a million friends and girlfriends who had nothing to do with Mom. It was like you figured out how to do new things after she died. And I only figured out how to repeat all her same shit. But that doesn't work anymore, because it turns out that, actually, I'm not like her in a lot of ways. Including some definite queer ways."

Seth looks at me, his brow now deeply creased. "You think I blossomed after Mom died?"

I shrug. "I mean, you came out after."

"I came out to *her*," Seth says. He pauses, then shakes his head. "She didn't want to hear it."

"What?"

Seth sits up a little taller and sniffs. He's trying to look strong. "She rejected it," he says coldly. "It was hard enough to even think about leaving her kids behind, she said. I was taking away one of her daughters before she was ready. So she just . . . didn't want to hear it. And that was that."

He looks at me again, this time with more of a glare. "Why do you think I let you have all of Mom's stuff? I didn't ask for anything after she died. You ransacked her drawers and closet and I just watched from the corner."

My cheeks burn. "I didn't know. I wasn't paying attention."

"The truth is, by the time she was gone, I convinced myself that I hated her," Seth says. A tear slips down the side of his nose. "I hated that she didn't see me, or didn't want to be part of who I was in the end. And after she died maybe I did sort of go into a cocoon, I guess. Or a seed pod—whatever blossoms do before they blossom. I was pissed and I was gutted. My own mom rejected me and there wasn't ever going to be a chance for her to undo that. Then, after a year, I finally figured that with all the surprise ways there are to die out there, life was too short to be miserable through the rest of it. So right after I turned eighteen I told Dad he could either have a son, or that I was leaving. And of course he freaked out that I might leave and he cried a bunch and said that he couldn't lose any more of his family and he would love a son. After that conversation, things just got . . . better. Though, to be fair, that was really the only direction to go at that point."

We're both quiet, each of us breathing shakily into our laps. Seth clenches and unclenches his hands.

"I don't really hate her," Seth says after a while. "I think there are a lot of great things she taught me that helped, even when I was doing exactly what she told me not to do with coming out and everything. Mom always had big dreams. She almost went pro at field hockey. She chased Dad instead of the other way around. She really wanted kids. She got all those things because she knew herself and went after them. So for me, I just rip off the label of what Mom was working for, and I look at her hustle instead. I work really hard at feeling like the person I want to be, and surrounding myself with awesome people, and exploring new places and communities. I try to hustle like Mom."

Seth stops, and it's clear he's said his piece now. But I can't respond right away. Everything he's put between us is still floating down through the air like ashes. Seth didn't even have the choice of following Mom's footsteps the way I did. Right away he was on his own. And even so, even in the worst possible situation, he found a way to move forward without leaving Mom completely behind.

I get up from the chair and sit next to Seth.

"Can I hug you?" I ask.

Seth flinches a tiny bit, and I know in that moment he must feel the same sort of weakness I do when it comes to being comforted. But eventually he nods and leans in to my side as I wrap my arms around him.

"I'm so, so sorry," I say into his shoulder. "I'm so sorry for everything that happened with you and Mom, and even with you and Dad, and how you had to do all that without any help."

"Mmph" is all Seth says into my hair.

I pull away and smile at him. "For what it's worth, I sure as hell didn't lose anyone when you came out. I was just happy to finally see you as you."

Seth sniffs again, then smiles back at me. "Me too," he says. "I was happy to see me too." He gently brushes my hair back down. "Might've gotten some snot in there. Sorry."

I laugh. "Then you're at least letting me take a shower before you send me home."

"I'm not sending you home," Seth says. "Not until you're ready."

He stands up from the bed, then holds out a hand to help me after. "We should get some dinner. Now you know the real story about my queer crisis. Let me help you get through yours."

Seth and I walk back down to Davis Square, studying the menus displayed in restaurant and café windows along the way.

"We can head over to Harvard," Seth says. "Charlie's is pretty good."

I shake my head. "No. Here's fine."

We end up in a Tibetan restaurant not too far past the T station. It's dark inside, and quiet, and the perfect place to settle in and confess.

I want to find a way to tell Seth about the panic attacks, and literally getting sick over the fear of not living up to my promise to Mom. I want to tell him about the whole rivalry with Van Darian: homecoming, the jacket, the final game at nationals. I want to tell him about my relationship with Caleb crumbling and my friendship with Katie fraying.

But the only way I can get to any of this is by first telling him every single detail of Rosa—from her winking at me on the field, to her ever-changing stacks of books, to the way she looks when she's balancing on a rail, silhouetted against the sunset. I tell him about all the ways we slowly came together, and the awful, twisted reasons we sprang apart.

"Damn," Seth says when I'm done. "You do need a seed pod."

"A what?"

He flaps his hand across the table. "Whatever blossoms use."

"I feel like the whole butterfly-and-cocoon thing would make a lot more sense."

"Too late," Seth says. "You're the one who said I blossomed after Mom died. Now it's your turn, seed."

I laugh. "Okay, whatever. So how do I do that, exactly? Do I just, what, start over and make myself like new things?"

Seth shakes his head and gives me a weird look. "No. You shouldn't make yourself like anything."

I lean back into the booth. "So I just like nothing, then? And be boring as hell?"

Seth gently pushes our empty plates to the side. He clasps his hands in front of him, elbows out, the way he always does when he's about to school me.

"Eve, you're missing the point entirely. Haven't you ever liked anything on your own, no other reason for it?"

I chew my lip, thinking.

"It's hard," I say finally. "I think I already liked field hockey . . . but then Mom died and I made it everything."

"Okay." Seth touches one spot on the table. "So keep liking it, but maybe don't make your whole future hinge on that. What else?"

I smile a little. "I like Rosa."

"Of course you do," Seth says. "She sounds like a total badass. Although with everything else that's happened . . . she might be a little too good for you at this point."

"No shit," I mutter.

He leans farther across the table. "What other things do you like?"

I throw my hands up. "I don't know! What else do you want from me? That's it! This is why I don't know what to do!"

Other people in the restaurant pause, forks almost to mouths, and look over. Seth pulls out his wallet and stands from the booth. He waves me after him and I silently follow as he pays the bill at the front counter. We head outside again and pull our jackets closed against the evening wind.

"I'm going to call Dad," Seth says as we walk. "Let him know you're hanging with me for a few days. I have class tomorrow, but I'm loaning you my T pass."

I look over toward the station across the square. "What am I supposed to do with a T pass? Go train hopping?"

Seth laughs. "Well, hopefully you'll actually get *off* a train somewhere and look around. Find something that seems cool, maybe even inspiring. You just ran into a dead end with Duke, but that doesn't mean you can't turn your ass around and find another way through the maze of life, or whatever."

I roll my eyes, but Seth catches my arm.

"I'm serious," he says. "You say you don't know what you like. So I suggest you do some exploring and figure out your next move. This time, on your own."

I sigh and fold my arms over my chest. Sometimes I really, really hate it when my brother is right.

CHAPTER TWENTY-SIX

The next day I chicken out on heading straight for the subway and instead follow Seth onto campus. I have no idea where I'm going, and after Seth shoos me away, I end up slipping behind another student into the main gymnasium.

Historic photos and giant trophies line the hallway, but right away I notice something odd. I only see pictures of the men's teams. A girl with a ridiculously oversized backpack walks toward me from the opposite end of the hall, and I can't help stopping her.

"Excuse me. Do you know where the women's trophies are?"

The girl blinks at me.

I gesture to the case. "Like, is there another hallway for those teams or something?"

She says nothing, but points to the lowest shelf—the one you would have to squat down to see properly—and keeps walking. I lean so far over I have to catch myself from falling before I can read any of the plaques or trophies at the bottom. I suck my teeth. The school has squeezed every single women's award or trophy down at the very bottom.

I sit on the floor, crisscross-style, and start reading everything in earnest. There are national-level titles down here. There are huge awards and certificates, and from as recently as last year. What are they all doing where no one gets to see them?

I look at a framed photo of last year's volleyball team—the national champion volleyball team—and imagine I'm one of the players. How would it feel, I wonder, winning such a big title for the school and watching it get tucked away out of sight?

It hits me as I'm basically face-against-floor staring at team photos and engraved plaques for people I've never even met, that this is something I sort of care about. This is something I sort of care about *a lot*. And it's not much, just a few trophies where no one can see, but it feels like a clue somehow. I might be working with only breadcrumbs, but I have to try to follow them as far as they'll lead me.

Seth meets me back at his apartment for lunch.

"Does Boston have any sports-themed museums or anything like that?" I ask over my bowl of lukewarm tomato soup.

"Just the Sports Museum," Seth says.

I raise an eyebrow. "It's literally called the Sports Museum?"

He nods and shows me a subway map so I can use his T pass to head there for the afternoon. I only get on the wrong train once, and manage to show up just in time for the museum's three o'clock tour. But the moment our tour group turns the corner from the foyer into the exhibit, my chest deflates. I see sports memorabilia everywhere. Posters and photos and gear and championship rings. But it's all for the Red Sox, the Bruins, the Patriots, the Celtics.

I turn on my heels for the exit before the group disappears down the first hall.

"Looking for something specific?" the man at the front counter asks me as I pass by.

"Yeah," I say, still heading out the door. "I'm looking for the women."

I give Seth his T pass back that evening and ask to borrow his library card instead. He laughs and shakes his head as he hands it over.

"Evie voluntarily heading into a library. I always love a good fastball."

"You mean curveball," I say.

Seth just grins. "Whatever."

I think of Rosa as I walk into the main library the following day. There is something undeniably comforting about being in a building completely surrounded by books. Most of the time when I'm in a building, the walls are just walls. But in a library, it really does feel like the walls are made of words. It's like I've stepped inside the crosshairs of a million people's thoughts and ideas and discoveries, and I get to figure out which ones I'll connect to. It's dangerous. It's intimidating.

It's exciting.

The librarian at the reference desk directs me to a section filled with catalogued books on different sports. I linger as

I run my finger down the spines. I don't want to read books about how sports are played or how to train to be the best out there. Those things barely count as books anyway. They're more like Gloria barking orders in written form.

The books on the histories of sports are a little more interesting, but they're still not exactly what I want. All the information in them seems so cut and dry. Here's the date when the first game was played. Here are some world records from the 1900s. Names and dates always seem to be the biggest things in history books, when they're obviously the most boring parts of history. It's the things people *do,* the risks taken and dreams gone after, that make the stories good.

I set another book back on the shelf and close my eyes. I can see Rosa sitting across from me at that diner, lighting up as she talked about the magic of fútbol. She didn't just know specific years or names of famous players. She talked about revolutions starting from the field. She talked about the whole world being shaped by one sport. I want to find something like that in here.

Near the end of the section, I manage to pick out one book on women's field hockey from the 1980s. It ends up being more of a photography collection than anything else, but I find myself flipping through photo after photo, like I'm looking through an old family album.

I imagine my mom there in the pages, setting records at a school that always paid more attention to the football team, no matter how much the girls were dominating their own fields. I imagine me, trying to sort out my roles inside and outside the game. I imagine Rosa, shoved from one sport to the other all because of some stupid, racist legacy students who couldn't share their spots on the field.

Then I think about Seth, who's missing from these pages. He's missing from so many stories he should be a part of. Growing up, Seth always joked that he was a theater kid, that he wasn't made for sports. But it's not his fault that so many sports are completely fucked up and hardwired into clear divisions based on gender. They don't leave much wiggle room for the people who don't fit into either category, or even people who transition. The whole idea of putting men to one side and women to another ends up leaving huge amounts of people out of the equation entirely. It's not right.

I close the book.

There have to be stories like Seth's out there. There have to be stories like Mom's and Rosa's. There has to be more to sports than this.

I march back to the reference desk. The librarian looks up from her computer and smiles.

"Oh good, you look hungry."

I stop. "Huh?"

"For more information," she explains. Then she pauses and gives me a once-over. "What year are you?"

Shit, I think. *Act cool. Just play it cool. You have a library card.*

I consider taking out Seth's card to prove it's okay that I'm here. Then I remember Seth and I only look alike the way a sister can look like a brother who's four years older than her. I sigh.

"I'm in high school," I murmur.

But the librarian's face lights up. "You're a prospective student?"

"Um . . . yes?" I say, unsure.

"Excellent. Perfect." The librarian pushes her rolling chair away from the computer entirely and gives me her full attention. "Hit me with your next question and let's see how I do."

It feels strange to have an adult at a college being the one to try to impress me. I turn my question over on my tongue like a hard candy, sucking on the words until they feel right.

"I'm interested in sports. . . ." I say slowly. "But I'm also interested in women in sports. And maybe trans women and trans men and nonbinary people in sports too, because I think that's all part of the history of women's sports in general. I want to understand why a lot of sports women play get overlooked compared to men's, and why most sports have to be split up by gender in the first place. I just sort of want to know all of it."

I flinch when I'm done, because that was the vaguest, stupidest non-question ever. But the librarian only looks even more pleased. She doesn't direct me to another aisle of books. Instead she starts looking up specific titles and writing them down on a piece of paper. She slides the list over to me.

"This is only a start," she says.

I look down at the first four titles, which don't look like they have anything to do with sports at all.

Badly Behaved Women
Not All Dead White Men
Trans*
Everyday Women's and Gender Studies

The librarian points to the fourth title. "I think you have a clear interest in gender studies," she says. "You should check out our program here. The GS department faculty are exceptional."

"Oh," I say quietly. And then again. "*Ohhh.*"

The sound feels like somewhere deep in my body finally exhaling. This is a *thing.* An entire college department–level thing. I always thought I had to split my brain in two when it came to sports and school. I didn't realize that one could make a perfect path for the other.

"Thank you"—I squint at the librarian's name tag— "Ms. Mihal."

"Please," she says with a smile. "Call me Adrianna."

She says it like she's planning on seeing me in here again.

And maybe she will.

I look over the list again. I wish Rosa were here, standing next to me. If I hadn't gone to Shipley or taken my teammates to the Lady Van Darian statue . . . if I hadn't been such a colossal idiot and ruined things between us, I know she would be so proud of me right now. She would see how much I listened to her, about seeing sports in the context of everything else. She was the one who said you could trace the world's history using soccer as a thread. But I think women's sports . . . gender and sports . . . might be that way too. That it can be a compass, or a lens, for seeing everything.

I head back out of the library with Adrianna's recommendations. I don't need the books just now. I only needed a start— a possible way out of the hole I've dug myself into.

I pause outside Seth's apartment.

If I do have what I came for, the start of my seed pod or whatever, that means my next move is to walk right back into the mess I ran away from. I'll have to see Katie and the team. I'll have to see Gloria. I have to see Rosa, too. Even if she never wants to see me again.

"The only direction is up," I tell myself.

And Seth's right: the phrase does kind of have a weirdly cheerful ring to it. Plus, don't seeds grow best when they're buried headfirst in the most disgusting, foul-smelling muck?

I ring the buzzer next to the front door and get ready to start packing.

It's time to slog back up through the shit.

CHAPTER TWENTY-SEVEN

My phone reminds me of one of those empty dirt roads in an old Western movie. Not a soul in sight. A tumbleweed rolls across the screen. Somewhere in the air, an ocarina plays that ominous three-note tune.

A showdown's coming.

Apart from Dad, no one has reached out to me since the finals game at Maryland. It would be one thing if I had my phone on airplane mode, or if I knew the people in my life happened to be super busy and off doing other things. But I can feel their anger waving in front of me like a hand in my face. I can only imagine how many times Katie has probably looked at her own phone and glared at my name on her contacts list. She might've even blocked me, the way I did with Rosa. I'm sure she hates me. I'm sure everyone hates me. I didn't just mess up my own title at nationals—I messed it up for our entire team.

I get home from Boston midday on Wednesday. Dad calls me from his office and asks if I'm heading to school.

"Not until tomorrow," I tell him. "I have a bunch of stuff to get done."

That much is true. With field hockey season finally behind us, all I have to look forward to before winter break is a slew of exams and essays. I make a peanut butter and jelly sandwich in the kitchen and pull open my laptop at the counter. My school inbox is filled with test prep and reminders I haven't touched. I lick a glob of jelly off my thumb and scroll down through the list.

For our history final, Mr. Mendenhall wants us to write a paper on an "unexpected momentous event from the last century." If I saw an assignment like this a few months ago, I would have rolled my eyes and waited until the night before the due date to start. Then I would have done my tried-and-true method of typing the assignment into Google's search bar and writing about the first result that popped up.

But this time I'm sort of intrigued. Unexpected *and* momentous. It would be super easy to talk about an event that surprised everyone at the time but was clearly huge the moment it happened. An attack starting a war. A natural disaster. A bombshell court case verdict. But what if the unexpected event still wasn't really thought of as momentous by the larger population? What if I had to convince the reader that the event fits both categories, even if people didn't pay attention to it at the time?

I drum my fingers on the counter. I don't want to open any other emails. I glance at my phone again.

"Four o'clock," I say to myself.

Rosa's out of class by now. She's probably carrying a huge stack of books to her dorm room, or to the library to browse through while she works the desk. Or maybe she's not in any of the usual places. Maybe she's off climbing a tree, just for the hell of it. Or taking a walk through the woods. Or gazing out across the water.

The keys are in my hand before I'm even fully aware I've made the decision to see her.

I stop by the grocery store on my way over and pick out a small bouquet of white tulips. The apology flower, apparently, according to some top result on Google. I make a mental note to actually start researching more instead of believing the first thing that pops up in a search bar. But the tulips are pretty, and I figure they'll be nice for Rosa to look at while every other living thing in Pennsylvania shrivels and curls back into winter hibernation.

The security guard at Van Darian waves me through the gate. I head straight for visitors' parking to find my usual spot.

For the first time since I started coming here in September, the spot's taken.

I pause behind the other car and shake my head. "It's not a sign," I say to myself. "Not a sign. There's another spot right there. Go park."

My skin tingles as I walk down the sidewalk toward Rosa's dorm. I want to reach for her. I want to place her hand on my chest so she can feel how broken my heart is too. I know I can't do those things. I know I have to stay on the other side of the room, be as respectful of her space as possible. I switch the bouquet of flowers from one side to the other. My fingers flex with the impatience of wanting her.

I slip into the dorm building behind another student and knock gently on her door. No one answers. I place my ear to the wood, but can't pick up any sounds one way or another. She could be out. Or she could be inside, silently reading in a corner.

"Rosa," I murmur. "Could you please . . . could I have a minute?"

I step into the communal kitchen just in case. But the dingy stove is off and cold. No music floats through the air. There are no hips swishing, no plates clattering over the table, no forks scraping up bubbling cheese.

I go back to her door.

"Rosa?"

The door directly across the hall opens.

"She's not there," another student says. She folds her arms over a ratty T-shirt and glares at me through large, round glasses. "And *some* of us have finals to study for."

I bow my head a little and step farther into the hall.

"Sorry. So sorry. Do you know where she might be, or—"

The girl's door closes before I can finish the question.

The flowers look slightly less perky as I carry them back out of the building. I tell myself to loosen up a little, to stop choking my peace offering. As the tulips and I get closer to the library, it occurs to me that this isn't even the first time I've had to come back here to apologize. This isn't even my first "so sorry I was an asshole" gift.

I stop in front of the statue of Lady Van Darian and gaze up at her serene face and open hands. It's too easy to remember Rosa's jacket up there, slung between the stone arms. A deep wave of shame fills me up, limb by limb. I hang my head and stare at the ground.

Seth's right: Rosa is too good for me.

One of the library doors opens and I watch a pair of students scuttle out into the cold, shivering as they clutch their books to their chests. I already came all this way. I take a deep breath and head inside.

The study tables, usually crisp and bare, are all filled with open notebooks and overheated computers. Every chair has a person in it, either poring over a book or typing madly away on a keyboard. I hear the soft mix of different voices all converging together as people whisper dates and names to themselves while flipping through note cards.

The atmosphere in the room is so hushed and so focused that it makes me want to drive home, grab my backpack, and come back with all my own assignments so I can slip right into the mix and get to work alongside everyone else.

Then I see Rosa at the circulation desk.

Her back is turned, and she's completely hunched over a book on the far counter. Her fingertip runs down the edge of the page as she reads. I take a deep breath and set the flowers over the checkout desk.

"Hi."

She doesn't look up from her book.

"I saw you when you walked in," Rosa says, her voice

almost disembodied from over her shoulder. "You shouldn't be here."

I pause and press my lips together.

"I—the guard saw me drive through," I say, as if that explains everything.

Rosa still doesn't turn. "I guess that means you're not here to destroy anything else, then? Or are you saving that for your next midnight visit?"

My cheeks get stiff and hot.

"God," I whisper. "I messed up so bad."

"Yeah. You did."

The book makes a small *thump* as it closes. Rosa leaves it and steps to the front desk. Her nails brush the plastic wrap around the bouquet, but she doesn't look down at the flowers. She only looks at me. Her eyes are cold, and piercing, and yet still almost stupidly beautiful. Her hair is swept back into an easy ponytail. Her eyelashes seem heavy as she blinks. I knew she was pretty before I liked her, before I even knew her. But the way she stands in front of me now makes my heart shudder in my chest. Why did it take me so long to get to her in the beginning? And how the hell could I have let her go so easily?

"I have finals." Rosa nods toward the massive study room behind me. "We all do. I'm sure you have them too. Not that you care about school."

"I do care about school," I whisper. I clear my throat and speak up a little. "More than I thought I did, at least. I went to the library at my brother's college, and the librarian there told me about the school's gender studies program. That might be something I do after all this. I could learn about women's sports and their history and a bunch of things I've never really thought about before."

Rosa's face stays blank. "Neat," she says, completely deadpan.

I can tell she doesn't want me to be here. I feel the signs pushing me toward the doors. But I've already come this far. I just need Rosa to hear a few more things, and then I'm gone. And then neither of us has to torture the other anymore.

"The thing about my mom," I say quietly, "is that she died from cancer. A really nasty, really shitty yearlong battle with cancer. And one of the last things she ever did was make me promise to keep going in field hockey after she left. She wanted me to go to Duke and then to go professional."

I pause for a moment.

"I think it was her messed-up way of trying to be immortal, kind of. Like, if I kept living her life, she wasn't really dying. And I was so young at the time. I didn't realize I could say no, or that I deserved to live my own life. So I promised her I would be exactly like her, would do exactly what she wanted me to do."

The tightness creeps into the back of my nose. My eyes sting at the corners. I'm going to fall apart here, in the middle of Van Darian's library, where half of the entire student population is currently congregated.

I keep going anyway.

"But you made me realize that I don't have to be a specific person, or jump through specific hoops, to feel close to her.

You made me realize I should get to be myself and have my mom still be proud of me, not because I'm just like her, but because I'm her kid."

A few fat tears slide down my cheek. I don't bother to wipe them away.

"You were the first person who made me think I could be loved outside of field hockey," I whisper. "And I'm not saying you loved me, because we're young and we haven't known each other that long and I haven't really earned that sort of feeling from you. But I think—I *know*—the feeling when I see you is love."

Rosa's eyebrows go up a little. I want to liquefy into a puddle on the floor, or better yet, disappear into thin air. This conversation is more painful than the hardest hit I have ever taken in the goal box.

Stay open, I tell myself.

"I fell too hard and too fast, and I didn't know what I was doing in that level of relationship. You just seemed too good for me, too good to be true, even. So when Katie said you were hooking up with Galen, I felt like it all made sense. Because how could I ever deserve you without there being a catch?"

Rosa opens her mouth.

"That's awful, I know," I say quickly. "I'm not expecting you to forgive me. I just wanted to say I'm sorry. I acted horribly and you deserve so much better than that. And thank you for stepping into my life at all."

I start to turn for the door before remembering.

"Oh," I add, "and I never should have taken your jacket

after you left it in my car. The other girls on my team wrote on it with the marker. But ultimately, the whole thing is on me. I lied to you, and I betrayed your trust. I wish I could take it all back. I'm so, so sorry, Rosa."

My last word echoes strangely across the foyer. I pause, sensing that something is different.

I hold my breath and slowly turn to the main room again. *Fucking hell.*

Nearly every person who had just been studying or typing or whispering to themselves is now completely silent. They're all staring at me. They've all been listening *this entire time.* I wouldn't be surprised if I looked down at this point and saw I was only wearing my underwear.

"Anyway . . . ," I say, hiking my shoulders up as if they could block out everyone else. "That's it. Thank you for listening. I'm sorry I didn't bring a vase for the flowers. I hope they cheer you up during finals."

"Thank you," Rosa says.

She stands there, looking stiff as cardboard. This is it between us. This is really it.

I nod and leave the library.

The December air hits me, sharp and icy. I should feel like absolute shit. I should be crying even harder out here than I was inside. But somehow, losing the girl of my dreams isn't as awful as I had imagined it would be. I feel lighter with everything said and out there. I came to tell Rosa I was sorry, and I said it. I never expected her forgiveness.

And yeah, even if I wish I got to hold her again, or sit and talk with her, or even laugh together as friends, I know that the apology was the thing we both needed most. We can each move on now. She helped me become a better person, and I'll always be grateful for that.

I walk down the path to my car, thinking of twin flames dancing around each other.

Llama gemela, Rosa's abuela had told her.

She was talking about me.

CHAPTER TWENTY-EIGHT

The next day, Dad practically boots me out the front door to get to school on time.

"You have a week and a half left until break," he says gruffly. "You can survive until then."

This is the only exchange we've had since I got home. I wonder if Dad's afraid I'll bring up the cancer stuff again. I wonder if he knows Seth's secret about Mom, the way she dismissed her own kid when he needed her most. Either way, I see the reserved, quiet way Dad moves around either subject. It's always been so easy to think about the best parts of the person we loved. It's harder to think about the rest.

There are things to figure out with Dad, but those are long-term things, lifelong things. I don't need to stick around the house and dig through more of Mom's past. I have to get my ass back to school and deal with my own future. And unfortunately, I can't fix my future without reckoning with all the selfish shit I've done over the past few months.

I arrive on campus and find that Heathclef's student council has set up yet another seasonal booth, this time just outside the senior parking lot. The same four council members sit behind a long folding table, bundled up in winter coats, smiling cheerily and waving students over.

"Give a *toast*-ed marshmallow hot chocolate to the holidays!" one of the council members yells out.

I can't help but smile, despite the awfulness of the pun, and wander over to the table. There's a large hot chocolate dispenser to one side, a small bowl of mini marshmallows, another bowl of chocolates individually wrapped in bright foil, and an array of clear cups filled with a creamy, frothy liquid.

"What's that?" I ask, pointing to the mystery drink.

One of the guys holds a cup out to me.

"Eggnog," he says as I take it from him. "Cheers!"

I look into the cup and sigh. "Cheers," I say dully.

I make my way into the main building. Once inside, I realize the usual world of high school has been turned on its head and tossed into utter chaos.

Thanks to upcoming finals and winter break, our class schedules are completely thrown out the window. The entire student body is set to attend a medley concert put on by the performing arts department over the morning. Then we have thirty-minute check-ins with every class during the afternoon to go over details for our last tests and assignments.

Every student around me seems to fall into one of two camps: There are the friend groups dressed in reds and greens, blues and silvers. The people laughing and ooh-ing as they exchange and open gifts. The ones singing "Jingle Bells" and checking outside the windows for snow. For this camp, school's as good as out. They'll be the ones singing along and clapping their hands at the concert. They'll be the ones groaning into their elbows propped on desks as teachers remind them that the last week of work is going to count for 40 percent of their semester grades.

The second main source of commotion, originating from the other camp of students, is the pure frenzy and fear of finals. While Van Darian's students seem to exude stress politely, whispering over notebooks in the library, the Heathclef students are flinging around their finals panic like softballs.

"I can't do it!" one girl cries out by the bathroom. "It's too much to remember everything all at once!"

Her friend gives her a quick side hug, then quizzes her on the next index card.

Across the hall, students are squatting on the floor, laptops balanced precariously over their laps as they mash their fingers into the keys. Other students are tearing through their lockers, ripping out loose sheets of paper.

"Where is that damned study sheet," a junior mutters, their head hidden behind the locker door.

I look back and forth between the celebrations and the panic. I don't know which group I fit into. Maybe I just don't belong to either.

Eventually the teachers emerge from their offices and grudgingly shove us all down the halls toward the main auditorium. The symphonic band is already positioned on the stage, their instruments waiting in their laps. The die-hard "Jingle Bells" fans congregate in the front rows. The study-obsessed sneak their books and notebooks into the back. I sit by myself next to the aisle.

The band teacher waltzes onto the stage wearing a full black suit along with a bright red scarf. He whips his baton in quick, jerky motions, as if tapping the air.

"A one and a two and a—"

The band jumps up together, sliding into a rendition of "Frosty the Snowman." The front rows of spectators jump from their seats along with the band. They flail their arms and shake their shoulders like they're at a rave and not a high school winter concert. I scan the rows of dancing kids, but don't recognize any of my teammates. I glance over my shoulder at the people burying their heads in textbooks in the back. I don't see my team there, either. Maybe there is a third camp at the school after all. Maybe it's just the camp of people who don't give a shit about any of this, one way or another.

I feel like every teacher would fit into that third camp. They stand along the side aisle, their arms stiffly folded between moments of not-so-discreetly checking the time on their phones. Two French teachers trade short whispers back and forth. My eyes adjust to the dark and I suddenly recognize the teacher standing directly behind them.

It's Gloria.

The band gets through three more songs before the upper-school choir marches out in their bright purple Heathclef robes.

As the choir gets into place, their long, satin sleeves flapping and tripping the band members trying to reshuffle, I make my attempt at escape. I slip out from my chair and head straight for the door, right past Gloria. As expected, she holds up a palm without taking her eyes off the stage.

"Mandatory event," she whispers. "Get back to your seat."

I shift so my head is poking out from where she's placed her hand.

"I need some air," I whisper back.

Gloria stares hard at me for a minute, and I'm not sure what she'll do next. But then the choir all starts clearing their throats at once and Gloria turns and ushers me out behind her.

We head into the main hall, right outside the bathrooms.

"This enough air for you, Feltzer, or are we taking a field trip outside?"

"No," I say, weirdly feeling shy. "This is fine."

I wait, trying to think of the right words to start. How do I even begin to talk about what happened on Saturday? How do you bring up calling a foul on your own teammate at nationals, or allowing a free hit to roll into the net, unchecked? How do you start a conversation about letting every single person on your team down?

Gloria bows her head. "I owe you an apology."

I jerk my chin back. "What?"

She looks up. "It was, and is, a fool move to only have one goalkeeper on a team—no matter how good that goalkeeper may be. I suppose I knew how badly you wanted to be like your mother. I wanted you to be like her too. I miss seeing her on the field, when we were the ones complaining about those god-awful purple jerseys. I miss so many things. . . ."

Gloria trails off. She sniffs. "And I didn't want to train another girl just to have her sit on the sidelines and watch you carry the team. But what I ended up doing was heaving every single game squarely on your shoulders. That was my fault."

I shake my head. "But we did great most games. And last year's season was good the whole way through."

"Right," Gloria says, folding her arms. "Which means you had years for that pressure to build up. I saw it after our homecoming game, and still I did nothing. I failed you, kid. And for that I am truly sorry."

My mouth hangs open, my tongue dry. I swallow, but a response doesn't come out.

"I thought . . . I'm the one who . . ."

Gloria clamps a hand on my shoulder. Her grip is stiff and firm, though I know her well enough to see this is her version of giving me affection.

"You're the one who played her damn best on the field. Every practice and game, Evelyn. You did your best. Your best is going to look different on different days, that's all. But you did your mom proud."

The urge to slip away and escape pricks at my fingers. I breathe and hold myself in place.

"Thank you," I murmur. I look into Gloria's eyes and manage a smile, even though I know she can see the tears gathering. "That's . . . that's what I've always wanted."

Gloria nods as the auditorium door cracks open. A senior

ducks out of the room, a laptop poorly concealed in his jacket. He holds the door until it closes silently behind him, then tip-toes *one, two, three* steps before he looks up and sees us. His face falls.

"Oh. I was . . . uh . . . I have to go to the bathroom."

"Uh-huh," Gloria says gruffly. She eyes the guy's hand clutching his jacket. "Go ahead, then."

He quickly skitters past us.

"Don't drop your computer down the toilet!" Gloria calls after him.

I smile and shake my head. "It's crazy how so many people are freaking out about finals," I say.

Gloria furrows her brow. "It's not just finals. You know that, right?"

I only blink back at her.

"College applications are due in January. A lot of seniors are scrambling."

"Oh." I turn toward the bathroom door, where we can hear the senior inside, typing away on his laptop. "So for ap-plications, people are . . ."

"Writing personal essays. Gathering recommendations. Applying for financial aid. All of it." Gloria pauses as she watches me freeze up. "You didn't have a backup plan after Duke, did you?"

I think back to my last meeting with Ms. Williams and sigh.

"No, I did not." I look at Gloria. "I'm completely screwed, aren't I?"

Gloria barks a laugh. "A lot of people would feel that way,

I'm sure. But as someone who shot out of this school way too fast from the gate, let me give you some advice: There's always time. Even if you have to carve that time out for yourself."

I imagine taking a knife to the next week of school and sawing it in half, carving out enough room to fit in the last three wasted months of college prep. I could have been looking up gender studies programs. I could have been asking which college libraries have books on women's history in sports. I could have been doing good enough work in my classes to earn recommendations that extend beyond my can-do attitude and reputation on the field. It's just too much. I can't get all that done in time, even with slicing an extra hour or two into each day.

"Thanks," I tell Gloria. I shove my hands into my pockets. "We can go back inside now."

"Ah, must we?" she moans, then throws an arm around my shoulders as we walk back into the concert together.

After another hour of forced caroling and poorly timed claps to "Sleigh Ride," we're finally released from the auditorium.

It's unpleasantly chilly outside, but I still peer through the windows for a free outdoor table to snag lunch before the speed-dating style of finals prep begins in the afternoon. I grab my sack lunch from my locker and push through the tightly packed throng of students. Another student and I collide head-on.

"Sorry," I say quickly.

"Yeah, me too."

We look up at each other.

"Hey, Katie," I say. "I didn't mean— I was only trying to—"

"Yeah," Katie says again. "Me too."

We laugh awkwardly.

Katie nods at the paper sack in my hand. "Where are you eating lunch?"

"Outside," I say. I wiggle the bag a little. "There's plenty to share."

She shrugs and follows me out to the central quad. We end up sitting on the same bench where we found Caleb during the homecoming mocktail hour. There aren't any leaves to kick around this time, though now the dried grass breaks off and crunches under our shoes.

I hold a small bag of chips open. Katie plucks one chip delicately and nibbles on a corner.

"I shouldn't have called that foul on you," I say. "Or pushed the ref to call the foul, I mean."

"Yes, you should've," Katie says. "I did run into Rosa. Really, I should have been thrown out of the game right then." She bows her head low. "I . . . I also took our field hockey sticks."

I turn to her. "What?"

"I hauled them to the dumpster so everyone would think Van Darian was messing with us again. I just wanted . . ." Her voice trails off. "We were so strong before homecoming. But then it was like you broke us apart, little by little. Every time you ran off immediately after practice. And then when you got mad at everyone at the pizza party. Even me, it felt like. I wanted to bring us back together one last time."

"Against Rosa," I say quietly.

"Yeah, against Rosa," Katie snaps. "I was freaking jealous, okay? You were never that close with Caleb. As your best friend, I had so much of you to myself. Then this new girl steps in and takes over everyone's role in your life: Caleb's role, Gloria's role, even my role. I guess I . . . hated her."

I bite my lip. "Is that why you lied about the hooking-up rumor?"

Katie shakes her head. "No. The rumor was real. I just passed it along to you."

"Which is also shitty," I point out. "It was incredibly homophobic, exactly like the talk at the pizza place. That's why I got so mad that day. I get what Mel was saying, about how it's really hard for people who aren't straight-passing, how there are tons of dangers and restrictions that come with being gay. But it's still harmful to dismiss bisexuality, or dismiss anyone who doesn't fit into a clear-cut label. I don't want to feel like there isn't a place for me on my own team."

Katie doesn't say anything.

"Also, no one deserves to be slut-shamed," I go on. "Even if they are hooking up with all their teammates. But Rosa wasn't. She was being affectionate with her friend, the way you and I are on the field. Or . . . were."

Katie nods slowly. We both sigh.

"But I am sorry I broke us apart this season." I shift one leg onto the bench so I can face Katie. "The truth is, I don't think I've been really *here* for a long time. Even before Rosa. And that's on me. I have a hard time talking about things I don't want to talk about. It's always been easier to be the one helping everyone else. I don't know how to talk about my stuff."

"Stuff like what?" Katie asks.

"Like . . . whenever I'm really missing my mom. Or when I'm so nervous about a game that I can't keep any food down. Or even the times being near Caleb made me queasy and I didn't understand why."

"Damn," Katie says. She gazes across the quad. "I never noticed any of that. I guess that makes me a pretty bad friend."

"Me too," I say softly. "I didn't let you in. And I could have been way more supportive about Bryce, or looking at sororities, or whatever else you've been going through over the last two months." I sigh into my arm. "I wish we could start the year over."

We polish off the rest of my lunch. A light flurry of snow begins to fall from the clouded sky.

"Well," Katie says after a while. "The season's done now. And we're seniors."

I nod. "Yep."

"Sort of a weird time to start over on a friendship."

"Yeah," I agree. "It is."

We look at each other, stone-faced at first. Then Katie slowly breaks into a smile. I smile back at her. She nudges her arm into mine and I rest my head on her shoulder. We don't even have to say it. I know we'll both put in the work. There's too much we owe each other, too much history and love to let things break between us.

The bell rings and we head to class for our last instructions on finishing the semester.

Luckily, every piece of information given during class check-ins seems to be stuff that's already up on the class pages online. In our history check-in, Mr. Mendenhall goes over the final paper assignment due next week. We'll need at least five sources for citation, he tells us. And a major part of the essay's primary thesis will be how our event qualifies as *both* unexpected and momentous, so we would be wise to choose something worthy of argument. I jot everything Mr. Mendenhall says down in my notebook.

We end up with ten minutes left over, and he has everyone use the time for researching our chosen topics. As we file out of the room once class is done, Mr. Mendenhall catches me by the door.

"Feltzer," he says. "What were you thinking of? For your event?"

I squeeze my laptop. "Um, I was thinking maybe of writing about when Nixon signed Title Nine and what that meant for women's sports. Or the Battle of the Sexes tennis match looked pretty cool. Or there was this female boxer named Jackie Tonawanda who sued New York State for the right to box men, and later she knocked out a male opponent at Madison Square Garden."

I shrink back a little. "I know those don't seem like big things. But maybe I could say why more people should know about them. Or whichever one I end up going with."

For the first time since I've met Mr. Mendenhall, he offers a genuine smile.

"You get it," he says, nodding.

He turns back toward his desk before I can ask what he means.

I stand in the hallway, holding my school stuff snug against me. A warm feeling sprouts from my toes and twists around my body like a vine. I've never really felt good at anything but field hockey before. But maybe this is where that all changes. Maybe this is how the rest of my life starts.

CHAPTER TWENTY-NINE

A week later, I walk out of my last final.

The students are supposed to leave the building quietly after we hand in our tests and essay packets. But the cluster of people around me explodes into whoops and laughter as soon as the cold air hits our faces.

I see Caleb up ahead in the parking lot holding hands with a junior. He spins her around and kisses her next to his truck. She nestles her head into his side.

They fit together, I think. I smile, knowing how good that feels, to really fit with someone else.

Instead of stepping into the lot, I turn and walk down the wide brick path toward the gymnasium and sports fields. The thick, darkened sky begins to open, and snowflakes as light as cotton slowly float down to earth. I watch the snowflakes gather over the path and landscaping. By the time I make my way down to my field, the world is covered in a thin sheet of white.

The blankness is ridiculously alluring. I plant one foot into the grass, then another, and another, leaving a perfect set of prints behind me. I wade out to the North Chamber goal posts and take my old stance in the middle. The snow keeps on falling. My footsteps leading out here are already fading.

I sit in the snow and stretch my legs out in front of me, then lean back until I'm spread open like a starfish. I swish my arms and legs back and forth, back and forth.

I stand up in my snow angel and study its outline.

"Not bad," I say to myself. "Not bad at all."

I stare at the empty space next to me, then leap across the snow and repeat the ritual of sitting, leaning back, and swishing my arms and legs. Now when I sit up again I can clearly see the two snow angels, lying side by side.

"Hi, Mom," I whisper to the other snow angel. I pull my legs in close and clasp my arms around my knees. "How's it going?"

The other snow angel shimmers.

"I finished my tests," I say. "We'll have to see how it all turned out, but I actually think things went okay. At least it was all interesting stuff. I never thought school was that interesting before."

The snow keeps falling softly over the empty silhouette.

"Like with my history paper, I got to write about this woman named Katherine Switzer, who crashed the Boston Marathon in 1967 by signing up as a guy. Over ten years later, she helped pressure the government into pushing Title Nine, which says that women can't be excluded from sports. The law kind of created the concept of women's sports, which I think is both a good and a bad thing. Like, women's sports are great. But it also separated women from men in some weird ways. And now Title Nine is actually being used to block trans women from participating in sports, which is so entirely fucked up. I don't know, I'm still thinking about it. I could have written a ton more. Which is really saying something, for me."

I lie back into my own snow angel, then reach for the other angel's hand.

"I wish you were still here," I say quietly. "But I'm also really mad at you—what you did to me, and especially what you did to Seth. I can't stop thinking about that. I want you to come back and make it better. Why can't you undo all the things you said to him? You put so much on him to forgive and move past because you couldn't be here to apologize. I wish you could come back and apologize."

A snowflake falls directly onto my eyelashes. I close my eyes against the cold.

"And by the way, apologies aren't about explaining yourself, or shifting blame. It's just about owning what you did and being genuinely sorry. That's it. That's what Seth deserves. Try to find a way to give that to him, okay?"

I keep my eyes closed. I can feel the snow dotting my cheeks, my ears, my forehead. I breathe in and out slowly, letting her be here. I can feel that she's here.

Something rustles over the ground, near the other end of

the field. I keep lying where I am, sinking deeper into my own outline. My right foot catches on something rolling straight for the net.

I sit up.

"That was good," Rosa says. "About the apology thing. You really do listen."

She digs her hands deep into her coat pockets and walks closer to me. I stare at the soccer ball pressed against the bottom of my shoe. It looks real. My foot arches back, like it would against a real soccer ball. But the moment feels like a mirage. Rosa seems almost blurred on the other side of the falling sheets of snow. Little specks of white sparkle on her coat lining, over her hair, on the tips of her ears and nose. Tiny pink roses bloom on her cheekbones. She looks like a dream.

She stops in front of my feet and points at the other angel. "Your mom?"

I nod, barely letting myself breathe.

"Yes," I whisper. I gesture to Mom's outline. "But you can sit here too, if you want. She would share."

"Okay," Rosa says. She carefully lowers herself to her knees, then twists onto her back and fills in the snow angel I made. She places her hands on her belly and threads her fingers together.

"You finish with school?"

I nod. "Yeah. Just now. You?"

Rosa nods. "Yesterday. Got my college applications turned in too. I'm going out for their soccer teams after all."

"Really? That's so great!" I pause. "It is great, right?"

She smiles slightly. "Yeah. It is. I thought about what you said before, back at the coffee shop. It really pissed me off at the time, just because I already had everything ready to go. But I don't want to be scared of going after what I really want."

"Well, I'm proud of you," I tell her. I squeeze my knees tight. "You're a hell of a lot braver than anyone else I know."

"Thanks." Rosa stares up at the sky. "I'm guessing . . . I don't know what's happening with Duke."

I shrug and watch the snow come down. "Nothing's happening with Duke," I say. "It was the place for my mom. Not the place for me."

"I think you're right about that." Rosa shifts onto her side so she's facing me. "So where are you applying?"

"Don't know yet."

The snowflakes are so tiny, but they keep filling in all the cracks on the ground. Uneven dips in the sidewalk slowly become leveled out. Patchy, brown lengths of grass over the field disappear. Everything melds together, leaving their differences behind and joining into one perfect blank sheet of paper.

I turn to Rosa. "My coach said something about there being plenty of time, if I just carve it out for myself. But I feel like there's no way I can turn in a good application by January. I want better recommendations than the ones I have now, which means I need time to do better work in school. Then there's the fact that I don't even know where I want to go. It's just . . . I'm not going to make it in time."

"Hmm." Rosa sits up a little. "Well, maybe that's what your coach was talking about."

I squint at her. "What do you mean?"

"I don't think she was telling you that a few weeks is enough time to apply," Rosa says. "I feel like she more meant you can give yourself extra time if you want. Like maybe you don't need to apply for programs that begin in the fall."

I think back to the concert from last week, and to standing across from Gloria in the hall. She told me I could carve out my own time. Maybe that's like the same thing as going at my own pace. Applying for college right now is what every senior feels like they have to do. But technically, I could wait another year, if I wanted. Or even just an extra semester. Everything's possible. It may not be conventional, or what's expected . . . but it is possible.

"Maybe I will take a gap year," I say slowly. "So that when I do head somewhere, I'm going where I really want, and doing what I really want. I feel like I've just started doing that lately. Listening to myself."

Rosa nods. "It will probably take a lot of practice."

I smile at her. "Good thing I like practice."

She looks at me, her expression unreadable. "Me too," she says softly.

Her lips stay parted open, just slightly, and I force myself to look away. I know she's not trying to torture me. But I'm only human. My heart begins to speed up in my chest. My breath comes out quick and shallow.

"I'm starting over with Katie again," I say, trying to distract myself. "We agreed the friendship needed a reboot. She's really, really sorry, by the way. Not that you ever need to forgive her."

Rosa brushes some snow out of her hair. "Yeah, that was shit." She stares down at the bits of snow turning to water droplets on her fingers. "But I do know the game can bring out the worst in people sometimes. Like we all take on a different part, or ego, and go there to the extreme."

"I definitely did that," I say. "I'd always pretend I was this bodyguard for my team. Like I had to protect our goal against everything, or else my actual life would fall apart."

Rosa gazes down the field and smiles. "I'd pretend I was a sort of agent, and I had to decode the other team's goalkeeper to complete my mission. Sometimes that meant pulling fake shots. Sometimes I would hide behind my teammates until the last second. And sometimes I'd just charge straight at the goalkeeper, like a bull."

"What was your strategy on me?" I ask.

Rosa bites her lip and a tiny part inside me explodes. She looks up at me, snow sticking to her lashes.

"To get as close to you as humanly possible."

I reach for the soccer ball at my feet and squeeze it close to my chest. I'm hoping Rosa doesn't see the ropes of tension looped around my fingers, palms, wrists. I breathe in and out.

"Maybe you and I can start over too," I say quietly. "From the game."

"Which game?"

"The first game," I say. I stand up with the ball and point to the invisible line in the snow that marks the goal circle. "Shoot this at me and we can go from there. Clean slate."

Rosa stands up after me and brushes the snow from her pants. She takes the ball uneasily.

"You're not wearing gear."

"And you don't have a field hockey ball and stick," I point out. "But this will do fine."

I stand in the middle of the goal box again, keeping my stance wide and arms spread.

Rosa takes the ball all the way to center field. She makes a dainty trail of footprints heading out in the snow, then turns suddenly and darts toward me. The soccer ball seems to be tethered to her foot by a string. She expertly kicks it down her path, forward and forward. I lick my lips. She's going to make this hard for me, I realize. Good.

I watch her closely as she dribbles the soccer ball one way along the goal circle, then pulls a switch and heads for the other side. I shift my weight from hip to hip, ready to leap in either direction. Then suddenly she swings her leg back and punts the soccer ball at me. I watch it rotate as it floats through a perfect arc through the air. I hold my right arm high. My fingers graze the very edge, but the ball slips through my hand. It swishes against the back of the net.

Rosa freezes where she is in the snow.

I turn to pick up the wet, slushy soccer ball and shove it under my arm.

"And Van Darian wins!" I call out in a mock announcer tone.

I march out of my goal box and meet Rosa at the circle.

"Good game," I say cheerfully. "You're . . . you're really good."

Rosa just looks at me.

I hold the ball out to her. "Maybe we can hang out sometime. Go on a walk or something."

Rosa tentatively takes the outstretched ball. Her skin just barely touches mine. She studies our hands. She's thinking about something. I'm not sure if my stupid pretend-scenario-small-talk is making it better or worse, but I don't know what else to say. I keep one hand held out.

"I'm Eve. I'd love to get to know you more. If that's something you might want too."

The question hangs in the air, unanswered. Suddenly my hand feels frozen, like I've plunged it into a bucket of icy water. The snow keeps blowing around us. My fingers go numb, one after another.

"I—"

Rosa clears her throat. Her voice sounds uncharacteristically tiny.

"I want it too," she says. She raises her gaze up to me, and something behind her eyes shifts. I feel the heat from her breath. I hear the huskiness and the hunger in her voice.

She doesn't shake my hand at all.

Instead, Rosa drops the ball at her feet and wraps both arms over my shoulders. I let my own arms rise and curl around her lower back. She pulls me in, and I pull her in. We melt into each other, sizzling over the snow.

CHAPTER THIRTY

Ten Months Later

I burst inside the locker room like a firework gone off too early.

CLANG! My stick bangs against a locker.

SWOOSH! My skort lands draped over a bench.

I dig my fingers under the hem of my shirt and pull it off in one fluid motion. By the time the next player comes into the locker room behind me, I'm nearly already in the shower.

"Damn, Feltzer!" my teammate yells. "The scrimmage is over. Don't you have any modes other than turbo?"

I laugh as I pull a clean towel from my bag.

"Look, when you're used to running in an extra forty pounds of padding, you can't help being fast when it all comes off!" I hang the towel on a hook and head into a stall.

"It's not my fault the BSSC doesn't have goalkeepers in the rec league," I add from behind the curtain.

I crank the handle and step into the spray before the shower has time to get warm.

The first ten seconds of water hit my body like a sheet of ice. It's a shock to the system—one that any normal person would probably avoid at all costs. But these days I need a slap in the face to calm me down after field hockey games. Once I get going, it really is hard to stop.

I thought the things I loved most about the field were all inside one goal box. Turns out, it's even more fun to venture outside of it.

I quickly scrub down and leave the stall so another teammate can step inside. But as I fling the curtain back, I see that people are still slowly sauntering into the locker room.

My teammates these days look a lot different from the ones at Heathclef. I play next to women and nonbinary folks in their thirties and forties, and even one killer midfielder who's turning fifty-three next week. I play with teammates who put their all into the game, but don't give two shits about winning or losing, so long as they leave everything out on the field.

I'm the youngest on the team. The buzziest, some say politely. Others, who remind me delightfully of Gloria, call me a Labrador puppy on acid.

The new reputation definitely took some getting used to. I've always been known as the serious one, the one weighed down by a million responsibilities. But that angle really gets put into perspective given that most of my teammates nowadays have actual kids and families depending on them outside of practice. I like being the puppy for once. It's a nice role reversal, although I can't wait until I'm not the only player drinking fucking club soda whenever we head out to the Burren Pub for sports trivia night on Wednesdays.

I shake out my wet hair and pull on my clothes. My locker key slips onto the floor, and I quickly shove it down into one pocket. I can't forget to hand it in this time.

Being a member of an adult rec league means that instead of having a gym or a home field, our team travels all around Boston for scrimmages and games. For one afternoon at a time, I get to hang out in different high school fields, or college stadiums, or even public parks if nothing else is open. It's sort of fun to move from place to place, knowing I don't have to land anywhere specific until I'm ready.

"Great defense, Feltzer."

Our center forward and team captain, Violet, gives me a thumbs-up. She pulls on her usual waterproof bonnet and fishes out a shower caddy from her bag.

"All right, team," Violet calls out. "Strategy meeting on Wednesday at the pub. Remember to get there early! Meeting's at seven. Trivia, eight!"

The others nod in agreement.

We're a small team, which means all of us sit down and contribute to our gameplays. Like Gloria, we like to change things up on the field. I've tried out being a forward, midfielder, defender—basically every position there is, aside from goalkeeper. But I won't be surprised if I take on defense again at our next scheduled scrimmage. It's pretty much my sweet spot.

Our senior midfielder pokes my elbow as I zip up my duffel

bag. "So you're sticking around the rest of the season?" she asks.

"Of course," I say. "Why wouldn't I?"

The woman shrugs and shakes her head. "You're destined for bigger things. Don't waste all your youth on us. I can see you playing with Women's FIH someday. You ever have anyone push you in that direction?"

My hand freezes on my bag strap.

"Um, yeah," I say after a moment. "My mom almost went professional. She played for Duke in college."

"That right?" the woman asks. "What's she doing now?"

I lift my chin and force myself to make eye contact. "She died when I was in middle school. Cancer."

I feel everyone else in the room pause. The midfielder looks at me. She presses her lips together and nods.

"Cancer is a damned *bitch*," she says.

I smile a little. "Yeah, it is."

Another teammate steps closer to us. "I'm sure the puppy already knows how good she is," she says, jutting her chin at me. "She doesn't need anyone to push her anywhere. Let her decide what to do with her time."

Violet pokes her head out of the shower curtain.

"Don't you dare scare Evelyn off the team, or we might have to actually start putting some effort into our games."

Everyone in the room, including me, laughs. The moment of tension seems to drift away, passing through all of us like water.

I wave goodbye to my teammates and turn in my locker key at Hormel's front desk.

The day outside is crisp and perfect. The chill of fall won't set in for another month, at least according to Seth, who's already been through four years of Boston weather. I let the sun soak over me and start my walk back to our apartment, dipping away from café awnings and avoiding the pools of shade.

A ridiculously affectionate couple canoodles over a shared bagel at one of the outdoor tables. In the corner of another café, a small group of college students gathers around a large plate of mostly demolished mini muffins. The students' hoods are all pulled up, their earbuds in, as they stare into their laptops. Two older women stop ahead of me along the sidewalk to point at a window display in a costume boutique. A man in a fancy leather jacket walks a miniature Italian greyhound sporting its own nearly identical jacket.

I keep waiting for the waning warmth of summer to drive people back into their houses like it does in Pennsylvania, but Seth tells me that doesn't happen here. The city becomes one connected, breathing home. People won't stop picking up groceries or catching a movie or heading for beers after work with friends. The veins of Davis Square will always be pumping with life and activity, even when the cold winds blow in and gray, sooty snow accumulates across every surface.

It's nice living with Seth again. It's also totally different from when we lived with Mom and Dad. Seth and I have this mutual understanding, an agreement that we both deserve to be adult versions of ourselves without anyone tying us down to our past. It's kind of funny to have the person I grew up with my whole life as my biggest supporter when it comes to starting over.

Over the summer, Seth followed his theater major post-graduation and got a job working at an interactive theater-slash-nightclub. They're currently performing an adaptation of Shakespeare's *A Midsummer Night's Dream* set in the 1970s disco scene. Of course Seth gets to play Oberon as the head male go-go dancer of the club.

Although it would be cool to strip down to a glittery underwear-and-cape ensemble like my brother, I end up paying for my half of the rent by working at the Tufts college library. My boss, Adrianna, still remembers the first time we met when I visited last winter and asked her about books on women's sports. I still have her list of recommendations. I've read all of them at least once. Adrianna's certain I'll end up at Tufts next year. I might even be able to skip a year ahead in the gender studies department, she tells me. But we'll see how I feel about applying in another month or two.

The narrow side street finally opens into the wider square. I check my phone and see the time, then head across another street to the main entrance for the T station.

I've barely stepped over the curb when I see the unmistakably shiny head of hair I know so well.

She floats up the escalator, emerging from underground like a city nymph. A book is balanced carefully in the crook of her elbows. Her hair falls over her face, twisting in the book's pages. I want to brush it behind her ear myself, but before I get close, she tosses her hair back and looks up. Her entire face breaks into a wide, crinkling grin.

"Well, hey there," Rosa says.

She tucks the book into her backpack. I cup her chin in

my palm and kiss her once, delicately. She inhales as she pulls back. Her eyes are soft and warm and inviting.

"Were you waiting long?" she asks.

I shake my head. "Just walked up, actually. Scrimmage went into overtime."

"I wish I could've been there."

"Next time," I say, looping my arm over her shoulders. "Speaking of, when do I get to watch you play?"

Rosa rolls her eyes. "The soccer season at Wellesley is so weird. Two games in two weeks, then nothing for the next two. It drives me crazy." She looks up at me. "I think our next home game is on the fifteenth."

"Then I'll be there." I plant another kiss on her head.

We walk hand in hand, making our way down the familiar route toward my apartment. The sun shimmers above us. I pause as we turn onto my street, tilting my head back and closing my eyes. Days like these are too good to be wasted under a roof.

"What's up?" Rosa asks.

I pop my eyes open. "Let's head over to Cambridge and rent a boat for the afternoon. We can head along the Charles. You want to?"

Rosa bites her lip and squeezes my hand. "Yes. I want to."

We run home and drop off our things just inside the door. Seth will understand when he sees the discarded pile. We'll catch him at dinner before his performance. Or we'll catch him tomorrow morning. There will be time.

Rosa and I trade stories about our weeks rapid-fire as we head back to the T. She tells me about the new book she's reading in her magical realism literature class. I tell her about the new book I ordered for the library about pioneering trans athletes. We slip into every topic like falling into potholes. One story leads right into the next. There are too many things to talk about to ever run out of steam.

"I told the team about my mom today," I say as we get off at Harvard Square.

"Really?" Rosa stops and swings herself onto a bike stand like it's a bench. Her legs dangle at my waist. "How did that go?"

"Fine. Good." I think for a moment, trying to explain the feeling from earlier. "The hard stuff doesn't follow me out of a room anymore. Like, people can label me or feel sorry for me or not, but their opinions aren't my problem, you know?"

Rosa looks at me and nods. "I do know," she says.

We stare at each other a little while. I wade between Rosa's knees and rest my head over her chest. She threads her fingers through my hair and scratches the base of my scalp. We fit into each other seamlessly. Like two halves of one whole.

"Do you still want to grab a boat?" Rosa whispers into my forehead.

I pull myself back up to standing. "Yeah. Let's do it."

Rosa shimmies off the bike stand and we turn again for the docks. The two of us join the crowd, blending in with the other lovey-dovey couples, the laughing groups of friends, the old ladies pointing at window displays along at every corner.

We make it to the river and check out a double kayak for the afternoon.

"Front seat!" Rosa calls as we pick up our paddles.

I laugh. "I wouldn't have it any other way."

We snuggle into the bloated life vests and shove our legs down into the footholds. Then the dock manager gives us one good shove and we're off, cutting through the current. All at once the rest of the world falls away and it's just the two of us, me and Rosa, gliding over the glassy surface.

I paddle for a few strokes, then prop my oar over my lap.

"Where should we go?" Rosa calls from the front.

"Anywhere. Nowhere," I answer. I smile at the glimmering water.

She looks over her shoulder and sees my oar, then follows suit with her own. I can hear the steady rhythm of her breathing ahead of me. I can feel the steady rhythm of my heartbeat inside me. The boat begins to turn, nosing its own path through the river. Neither Rosa nor I make any move to paddle off the boat's chosen course. Instead, Rosa reaches one hand behind her back. I lace my fingers through hers.

I don't know where we'll end up, floating along like this without a plan. Maybe we'll get tangled in the brush, or beached on a sandbar. Maybe we'll drift into a part of the city we've never seen before and discover something wonderful. Either way, it feels better to surrender to the water than wear myself out trying to overpower it.

Rosa starts humming a tune from her cooking playlist.

I lean my head back, soaking in the sun through my cheeks, and nod along.

Everything about this moment is new and different.

Mom and I never listened to music together. We never went out on the water. I don't have a single childhood memory to ground me to this spot. I'm not on the road Mom forged for me anymore. These days, I sort of meander down any side path that looks interesting.

But I'm still a person figuring out my life, just like Mom was. We both made huge mistakes and failed the people we love the most. But I think she and I can be more than our mistakes. I think that underneath everything else, under all the pain she put on Seth and all the expectations she put on me, Mom was just trying to figure herself out. That's what I'm doing now. And Duke or no Duke, field hockey or no field hockey, that's enough for us to be connected.

I catch on to the melody and sing alongside Rosa.

I know in my heart that Mom is listening.

ACKNOWLEDGMENTS

It is a truth universally acknowledged that acknowledgments are easy to fantasize about when working on a fledging manuscript and yet nearly impossible to write when the time comes to share that finished book with the world.

The first thank-you must go to my editor, Alison Romig, who is most definitely the love interest in the story of this book's journey to publication. From the very beginning, Alison *got* every aspect of the world and characters, and right away, Evelyn, Rosa, and I were smitten. Thank you, Ali, for loving this book through all its stages. Thank you to my agent, Lauren Spieller, for pushing me to expand my horizons as a writer. You singlehandedly ushered me into my "Chameleon Era," which I'm in no hurry to walk away from anytime soon. Thank you for sending me random prompts and telling me to do the thing, even when it seemed completely out of my wheelhouse. You believed in me as a YA writer before even I did.

Thank you so much to everyone at Delacorte Press. Writing can sometimes feel like a solitary sport, but book production is always an intensive team effort. I am endlessly grateful to Sarah Maxwell, the cover artist of my dreams, for doing Evelyn and Rosa so right. Immense thank-yous to the brilliant cover designer duo Angela Carlino and Liz Dresner, and to the freelance cover designer, Lesley Worrell. Cathy Bobak, you've created magic in this book's interior design and typesetting. Colleen Fellingham and Katy Miller, thank you for triple-checking every word. Joey Ho, thank you for every platform and opportunity you've found to promote this love story. Beverly Horowitz, Tamar Schwartz, and Shameiza Ally, none of this would have happened if not for your flawless stewardship. I appreciate every single one you. I love working alongside you. I am so, so proud to be a Delacorte author.

I owe nearly everything I am as a writer to my dear friends and critique partners. Alder Van Otterloo and Erica Watters, thank you for having a good feeling about this story from its earliest drafts. Wendy Heard, thank you exuding the sexy gay energy I'm always trying to capture on paper. Brian Kennedy, thank you for leading me down the rom-com path, and for your immense kindness and support in helping me along behind you. Loriel Ryon, thank you for being my sounding board, and for getting up to write the words every day. To say I look up to you is a vast understatement. Becky Albertelli, thank you for the thoughtful and loving conversations on what it means to be enough in this community, as both a writer and as a person.

Marken, thank you—truly—for kissing me so hard I nearly lost consciousness and then ghosting me as soon as I tried to reach back. It's no wonder I had to use my experiences with you in my first YA book. Kyle, you are absolutely nothing like Caleb. You're one of the best friends I've ever had, and thank God we didn't hold each other back in the long run. To all my other twin flames—Josephine, Collin, Sandra, Charlie—thank you for teaching me about love and about myself. I hope you are all finding your deepest happiness in life.

David, you're what happens when a relationship turns out exactly right. You've been the best teacher and friend and the only other half to my orange in this entire universe. You know how much I wanted to marry a woman, and still, I married you. Because you're that great. Thank you for insisting I chase my dreams, and for shifting heaven and earth to make sure I get to keep working even as our family grows. I have never known support like yours. You've made writing, and my career, a love language between us.

August and Rowan, damn it if you haven't turned my world completely upside down and filled it to the brim with so much love that it makes me dizzy. I wrote this book while August slept on my chest and Rowan did somersaults inside me. You kids know my heart inside and out. You *are* my heart. Mom and Dad and Brooklyn, I don't know if you'll be able to read this story, and that's okay. I wrote it as an escape for myself when the four us were confronted with the hardest year of our lives. So many of these chapters were drafted in hospital waiting rooms. Thank you for providing a safe place, for being a stable and loving family that lets me explore all the possible situations and dynamics for my characters. Only the good parts are inspired by you.

Finally, thank you to everyone who reads this book and

finds themselves somewhere in the pages. Queerness is such a strange nebula, ever-changing and expanding as we all add our unique experiences to it. I fell in love with Evelyn as a character because she gave me a world to explore my personal feelings on the connection between sexuality and gender identity. Someday I'll write a whole book on that, on what it feels like to want to be everything all at once, but even opening the door to that path has been the most wonderful breath of air. I hope every reader finds their door and path, as Rosa says, using labels when they help and eschewing them when they don't. You are precious and whole and enough, exactly as you are.

Delacorte Romance

IT'S A LOVE STORY.